# Her Mother's Killer

## Pam Crooks

Cover Design:  Book Cover Express
Background Photo:  © andreiuc88 - Fotolia.com
Author Photo:  Britson Sommer Photography

Her Mother's Killer is a work of fiction. Names, characters, places, brands, media and incidents are either the product of the author's imagination or are used fictitiously. The author acknowledges the trademarked status and trademark owners of various products referenced in this work of fiction, which have been used without permission. The publication/use of these trademarks is not authorized, associated with, or sponsored by, the trademark owners.

# PROLOGUE

Adrienne Morelli leaned back in the chaise lounge, tantalized by the aroma of Porterhouse steaks sizzling on the grill. A picnic table draped in a red and white checkered tablecloth had already been set for three. A large pitcher of iced tea, its sides beading with moisture, sat in readiness for dinner to begin. She sighed in contentment.

Her father finished turning the steaks and closed the lid on the grill. Laying aside his tongs, he maneuvered his wheelchair at an angle to the chaise.

"Just a few more minutes," he said and winked.

"Good. I'm starved." She smiled and reached toward him, taking his hand in hers. "I'm glad to see you looking so relaxed, Dad. Mom says you haven't slowed down since the election."

He pressed a kiss to her knuckle and shrugged. "There's a lot of work to do for our fine state. But it does my heart good to see my little girl again, even if it's only for the weekend."

She huffed a breath in good-natured exasperation and withdrew her hand. "Dad. I'm not little anymore. I'm a woman. All grown-up."

"And a beautiful woman at that."

She rolled her eyes. "Yeah, whatever."

She didn't consider herself blessed with an abundance of beauty, not in the way her mother had been. As her parents' only child, Adrienne definitely took after her father in the looks department--average features, lean, long-legged and athletic. Well, her father *had* been athletic until a skiing accident the year before crippled him.

But at least she could claim she'd inherited his brains-- and his love for the wonderful state of Tennessee.

Her gaze lingered on the dense forest bordering the mountain chalet her parents had rented. Maple, oak and yellow poplar trees grew lush and thick on the mammoth slopes of the Great Smokies. Wildflowers colored the woods with nature's crayon in vibrant shades of purples, pinks and oranges, and hundreds of species of wildlife called the forest home. Adrienne marveled at all of it.

"Quite a view, isn't it?" her father asked.

"Spectacular as always."

"It's important to keep the Tennessee wilderness untouched, Adrienne. The thought of developers coming in to build their golf courses, swimming pools and tennis courts makes my stomach turn."

"Mine, too."

"Your mother has been working with Murdock, Inc.. They're ready to deed us another two thousand acres of wilderness in Scott's Gulf."

The project had been Julia Morelli's passion, Adrienne knew. Saving the Tennessee wilderness. After her father's skiing accident, she'd stepped in to win the Murdock corporation's confidence and subsequent approval to donate the land to the state.

Adrienne thought of the conservation group who labored tirelessly with her mother to preserve the beauty in their part of Tennessee. "I'm sure the Scott's Gulf Alliance is thrilled."

"Ecstatic is more like it." Julia smiled and set a bowl of lettuce salad, covered in plastic wrap, on the picnic table.

She moved toward the wheelchair, and her father shifted, giving her room to perch on the armrest. He slipped his arm around her hips and patted her thigh.

The gesture struck Adrienne as intimate in its simplicity, familiar and loving and one of many she'd witnessed throughout her life. Julia was a wife who preferred to be close to her husband any chance she could. Her devotion ran deep and genuine, and a sudden pang of longing stung Adrienne. She wanted a love of her own someday, a man to cherish forever, like her parents cherished each other. They made 'happiness' look easy, she mused, and because of them, Adrienne's expectations had always been high. Maybe too high. She had plenty of male friends, but none of them had stolen her heart. Some days, she wondered if any one would.

"Your mother has done a fantastic job with Murdock. She's charmed the Board of Directors to her way of thinking," Daniel said proudly.

"Not all of them," Julia said with a sudden frown, giving Adrienne an inkling that someone had been resisting her efforts, and the schmoozing hadn't been entirely easy. "But now that all the squabbling is over, everything has fallen into place."

"Squabbling?" Adrienne asked.

"You know the saying," her father said. "'One bad apple' . . .."

Julia tapped a manicured finger on his lips, hushing him before he could finish. "We don't want to bore Adrienne with state business. Not another word about bad apples or Scott's Gulf for the rest of the weekend. Okay?"

"Okay." He nipped at the red-painted fingernail, and she snatched her hand away with a soft laugh, then stood. "How are those steaks coming?"

"Done by now, I think." He rolled the wheelchair toward the grill.

"Adrienne, I've left the salad dressings in the 'fridge. Ranch and Roquefort. Bring them both out, won't you?"

"Sure."

"We should have a nice bouquet of flowers to enjoy during dinner."

"The table already looks nice," Adrienne said, but her gaze slid toward the wildflowers again.

"Flowers will be festive. How often does our little girl

come to stay with us for the weekend?"

Adrienne's mouth softened in amusement at Julia's teasing, and she ignored the urge to state her evolution into womanhood again. Her mother strolled across the lawn toward a patch of wild blue phlox growing at the edge of the forest.

Adrienne considered the trim figure sheathed in designer jeans, silk shell and skimpy Italian sandals. Some would call Julia Morelli a trophy wife, a vision of well-groomed perfection to complement her husband in his gubernatorial seat with the state of Tennessee.

But she was more than that. She worked hard to help him be the best he could be. Her determination to win the land deed would be an asset to his leadership position in the state, and as a former beauty queen and film star, she had grown to be a favorite of the media, a photographer's delight. Her radiance charmed the most hardened of the opposition.

Everyone loved Julia Morelli. But none more so than her husband and daughter.

Something glinted from within the depths of the forest. A flash so quick and bright, Adrienne's eyelids reacted in a sudden blink. Only a few dozen yards away, her mother knelt, gathering the wild phlox. Adrienne's heart fell into uneven rhythm.

Her stare clawed the trees, her mind rushing to form images of black bears and wild boars, drawn by the scent of grilling steaks. She rose uneasily from the chaise lounge.

Movement stirred within the shadows. Her mother finished her picking and straightened, cradling the bundle of flowers in her arm; her fingers busily arranged the stems.

And before Adrienne could warn her, before she could scream her mother's name, a gunshot sliced through the mountain air, and Julia Morelli fell into a bloody, lifeless heap.

# CHAPTER ONE

*Memphis, Six Months Later*

"I want your best man for my daughter, Grif. Your absolute *best*."

Griffin Silverhawk, sole owner of Silverhawk Investigative Services, eyed the state's governor with cool intensity.

"And we both know who that would be, don't we?" he said.

The other man's penetrating gaze never wavered. "Yes."

Daniel Morelli, Governor of the state of Tennessee and a long-time acquaintance of Griffin's, arrived only moments ago--alone and in person when anyone else in his position would have simply phoned. Or assigned some administrative assistant the task of hiring a top-notch bodyguard for his only daughter.

Griffin pulled open a desk drawer and chose a cherry-flavored Tootsie Pop from his stash. After offering one to Morelli, who declined with a brief shake of his head, he tossed the wrapper into the waste receptacle and popped the sucker into his mouth.

"Adrienne's grown into a sophisticated woman, hasn't she?" he said after a thoughtful lick.

A shadow crossed the governor's features. "As sophisticated as her mother was."

At the mention of his wife, a moment of grim silence passed between them. The entire state had mourned Julia Morelli's death, a death she never deserved. Sharp regret shot through Griffin.

Worse, her murderer had never been found. Not a trace of evidence had been left behind, except for the bullet found in her back. The Great Smokies was a huge pile of mountains. Thousands of acres of dense foliage and rough terrain proved nearly impossible to investigate. Though Morelli stamped the case Top Priority and called in the FBI, law enforcement officials failed to solve it.

"There's been a few death threats, Grif." Daniel's mouth twisted. "Clever little poems that warn me to walk away from two thousand acres of Scott's Gulf. Or else."

Griffin stiffened in alarm. "Julia's killer is still out there."

"And Adrienne has to go back to the mountains in my place."

"Find someone else to go instead."

"We're ready to close the deal, and she's the only one qualified to cinch it for me."

"It's too dangerous for her."

"Which is why I need your best bodyguard!"

Griffin's fist tightened over the sucker stick. "Scott's Gulf is pure wilderness, Daniel. A bodyguard's nightmare. There's a million places for a killer to hide--in the forest, caves or any of those damned hollows. If she goes traipsing up those mountains, she'll be an easy mark for any sniper."

Morelli leaned forward. "I want those two thousand acres, Grif. The state of Tennessee *needs* them. We're going through with the deal, and I need your help to do it. For Adrienne's sake."

"Look, sir. I'd like to--"

"Cut the 'sir' crap, Grif." Morelli reached inside his suit coat and withdrew his checkbook. The pen scratched across the paper; he signed his name with a clipped flourish. "Here's your fee and then some." He yanked the check along the perforated edge and tossed it toward him. "Give the extra to your man. Convince him to take the job."

"The money means nothing to him."

"I don't care what it takes. Just convince him. You're

his boss, damn it."

"He's protecting another client right now."

"Pull him off that job and put him on mine." Morelli leaned forward in his wheelchair. "I want him with Adrienne twenty-four hours a day. He's not to let her out of his sight. Ever."

Griffin's eye narrowed. "Twenty-four hours is grueling for any bodyguard, no matter how good he is."

"Have him meet me in Nashville in two days," Morelli said as if Griffin had never spoken. "That's when Adrienne is scheduled to leave. If he has any questions, you know where to reach me."

Griffin gritted his teeth to keep from arguing further. Morelli slid the checkbook back into his suit coat and wheeled away from the desk. Within moments, the door slammed shut behind him.

For a long moment, Griffin sat in the silence and glared at the telephone. He dreaded making the call to his best bodyguard.

Mick Corrigan would *not* be happy.

* * *

*Nashville, Two Days Later*

Adrienne burst into her father's office at the State Capitol Building and tossed a sheaf of papers onto his desktop.

"What's this about you hiring a bodyguard for me?" she asked, setting her hands on her hips. "Tell me Renee is joking."

"Renee would never joke about something like that," he said of his executive secretary. He met Adrienne's outrage head on. "She's much too efficient."

"It's true then?"

"Your trip to Scott's Gulf won't go unnoticed by the press or the people in the mountains. You have the officially documented and most up-to-date endangered species list"-- he indicated the sheaf of papers she'd dropped on his desk-- "for Murdock. Once they have that, they'll deed the land to us and prevent the land developers from moving in. Those two thousand acres will be big news to this state."

"Look. I know there's opposition to this acquisition. There always has been. We'll deal with it. It's what Mom would've wanted." She paused, letting her words sink in. "You don't have to do this."

"Word will spread you're in the area. I want you safe."

"If the murderer wanted to kill me, he would have done it by now."

"Adrienne!"

The sharp reprimand stopped her protests cold. She understood her father's reasoning, his fear of losing his only child. Neither of them could forget Julia Morelli's murderer had never been caught.

All the old memories came crashing back. She didn't want to think of being afraid, not now, when she'd only started to heal after all these months. Adrienne stepped to the ceiling-high window and stared unseeing into the busy city outside.

After her mother's death, her father ordered round-the-clock protection for them both. When the leads grew cold, the protection ended. But she had to admit having a bodyguard back then left her feeling incredibly safe.

Especially having one bodyguard in particular.

Her breath hitched in horror. She whirled back toward her father. "What agency did you hire?"

He met her demanding gaze without flinching. "Silverhawk."

Her fingers flew to her mouth. "Not Mick--"

"Corrigan. Yes."

Oh, God.

"Sorry you're disappointed, Adrienne."

At the low, masculine voice--that voice which had haunted her dreams for months--she whirled again, this time toward the other side of her father's office, to the tall, mahogany bookshelves where *he*, Mick Corrigan, leaned with one broad shoulder and a thumb hooked in his waistband. A frown slashed his hard mouth.

Resentment emanated from him. He didn't want to be here anymore than she wanted him to be, she realized. Her cheeks heated with indignation, and she spun back to her father.

"The least you could've done is told me he was here," she hissed.

"The way you came storming in here, I didn't have a chance. And neither did he." Daniel frowned. "He's greeted you civilly, Adrienne. Please respond in kind. After all, you two will be together constantly for days."

Adrienne clamped her lips tight. She couldn't remember the last time her father had been angry with her. He spoke to her now as if she were a rebellious teenager.

Well, she *was* feeling pretty rebellious right now, damn it. Mick Corrigan aroused in her emotions she shouldn't feel. Memories she needed to forget.

But thoughts of her mother overrode them all. Julia Morelli would never have allowed her irritation to show. She was the epitome of graciousness, of manners and good taste, and, for her father's sake, Adrienne had tried hard these past months to emulate her.

Adrienne lifted her chin. She faced her new bodyguard squarely and extended her hand.

"Good to see you again, Mick," she said stiffly.

He made no comment to her blatant lie. Instead, he strode toward her, all male grace and coiled power, and took her hand in his.

Her knees went weak.

Dear God. How was she going to get through this?

* * *

"Why are you so upset?" Renee demanded, the heels of her career-style pumps a tattoo of sound on the marble floor as she hastened to keep up with Adrienne's longer-legged stride. "Just because your father insists you have a bodyguard is no reason to get mad."

"The whole thing is ridiculous." Adrienne shoved the

door of the Capitol Building open. Bright afternoon sunlight blasted into her face; she rooted inside her carry-all for her sunglasses.

Renee slipped through the door before it closed again. She clutched a briefcase in one hand; in the other, a piece of Adrienne's luggage.

"The outside pocket," she said, watching her. "The zippered one."

Adrienne made a strangled sound of frustration and found the sunglasses, right where Renee said they'd be.

"You're frazzled," Renee said, amused and a bit winded as she followed her down the steps toward the parking lot. "*He* frazzles you."

Adrienne paused on the landing above the next set of steps and sighed.

"He's going to drive me crazy," she said and took the luggage the other woman held. "I don't want to be with him."

"Ye gods. Why not?"

"Because."

"Well, that told me what I wanted to know."

Adrienne glared at her. They'd become fast friends from the first day her father had hired her as his secretary. With a quick smile and sunny disposition, to say nothing of a razor-sharp efficiency that never failed to make Adrienne's head spin, Renee was one hundred percent professionalism. Adrienne trusted her implicitly.

Maybe someday she could confide all that was in her heart regarding Mick Corrigan. But not now. Not when she'd be climbing into a new SUV to drive with him to White County in the next ten minutes.

"So you had an affair with him," Renee said and shrugged. "Don't torture yourself over it."

Adrienne bit her lip. Was it so obvious? "We broke the rules. It should never have happened."

"You were still grieving over your mother," Renee said quietly. "You needed him, and he was there for you. What's so wrong with that?"

"It's not as simple as you make it sound."

Renee wrapped an arm around Adrienne's shoulder in a brief, fervent hug. "It'll be fine. You'll see. You have a job to do. So does he. Just roll with it. What other choice do you have?"

"Absolutely none." She stepped back, tucking her hair behind one ear. In all her discomfiture, she'd forgotten to bring her hair clip.

"Well, he could guard my body any day." Renee's gaze slid over Adrienne's shoulder. She purred in pure, feminine pleasure. "He's waiting for you by the Range Rover. Hubba, hubba. Is he one gorgeous man or what?"

Adrienne dragged her gaze across the parking lot, too. Mick stood next to the luxury vehicle while talking to several members of the Capitol Police, his garment bag on the blacktop, ready to be loaded. Though his stance appeared relaxed, she sensed the control in him. That ever-present vigilance of his surroundings that made him the best of the best.

As if he sensed their perusal, his dark head lifted to swivel in their direction, and his glance locked with Adrienne's. A jolt went through her. She started guiltily and jerked away to fumble at nothing in her carry-all.

"Is it true he's part Cherokee?" Renee asked in a loud conspiratorial whisper, nudging her toward the last flight of steps.

"Yes," Adrienne said, refusing to look at him to see if he still watched her.

She purred again, low in her throat. "Sounds so primitive."

Renee, a city girl born and bred in California, was oblivious to the fact the Cherokee were one of the first settlers of Tennessee. Thousands of them still lived in the state.

"It's not--I mean, he's not. Primitive, I mean." *Except in bed. Oh, God. Especially then.* "He's a gentleman, through and through," Adrienne said through clenched teeth.

"Well, shoot. What do you have to worry about then?" Renee said and flashed a wide smile.

They reached the bottom of the steps and strode across the sidewalk toward the parking lot. Renee's smile brightened as they drew closer to the Range Rover, gleaming metallic red in the sun.

"Here she is. All packed and ready to go." Renee reached toward Mick, a ring of keys between her fingers. "You'll need these, Mr. Corrigan."

When she would have dropped them into Mick's outstretched palm, Adrienne snaked out a hand and took them first.

"I'll drive," she said firmly.

But just as fast, Mick's hand closed over hers, hard enough to prevent her from tugging it back. Her gaze slammed into his.

Those black eyes glittered down at her in unspoken warning. For appearance's sake, she knew, he voiced no protest, but the unyielding set of his jaw revealed he wouldn't tolerate her rebellion, not when he was in charge, hired by her father to protect her.

"Sure," he said smoothly. "Whatever you say." Only then did he release her, and Adrienne took a hasty step backward.

"Let's get moving then. It's getting late." As pathetic as it sounded, she felt a need to assert her authority. With fingers not quite steady, she pressed the button on the SUV's door handle; the vehicle chirped, the lights flashed, and the locks released.

"The camera and maps are in the carry-all with your laptop," Renee said while Mick loaded their luggage. "The cell phone charger is in your briefcase, along with a credit card and the itinerary. Remember, dinner is at seven tonight in Sparta. The Golden Eagle."

"I know," Adrienne said. Their plans were of her own making. She knew exactly where she needed to be and when.

"We're expecting regular updates," Renee added as Adrienne slid behind the wheel. "Call us. Often."

"Yeah, yeah." She waved a hand and shut the door. The passenger side opened, and Mick's muscular frame filled the seat.

He was dressed completely in black. From the fine knit, mockneck sweater that accentuated the breadth of his shoulders to the way his slacks clung to his thighs, he dominated her senses. His cologne mingled with the smells of a new vehicle and its leather. Though the Range Rover boasted an expanse of room, his bulk seemed to take the majority, and Adrienne began to doubt the wisdom of her decision to drive. He rattled her concentration, and they'd yet to leave the parking lot.

"Daddy spared no expense for his little girl," Mick murmured with cool sarcasm, his gaze roving over the state-of-the-art dashboard, console and grained leather upholstery.

The taunt stung. "It's rented."

"Some people could buy a house for what this thing costs." He slid on a pair of sunglasses, their lenses as black as his clothing.

Her nostrils flared. "Look, Mick. How about if I drop you off at the nearest Avis? You can rent your own itty bitty car and go back to Memphis. *Daddy* will never know. I'll go on to Sparta without you, and we'll both be happier."

"No chance, sweetheart. The job's paid for and then some. We're stuck with each other. Wasn't my idea, believe me."

"You bastard."

A muscle moved in his cheek. He turned away and stared out the window. The late afternoon sun profiled the hard set of his jaw, glinted on the sheen of his dark hair, hanging in a queue past his shoulders.

"I'm sorry," he said finally and turned back to face her. "You didn't deserve that."

"Neither of us deserves *this*." Her hand made a frustrated movement in the air, a gesture of them being together, and his lips thinned in agreement.

In the rear view mirror, Adrienne caught a glimpse of Renee and the group of Capitol Police waiting expectantly for their departure. Sighing heavily, she pushed the ignition button and drove out of the parking lot.

\* \* \*

The Range Rover cruised eastward along Interstate 40 toward White County. After repeated checks in the side mirror, Mick was convinced no one followed them, and he allowed himself to relax.

A keen awareness of Adrienne took over. The same awareness that had hummed in his veins from the moment he saw her in her father's office. She seemed engrossed in a popular country music radio station, tapping a finger to the beat of the latest Tim McGraw song. Mick was glad for the lenses that shielded his eyes. They gave him an opportunity to study her without her knowing it.

She'd matured in the months since her mother's death, carrying a refinement about her that hadn't been there before. A confidence. A sultry, feminine appeal that shook him to the core.

He still wanted her. As much now as he had then.

It wasn't fair a man should want a woman he had no business having. Adrienne Morelli was destined for great things. She had brains. Ambition. A devoted father who knew important people but who had enough influence and power to help the little people, too.

Mick would always be in the background. He preferred it that way. He'd been born a country hick who managed to save himself from the Tennessee backwoods, but he never had any aspirations for being in the limelight.

People who did usually found themselves in some kind of trouble, whether they went looking for it or not. They gave men like him all the jobs they could handle to protect them. And paid big bucks to do it.

Adrienne was different. Through no fault of her own, she lost her mother to a cruel, senseless death. And because of it, she'd been forced to step into the glaring eye of a sometimes hostile public.

Or a loving and curious one. At times, the paparazzi had been merciless in their quest to know her better. After Julia Morelli's death, condolences poured in from all over Tennessee and half of the United States. Adrienne had been profoundly touched. Often overwhelmed. Yet despite all the love and compassion she received, she was deeply afraid of her mother's killer.

It had been Mick she turned to for strength. Her vulnerability had touched him in parts he didn't know needed touching. His cynical heart melted, and she'd tumbled inside.

She'd trusted him with her life, trusted him more than any other man on the earth, up to and including her father. It was a blind trust. Fresh and pure. Total and complete.

But they both knew he couldn't go on protecting her forever. That had scared her, too, and one night, they made love. He hadn't known she'd never been with a man before, and the realization of what he'd done, the immensity of it, had been a real sucker punch to the gut.

He'd broken his number one rule: *Never get involved with a client.* Grif could have fired him. Hell, he should have. Mick would've deserved it. Adrienne had become too much of a distraction. She clouded his mind when he needed to be alert, ready for anything. Detached.

For her sake. For his own. Without his senses razor-sharp, she could be killed. They both could.

He cut out the next day, before dawn, leaving Adrienne still naked and warm in the sheets. By the time she awakened, another of Silverhawk's bodyguards had been assigned to her. And Mick hadn't spoken to her since.

But he thought of her. Nearly every minute of every day.

"You're staring at me," she said. "What am I doing wrong?"

His thoughts scattered. So much for the dark lenses hiding his stare. He dropped his gaze to the speedometer.

"You're driving too fast," he said. "Slow down."

"What?" Her glance dropped, too. "I'm four miles over. Maybe five. That's not speeding."

"The hell it isn't. Slow it down, Adrienne. We don't need a cop on our tails when we pull into town."

She rolled her eyes and tapped the brake, then re-set the cruise control. "Is it going to be like this from now on, Mick? You nagging me over every little thing?"

"Not if you do things the way I tell you." Out of habit, he checked the sideview mirror again and saw no one.

"Your way."

"Yep."

She propped her elbow on the window ledge with a dramatic sigh. "Lord, spare me from a fanatical bodyguard."

"I told you. This wasn't my idea."

"Have you ever been to Sparta before?"

"Yes. Here's your exit."

"I know it's my exit." She lifted the blinker lever with a finger and slowed to make the turn off the interstate onto State Road 111. "I've never been to the Golden Eagle."

"Neither have I."

"So neither of us knows where we're going."

"We'll find it."

Sparta was a small town. A kid on roller blades could navigate his way around the place.

She kept her speed moderate and touched several buttons on the SUV's navigation system in the dashboard. A map appeared on the screen, showing the location of the motel, and she sat back in satisfaction.

Mick eyed the information displayed in front of him. In off-road mode, that same global positioning system could track their location anywhere. He frowned.

"What's the matter, Corrigan? Don't like modern technology?" she asked, her brow arched.

"It has its advantages."

"But you think it has disadvantages, too."

Grim, he glanced at her. "I know it does."

He didn't have to tell her why. She pulled her gaze from

the road and studied him for a long moment.

And for the first time since they left her father's office, worry shadowed her features.

# CHAPTER TWO

Mick scanned the cars and pickups lining both sides of Main Street. Nearly all of them were older models, showing wear and tear from hard use on rough mountain roads.

If the citizens of Sparta didn't know someone important had come to visit their little town, they did now. One look at the shining red Range Rover, at the top of the line in luxury for SUVs, said it all. M-O-N-E-Y. Annoyance rolled through him.

Adrienne turned off the ignition in front of the Golden Eagle Motel and Restaurant, unfastened her seat belt and reached for the door handle. Mick's hand snaked out and captured her wrist.

"Now that we're here, I'm laying down a few rules, Adrienne," he said. "From now on, I go everywhere with you. If you want a roll of breath mints, we buy it together. If you have to use the bathroom somewhere, I'm right outside waiting for you. If you want to go for a stroll, we walk together. We eat together. We--"

She pulled her arm away. Her gray-green eyes flashed. "I know the routine, Mick. As I recall, the last time you were my bodyguard, we even *slept* together."

His chest tightened at the bitter hurt in her tone, a hurt for which he was responsible. "Adrienne."

"But we both know that was a mistake, so we won't do it again, will we?"

"No," he said, his teeth clenched.

She tossed her head haughtily. "Let's see if I know the

drill. When we enter a building, you'll go in first. I always follow. If we're in a crowd, you'll be at my side, refusing to let anyone touch me. If we're on a sidewalk, I walk on the inside. You walk curbside. Have I forgotten anything?"

"You're a smart lady, Adrienne."

"That's right." Her tone chilled him. "Smarter now than I was then."

Her meaning wasn't lost on him, and she was out of the SUV before he could stop her. He longed to keep her strapped in her seat to give him a chance to explain. He wanted to convince her of all the times he thought of her. Worried for her. Lost sleep over her.

But given how much he hurt her, she wouldn't listen if he tried. Resigned, he hurried to catch up with her.

The Golden Eagle's rooms lined the north and south sides of the motel, with the restaurant in between. After checking in at the front desk, they located their rooms on the far northern end and parked the SUV directly outside. Mick unlocked the door to Adrienne's room first and stepped inside.

He ran a sweeping inspection about the sleeping area, then did the same with the bathroom. Everything appeared normal. The Golden Eagle was brand new, the one and only motel in Sparta, but the rooms were nothing out of the ordinary. Clean. Generic. He'd bet his own quarters would be an exact duplicate of Adrienne's.

He frowned at the realization no interior door connected them. "We need adjoining rooms."

"They don't have them. Best they could do is book us side by side."

"This isn't acceptable. Can't watch over you when a wall separates us."

"If I need you, I'll scream loud."

He was not amused. "Is that supposed to make me feel better?"

"You're just going to have to deal with it, Corrigan." She held the door open. "Now out. I have less than an hour to get ready."

Daniel Morelli made it perfectly clear Adrienne was to have twenty-four hour protection. Impossible, unless Mick slept in the same room with her--which was obviously out of the question--or at least had quick, easy access to it. And, unless he personally sawed a doorway out of the wall, Adrienne was right. Mick would have to do the best he could under the circumstances.

"My room number is 114," he said. "If you need me, call. Just put a '2' in front of--"

"I think I can figure it out."

His patience wavered. He had a job to do. Under the circumstances, *she* would have to deal with it, and that meant listening to--and obeying--the rules he made.

"I'll be okay, Mick," she said, as if she could read his thoughts. "It's only for an hour."

He didn't like leaving her where he couldn't see her, but he laid her briefcase and luggage on the bed, pocketed her extra room key and left.

* * *

Adrienne released a long breath. Now that Mick was gone, the tension seeped from her body. She didn't realize how uptight she'd been.

If only he didn't have this effect on her. If only she could put him from her mind, forget how she came dangerously close to falling in love with him six months ago. If only . . ..

Spearing a hand through her hair, she closed her mind to 'if onlys'. Minutes were ticking away. It would be seven o'clock before she knew it, and she couldn't let thoughts of Mick interfere in tonight's dinner. Too much was at stake. If she hurried, she could shower and dress and still have time to review her notes before she met with the representative from Murdock, Inc., and the Scott's Gulf Alliance.

Twenty minutes later, clad only in her bra and spandex slip, she stood in front of the bathroom mirror and applied her make-up. But only when she searched her cosmetic bag, dumping its contents on the sink to make sure she hadn't missed it, did she realize she'd forgotten her lipstick.

She needed lipstick. Never went without it. She wasn't particularly vain, but color on her lips ranked near the top of her must-have list, especially on a night like tonight.

Adrienne recalled seeing a drugstore on the corner. She had just enough time to run over and buy a new tube.

*I'm laying down a few rules, Adrienne.*

She glanced at the telephone. She had to call Mick.

*From here on out, I go everywhere with you.*

Through the shared plumbing of their bathrooms, she could hear the water running. Mick was taking a shower. If she called him now to go with her to the drugstore, he wouldn't hear the phone anyway, and never mind the time delay.

"This is ridiculous. I'm perfectly safe buying myself lipstick," she muttered out loud. She could be gone and back in less than ten minutes. He'd never know she left the room.

She rushed from the bathroom, plucked her black dress from its hanger and shimmied into it, then slid her feet into her shoes. Grabbing her room key and purse, she dashed out the door. Six minutes later, she stood at the cash register, a tube of lipstick on the counter in front of her.

The cashier eyed her with curiosity. "You new in town? Don't recall seeing you 'round these parts before."

Adrienne smiled politely. The woman appeared to be in her mid-forties, plain looking with brassy blonde hair that clearly came out of a bottle. "I'm here for a meeting."

"You must belong to that fancy SUV parked at the motel. Don't recall seeing any of those 'round here before, either."

"Yes, it's mine." Adrienne didn't bother explaining it wasn't really hers, but a rental. She extended her hand, a ten dollar bill between two fingers, and hoped the woman would take the hint.

"I can't imagine owning something that fancy. Why, all I got to drive is my ol' man's '79 Chevy pick-up. It don't look so good, but gets me where I need to go, I guess." She laughed.

Adrienne kept her smile in place and refrained from checking her watch.

The cashier scanned the bar code on the back of the packaged lip color. "What kind of meeting are you here for?"

"I'm with the state of Tennessee." Was the woman this friendly with all her customers?

"The State?" She halted, holding a plastic sack in mid-air. "Why, you ain't the Governor's daughter, are you?"

Adrienne eyed the sack. If the cashier didn't drop the lipstick inside real soon, Adrienne would do it herself. "Yes. I'm Adrienne Morelli."

"Why, you are, aren't you?" She was clearly awed. "Saw your picture in the weekend paper. You're here about that deed to two thousand acres of Scott's Gulf, aren't you? Wait 'til I tell my ol' man I met you. He'll be plumb tickled! You're *famous*!"

Her excitement would have been charming if Adrienne would've been of a mind to enjoy it.

"I'm not, but you're very kind to think so. Really,"--she made a show of peering at the woman's name badge--"Bess, I'm in a hurry. My meeting will start soon."

"Why, sure, Miss Morelli." This time, Bess moved a little faster, bagging the lipstick with a rustle of plastic. She took the ten dollar bill and made change, but in her fluster, had to count it out three separate times.

Adrienne stuffed the bills and coins into their proper compartments in her billfold and relayed her thanks.

"Wait, Miss Morelli."

Nine minutes since she'd left the motel. "Yes?"

Bess riffled through some papers stacked against the cash register, then opened the drawer. Clearly, she was in search of something. Finally, she settled for a pad of refund slips.

"Would you mind giving me your autograph?" she asked, ripping one sheet off and turning it over to its blank side.

"My Eugene just won't believe I met you!"

How could Adrienne refuse her? "Of course." Taking a pen, she wrote a brief message, offered her best wishes and signed her name. "There you go."

"Oh, Miss Morelli. *Thank* you!"

"You're quite welcome." Adrienne headed for the door.

Eleven minutes to buy lipstick. She was beginning to feel harried.

"Wait 'til I tell Eugene," Bess gushed behind her. "Have a nice evening, Miss Morelli."

"Thank you. You, too," she said in automatic response and practically ran out the door. She returned to the motel in less time than it took to leave it and darted a quick glance toward Mick's room. The drapes were still pulled; the door closed.

The last thing she needed was to alert him she'd been gone. He'd be done with his shower by now, she knew, sliding the key in her door as quietly as she could and envisioning him standing before the mirror, a towel wrapped around his lean hips. He was shaving perhaps, or pulling his wet hair back into its usual queue. There would be droplets of water on those strong shoulders of his, a fog of steam on the mirror. Maybe droplets on his chest, too, the skin glistening in places he'd missed with the towel.

Her belly curled at the image, and she stepped into her room, darker now than when she'd left it. She closed the door and turned the lock.

Adrienne frowned. She'd left the bathroom light on. She was sure of it. She distinctly remembered being in such a hurry that she didn't take the time--

A large hand clamped over her mouth. The nose of a gun pressed hard and cold against her temple, and Adrienne's eyes widened in terror. A scream shot upward into her throat; a man's iron-muscled arm hauled her against his body, jerked her head back against his shoulder, and pushed her roughly toward the bed.

Her mother's killer.

He found her, she thought in horror. After all these months, he *found* her, and now it was her turn, just as she'd always feared. Her turn to be killed in cold blood.

With the knowledge, the chilling reality of it, some hidden part of her found the will to fight back. Clawing at his forearm with her fingers, she writhed and twisted and lashed out with one leg, tangling her foot with his. They fell sideways onto the mattress, and he tossed the gun aside. She barely landed on the bedspread before those powerful arms twisted her from her front to her back, and he held her pinned beneath him on the bed.

She gaped up at him.

Mick.

*Mick!*

She cried out her outrage and pounded his shoulders and chest with her fists. He swore, grasped both her arms and held them high above her head.

She sucked in air. Her chest heaved from her exertions, from absolute fury, but he was breathing hard, too.

"Damn you, Corrigan!" she grated.

"Do you understand what it would've been like if it'd been your mother's killer waiting for you instead of me?" he demanded. His fingers tightened over her wrists. "*Feel* what it would have been like, Adrienne. You're powerless right now with me. You'd be powerless with him, too."

"Stop it, Mick." Her voice quavered, the ferocity of his words sinking into her comprehension like ice against her anger.

"It's my job to take any bullet intended for you. The killer would have had a gun. How can I protect you if I'm not with you? How can I protect you if you leave this damn room *and I don't even know it?*"

Adrienne had never seen him so furious. She knew she was in the wrong and hated it. "I'm sorry."

His breathing slowed. His control returned in degrees, and his fingers loosened over her wrists.

"I called you," he said, his voice still rough, but quieter.

"I couldn't hear your shower running anymore. Think of what I felt when you didn't answer. Or when I ran over here and found you gone."

She inhaled his heat, absorbed the weight of his body over hers. "I said I was sorry."

"Can you imagine what went through me?"

He was relentless in driving his point home. "Yes."

"I found your makeup all over the bathroom sink. Your purse was missing. I had a pretty good idea what you'd done. At least, I *hoped* I knew what you'd done."

"It was stupid of me." Guilty and humiliated, she wallowed in remorse. "I won't do it again."

"Damn right, you won't."

He shifted from her, easing onto his side. The air shimmered between them with volatile awareness, a delayed reaction to what just transpired between them.

And what might have been.

His knee wedged between her thighs. Her dress had hiked up near her hips, her bare skin sensitized to the fabric of his slacks against it. His face was close to hers. Too close. His dark, troubled eyes roamed over her face, drifted downward and settled on her mouth.

Adrienne turned her head away. She didn't want to know if he intended to kiss her. She didn't know if she could resist him if he tried when every brain cell in her head warned that she should.

She could so easily fall under Mick's spell again. She didn't want to need him like she'd needed him before. She didn't want to drown in his protective masculinity.

Like she was doing now. She scooted away from him and off the bed, then tugged her dress back down past her thighs and drew in a long, steadying breath.

"It's nearly seven. I have to finish getting ready," she said.

He got up, too. He was barefoot. Only a couple of buttons held his shirt together, a clear sign of his haste in throwing it on. He hadn't taken the time to tie his hair back, and it hung loose and wet on his shoulders.

"I'm going to finish dressing in here--with you," he said, his expression daring her to argue. Adrienne's brow rose, but she said nothing. He retrieved his Beretta. "I have to go next door to get my stuff. I'll be back in three minutes."

He made it back in two, but it was long enough for Adrienne to apply her lip color, then begin to work on her hair. While she wielded the straightener down the long strands, his image appeared next to hers.

She moved over to give him room. In a few deft strokes, he combed back his hair and tied a leather strip to hold the queue. He set the comb down and reached for his cologne.

"This is just a little too cozy, Corrigan," Adrienne frowned, watching him.

"Get used to it." The air filled with the expensive scent he rubbed onto his throat and face. "It's six thirty-two. Anything I can do to help you get ready?"

He put the bottle on the sink next to her body lotion and left the bathroom. An intimate thing, a man's cologne mixed in with a woman's toiletries. Adrienne refused to dwell on it.

"You can read my notes to me." Now that he was out of the tiny room, she set to work on her hair in earnest.

"Where are they?" He strapped on a shoulder holster and shrugged into his jacket.

"In my briefcase. There's a folder labeled 'Scott's Gulf.'"

After he located the notes, he sat on the side of the bed, facing her while she stood in the bathroom. He recited from the neatly typed pages, asking questions now and then, refreshing her memory on the more technical points of the deal. By the time he finished, she felt better prepared for the important meeting ahead of her.

But on an afterthought, Mick flipped back through several pages.

"What is this 'Mountain Crest Resort' you've noted?" he asked. "Someone wants to build a recreation area in Scott's Gulf?"

"Yes. The effort is backed by Bernard Webster, the

mayor of Sparta. The mere mention of the man's name raises my father's blood pressure. Webster will not be a happy man when Murdock, Inc., signs over the two thousand acres to us."

"He wants the money the resort will bring in for the area."

"Exactly." She glanced at her watch. Two minutes after seven. She grimaced. "I'm late."

"You're fine." He held her jacket for her, and she slipped her arms into the sleeves, then stole a few seconds to check her reflection.

There was a lot to be said for the 'little black dress,' her mother always claimed. Adrienne admitted her waist-length jacket lent an elegant touch to hers. With her auburn hair smoothed against her scalp and pulled back with a wide hair clip at her nape, she supposed she looked presentable enough.

"Nice," Mick murmured. "Very nice."

"This is as good as it gets." Adrienne had no illusions about her looks. Or her perception of them. She would never be as beautiful as Julia Morelli and had long since given up trying to be. She took her purse and briefcase and headed for the door, pausing while he locked the room behind them.

The restaurant required a leisurely walk from the outside. She fell into step with him and sensed his shrewd gaze upon her.

"You find your appearance lacking, Morelli?" he inquired.

"Let's just say my mother had the ability to knock the state of Tennessee's socks off when it came to dressing up. The press showed up in swarms just to photograph her."

"But if your mother stole the limelight, it was your father who put her there."

"Yes. In the short time he's been in office, he's done some wonderful things for the state. They both have." She glanced up at him, strong and tall in the evening light, and marveled at his perception. "She made him look good. They were the perfect team."

"And since then, you've taken her place."

"Yes. For Dad's sake. He needed me to." Adrienne had stepped into her mother's role, but it'd been a big role to fill. Adrienne had never favored the limelight.

"You've come a long way since she died, Morelli."

She opened her mouth to ask him how and why he would know such a thing, but his attention was diverted to the crowd hovering in front of the Golden Eagle Restaurant.

Adrienne's pulse faltered from an instant flare of panic before she repressed it. She always endured the panic, along with a deep-seated fear of a large group of people where her mother's killer might lurk.

She sensed the tension in Mick. The absolute alertness. He took her elbow and moved closer.

"Your fans await," he drawled.

"Or an enemy," she murmured.

A tiny muscle in his cheek moved. The crowd seemed to sense her arrival and turned, smiles breaking out on their faces. Someone held up a sign that read 'Save the Wilderness!'. Several chanted, "Thank you, Miss Morelli!"

Mick and Adrienne turned onto the sidewalk leading to the restaurant's brass-trimmed glass doors. The crowd pressed forward. Mick angled his body toward Adrienne's, his left hand still holding her arm, the right extended outward, preventing anyone from getting too close.

"Excuse us," he said again and again.

Suddenly, out of the blur of faces, a man in faded denim overalls appeared in front of them, and Adrienne halted with a startled gasp.

"Stay back, sir." The respectful command in Mick's voice held an underlying vein of steel.

The man stepped aside only a few feet. He stared at Adrienne beneath the brim of a battered straw hat, sweat-stained and worn through in places. Suspicion emanated from his sharp eyes.

"You're the one layin' claim to them two thousand acres

of Scott's Gulf, ain't you?" he demanded.

His hostility was a volatile thing. Adrienne chose her words with care.

"The state plans to acquire the land, yes," she said.

"Keep moving, Adrienne," Mick said, his voice low.

She gave the old man her full attention. She wondered how long it'd been since he bathed. He carried a definite odor about him. "Does this matter concern you, Mr.--?"

"Folks just call me Farley," he said, still glaring.

"Mr. Farley."

"And damn right it concerns me."

"Let me assure you the state's ownership of the land will mean nothing but good for all of us. The benefits are enormous." Daniel Morelli believed every Tennesseean's opinion mattered, and he'd taught Adrienne the same. She absorbed Farley's words and respected them.

"Hogwash!" he snapped. "Them benefits are just as good when it comes to linin' someone's pockets." He jabbed a knarled finger toward the range of mountains behind them. "Them hills up there is a gold mine. You claimin' to tell me and the rest of us that you and your pa and them government bigwigs you're workin' with ain't gonna do some benefittin' of your own?"

Adrienne's hackles rose at his accusation. Keenly aware of the crowd hanging on to every syllable, she kept her expression composed. "I assure you nothing of the sort will happen."

"Figured you'd say that." His weathered features showed his contempt. "They all do."

Her chin lifted. She was failing miserably at her attempts to placate the man. "Mr. Farley, I'll be happy to visit with you further at some point during my stay here in Sparta. "I'll--"

"Like hell you will," Mick muttered, low enough that Farley or the crowd didn't hear. His grip on her elbow tightened, and he forced her forward with a firm tug. "Excuse us, Mr. Farley. Miss Morelli is late for a meeting."

"Mick, wait," Adrienne protested, but already her feet were scurrying to keep up with him. She twisted to peer over his shoulder at the old man. For an instant, their gazes locked.

"You ain't heard the last from me," Farley shouted, his clenched fist punctuating the vow. "Y'hear me?"

Mick yanked the restaurant's glass door open and pushed Adrienne inside. The door swung closed behind them, and though Mick kept her moving, Adrienne twisted again, her eyes searching the faces of the crowd.

But Farley was already gone.

# CHAPTER THREE

⟡

"It's a good thing y'all are doing for us, Adrienne. I'm just so excited, I can hardly sleep at night." Izzie Stockton beamed and gave Adrienne's hand a grateful squeeze.

"I'm not the one to thank, Izzie. If not for Mr. Kershner and Murdock, Inc., none of us would be sitting at this table now." Adrienne smiled back. She genuinely liked the white-haired woman with the soft Southern drawl. Along with her husband of fifty-two years, Dietrich, she'd co-founded the non-profit corporate structure of Scott's Gulf Alliance.

"Murdock should be commended." Dietrich nodded. "With the signing of this deed, we'll have surpassed the half-way point of our goal to preserve what we feel is one of the few pristine areas left on the Cumberland Plateau."

"Well, we certainly see it as an ideal opportunity for the state of Tennessee to create a wilderness 'green belt' so to speak," Ronald Kershner, Murdock's representative, said. He unclasped his fingers from where they rested across his rounded belly and reached for his coffee cup.

"One that will join four separate counties," Izzie added.

Kershner sipped. "You all know how important it is to keep the momentum going."

Adrienne pushed aside her plate, her dinner finished. "You have my assurance we will cooperate with you and our state's Conservation Fund. Together, we can develop a long-term plan that will manage the environment, not only for these two thousand acres, but also for Murdock's property adjacent to the area."

"Very good." Kershner's smile competed with Izzie's for radiance.

"Plans for the Hickoryville ceremony are set. After tomorrow, the signing of the deed will be official." Izzie wiggled in her seat. "Don't know's that I can wait that long."

Adrienne had to agree. If it'd been up to her, the signing of the deed from Murdock to the state of Tennessee would have been done tonight, at this dinner. But the Scott's Gulf Alliance had campaigned for a different sort of ceremony, one that would be held in the tiny mountain town of Hickoryville, north of Sparta and the last patch of civilization before the wilderness.

It would be appropriate, she supposed, to have the deed officially transferred when they were surrounded by those who loved the area most and who would see the area unspoiled in its natural beauty for generations to come.

"So long as nothing goes wrong, tomorrow will be here before we know it," Dietrich assured her. "Weather promises to be fine, too."

"Farley had better not stir up trouble for us," Izzie said. "The old coot." Her sympathetic glance touched on Adrienne. "I know he was a bit of a bother to you tonight, but don't let him worry you, dear. Everyone knows he has a chip on his shoulder a mile wide, especially when the government is involved. Mostly, he just wants to be left alone. Don't reckon there's much that pleases him these days."

"He wasn't a bother at all. He just doesn't trust me." Adrienne hoped to meet with him again soon to smooth over his concerns. After all, he lived in this part of the country. He was entitled to her time and an explanation of the state's point of view.

"You're from Nashville and the Capitol building. That's reason enough in his mind not to trust you," Izzie said. "You haven't seen the last of him. I guarantee it."

"I'll be ready for him when I do." Adrienne smiled, as

much for Izzie's benefit as her own.

"Speaking of trouble," Dietrich grumbled. "Here comes the mayor."

Adrienne glanced up at the man approaching their table. For months, Mayor Bernard Webster had been a real thorn in her father's side, stopping just short of harassment in making his opinions against the Scott's Gulf land deed known.

He fought the state's--and Daniel Morelli's--plans to preserve the Tennessee wilderness with every weapon at his disposal. His desire to have a resort built in the Cumberlands clashed violently with Daniel's vow to prevent it. Intense lobbying and thousands of dollars had been poured into the effort from both sides.

Webster extended his hand. "Miss Morelli. Bernard Webster."

Despite his brusqueness, Adrienne gave him her brightest smile. "So pleased to finally meet you."

Bracing herself for his purpose in coming, she placed her hand in his for a firm handshake, keeping her appraisal of him discreet. He was a rather dowdy-looking man, given his worn leather shoes and ill-fitting suit. Or perhaps it was the graying sideburns, decades out of fashion, growing thick near his ears.

After seeing him, she wondered where he found the money to fund the intense lobbying. Certainly not with his own; it appeared as if he didn't have a spare dime to his name.

His glance took in the Stocktons and Ronald Kershner. "You're meeting about the Scott's Gulf deal, aren't you?"

"We are," Adrienne said.

"Let me remind you, Miss Morelli, our little town is desperate for the money a resort like Mountain Crest could bring in."

"My father and I feel it's far more important to keep this part of the country in its natural state. Murdock believes in the endeavor as strongly as we do."

"I suggest you rethink your position."

"It's too late for that, Mayor."

"Mountain Crest will put Sparta on the map!"

"And destroy part of Tennessee if it does," she shot back.

The mayor drew back with a sharp inhalation of breath.

"I'm sorry. Truly, I am," Adrienne said, wanting to make amends for her outburst. "In time, you'll see we're doing the right thing for our state. When I return to Nashville, I'll speak to my father about your concerns."

"He won't listen." The mayor's sideburns quivered with his indignation. "Let me warn you, young lady. There are men more powerful than your daddy who want a resort in these mountains. They'll do what they have to so's they get it. Back off now while you still can. Otherwise, you just might regret it."

He spun on his heel and stormed off. Adrienne stared open-mouthed after him.

"Well!" Izzie huffed. "First Farley, and now *him*."

"We're signing the deed tomorrow. The mayor will just have to accept it," Kershner added firmly.

"His bark is worse than this bite. Always has been," Dietrich nodded with an encouraging smile. "Don't you pay him no mind."

"That's right, dear." Izzie squared her shoulders. "Now, where's Denny Ray?" With the sudden change of topic, her gaze swept across the crowded restaurant. "Here it is, time for dessert, and that boy still hasn't showed up."

"Smart as he is, he never could tell time. Leastways when it came to being on time," her husband said, shaking his head. "He'll get here when he's good and ready."

Adrienne shook off the troubling thoughts the mayor invoked. Her glance touched on the empty chair at her left which had been reserved for Denny Ray Greer, a Tennessee Park Ranger. According to Izzie, he joined the Alliance nearly a year ago and was one of their most enthusiastic members. He'd insisted on being included in this dinner meeting, and her mouth pursed in disapproval of her own.

The least the man could do was show up.

The waitress removed their plates, then took orders for dessert. As if the end of the meal signaled an end to the business portion of their meeting, too, conversation drifted onto other subjects, most of them involving Izzie and Dietrich's grandchildren.

Adrienne was glad for the reprieve. For the first time since she arrived in Sparta, she allowed herself to relax and didn't join in with the others' chatting. Involuntarily, her glance slid across the room to find Mick.

He stood against one wall of the restaurant. Tall, feet spread, hands clasped behind his back, he could have passed as a member of the Golden Eagle's management. His scrutiny continually ran over the dinner crowd, those dark eyes seeming to miss nothing as they touched on everyone in an unobtrusive investigation of their presence in the room. Adrienne doubted the patrons even realized he was there.

She couldn't help it, but her gaze clung to him. The dim lighting accentuated his Cherokee heritage--the sun-bronzed angles of his face, the square set to his jaw, his silent strength. Her blood warmed just looking at him.

The man still had power over her. She found herself wishing he would come over and join her, to sit in the chair saved for Denny Ray and have dessert with her.

But, of course, he wouldn't do that. He had a job to do. He'd stay in the background and remain detached, one of the rules in his strict code of conduct while being her bodyguard.

Well, she'd remain detached, too. She became involved with Mick once before and suffered from it. It wouldn't happen again.

The restaurant's brass-trimmed doors opened, and a man dressed in a navy pin-striped suit rushed in. Tanned and muscular, he spoke briefly to the restaurant's hostess, and she turned, leading him to Adrienne's table.

Mick's stare pinned on him from the moment he arrived. Adrienne wondered if she saw a glimmer of recognition in his features. If it'd been there, though, he banked it as quickly as it appeared.

"Why, Denny Ray, doggone you, I was beginning to think you'd forgotten all about us," Izzie said, exasperation evident in her tone. "Glad to see you could join us after all."

Denny Ray bent down and pressed a kiss to her wrinkled cheek. "Sorry, Izzie. I had a flat tire on the highway coming in. Forgive me?"

He flashed her a dazzling smile, and the exasperation dissipated from the older woman.

"I'll forgive you, just like I always do, you rascal." She chuckled, as if she knew how easily he'd charmed her. "Got the tire fixed okay?"

"Just fine." He turned to Adrienne. For a moment, he didn't say anything, but studied her in a way that might have stolen her breath if she'd been easily swayed. "So this is Adrienne Morelli."

Her mouth softened at the huskiness in his tone. A woman had to keep her guard up with this one. "So it is."

"I see you in the papers and on the news." Hazel eyes melded with hers. "The cameras don't do you justice."

The man was smooth. Very smooth. She allowed herself a small smile. "Why, thank you."

"You're welcome." He maneuvered his chair at an angle that kept her in his full view. He crossed his arms over the table top and lavished her with his complete attention. "Tell me about this meeting I've missed."

She exchanged an amused glance with Izzie, and between the two of them, brought him up to date on all that transpired during dinner, ending with the encounter with the mayor. Denny Ray was keenly interested, and she found herself liking him, despite his flamboyant manner.

Conversation remained animated through dessert until it was time to leave. Engrossed in a discussion with Adrienne on the state's continued efforts to cultivate the near-extinct species of the Tennessee coneflower, Denny Ray kept close to her side as they left the restaurant. Her senses clued her in when Mick followed closed behind.

Dusk had fallen. Blended hues of red and orange blanketed the horizon, the final traces of a sun that would be gone in but a few minutes' time. Denny Ray pulled his shirt cuff back, revealing the gold watch strapped about his wrist. Adrienne couldn't help noticing the fine quality of the piece, strikingly unique with an engraving of a peregrine falcon carrying a branch in its beak.

He released a low whistle. "This late already?" Gleaming white teeth showed in yet another radiant smile directed at Adrienne. "Time flies with a beautiful woman."

"Well, figuring you missed three-fourths of the meeting and didn't even eat, no wonder the night seems short for you." Izzie shook her finger at him.

"Don't scold me, darlin'. I already said I was sorry, and you promised to forgive me."

"If you want to be in on the doin's at the Hickoryville ceremony tomorrow, you'd best try a little harder to be on time. You won't get another chance for a celebration like this one."

"I will, Izzie." Denny Ray's features appeared genuinely contrite. "Promise."

She turned to Adrienne. "You're planning on staying at our cabin tomorrow night, aren't you?"

Adrienne's mind sifted through the itinerary she and Renee had arranged. "I am."

Dietrich withdrew an envelope from inside his suit coat. "Here's directions up the mountain. Our place is a tad hard to find if you don't know where you're going. Key's in here, too."

"This is very generous of you," Adrienne said, taking the envelope from him. "Thank you."

"Hickoryville isn't big enough to have its own motel, so we're happy to let you use it. The refrigerator is stocked. Help yourself to anything you need." Izzie cast a pointed glance toward Mick, standing discreetly in the shadows of the Golden Eagle. "The place has two bedrooms," she added, lowering her voice. "One for each of you."

"That's good to know," Adrienne said soberly. *More than you realize.*

"We'll see you tomorrow then."

Adrienne shook hands with both the Stocktons and Ronald Kershner. After exchanging pleasantries, they departed.

"So who's the goon?" Denny Ray asked, in no hurry to leave with them.

"Goon?" She glanced over her shoulder. "You mean Mick?" She resented the term being applied to him. "He's an associate of mine."

"Your bodyguard, you mean."

Her chin lifted. Why did he have to sound belligerent about it? "Yes."

"Because of what happened to your mother?"

"Yes." He would know of her death, of course. Most everyone in Tennessee did. She extended an arm toward Mick, an invitation to join them. "Mick, I'd like you to meet--"

"I know him." Mick moved into the glow from the restaurant's gaslights, halting beside Adrienne. He made no effort to shake the other man's hand.

"Corrigan." Denny Ray appeared taken aback.

Animosity shimmered between them. Adrienne regarded Mick uncertainly. "You two have been acquainted before, then."

"A while ago." The set of his jaw seemed more taut than usual.

"Been a long time, buddy."

"Yeah."

"Didn't know you were still 'round these parts."

"I'm not, most of the time."

Clearly, Mick was in no mood for polite conversation. Denny Ray turned back to Adrienne.

"He never was much of a talker." He flashed a disarming grin. "Mind if I walk you to your room?"

"Of course not."

And she didn't, not when a stubborn side of her wanted to rebel against Mick for his rudeness. Denny Ray turned in the direction of their rooms, and she fell into step with him, their stroll unhurried.

"I'd like to get together with you in Hickoryville," he said. "I discovered a cluster of roosting cavities of red-cockaded woodpeckers near there the other day. Far as I know, the cluster isn't documented. Thought maybe you'd be interested in seeing it with me."

"I'd love to."

"The species is on the endangered list, and the cavities are a real find since no one knows they exist."

"I'm thinking of the photo op. The media will have a heyday."

"Shhh." He draped an arm casually about her shoulders and put a finger to his lips. His eyes twinkled. "This is our secret. I haven't told anyone yet. Let's just wait until we can take some pictures for the press, okay?"

"Sure." She smiled. She held no doubt women were not a problem for this man. He had flirting down to a science. "We'll plan on it."

"Shall we set a time?"

The sudden screeching of brakes startled her from making a response. Mick yelled her name and grabbed her arm, yanking her away from Denny Ray on the sidewalk to safety on the grass with him. Tottering on her dressy heels, she stumbled awkwardly, and his arms tightened around her, keeping her steady.

An aging Studebaker pickup the color of a Cumberland forest careened from the street and headed toward the curb. Denny Ray spat an epithet and jumped back. With its cargo of small animal cages wobbling in the back end, the green truck veered sharply again, away from the sidewalk and back onto the street where it belonged. The Studebaker disappeared around the corner, and within moments, the roar from its battered muffler faded.

"Oh, my God." Adrienne pressed a hand against the

thundering in her breast. "Did anyone get a license number?"

"I know who it was," Denny Ray said. "Everyone around here does." Anger darkened the hazel of his eyes. "That damn rattle-trap ought to be hauled to the junkyard, and Farley right along with it."

"Does he always drive like that?" Mick asked. "Or was his recklessness intentional?"

"Both," Denny Ray said.

Adrienne gasped. "But he could have killed you."

His glance burned into her. "Or you."

"Me?" Her blood ran cold.

Mick stiffened and swore.

"You're the important one in town." Denny Ray's gaze remained serious. "He knew what he was doing. Don't think he didn't. Consider this little episode a message. A warning of sorts." He hesitated. "Do you know why he might be upset with you?"

She thought of the incident in front of the Golden Eagle before dinner, Farley's suspicions regarding the state's acquisition of the deed to Scott's Gulf. She thought, too, of Mayor Webster. "Well, yes, but--"

"Adrienne has done nothing to upset anyone, Denny Ray," Mick interrupted. "Quit insinuating that she has."

Irritation darkened the other man's expression. "I'm not insinuating anything, Corrigan."

She turned toward Mick. "You know Farley was upset with me and the government in general. You heard him yourself."

"I don't know anything at this point. Neither do you." His glance slammed into Denny Ray's. "Or you." He took Adrienne's arm in a firm grasp. "So let's quit speculating and get back to our rooms."

He planted his hand on the small of her back and urged her onto the sidewalk. She refrained from arguing, but worry had set in, and she wouldn't forget Farley until she was safely back in Nashville.

"Now, where were we?" Denny Ray smiled down at her.

"Hickoryville, wasn't it?"

"Yes." Adrienne's brain scrambled to focus on the conversation they'd had before Farley nearly ran them over. "And the red-cockaded woodpeckers."

He took her elbow and tugged, but Mick's hand stubbornly tightened on her waist. Denny Ray speared him with an irritated glance. "Do you mind, Corrigan?"

"As a matter of fact, I do."

"Mick." Adrienne pushed against him, not bothering to hide her impatience. He was taking this bodyguard thing too far. She had state business to do with Denny Ray, and right now, Mick's opinion of the man was irrelevant.

He released her, but anyone could see his displeasure from doing so. They resumed walking toward the far northern end of the motel where their rooms were located.

"How about I meet you in Hickoryville at 2:00 tomorrow afternoon?" Denny Ray asked. "There's a little café everyone just calls 'The Diner'. You can't miss it. It's the only one in town."

"The Diner at two." She nodded and filed the information away in her head.

He bent closer. "Leave your goon behind, will you?"

If he used that word for Mick one more time, she'd smack him for it. "I don't think so."

Mick would never allow it, and did she really want to be alone with Denny Ray anyway? He had 'womanizer' written all over him.

"We won't need him there," he insisted.

She strove to be gracious and managed to smile. "The decision is mine, Denny Ray. Where I go, he goes."

He shrugged, giving up. "Hey." They drew closer to Rooms 114 and 116. "A Range Rover. This yours?"

Adrienne had never driven a vehicle that drew more attention than this one, but she was glad for the distraction it provided. "Yes."

He whistled in appreciation. "Nice. Red?"

Nightfall darkened the true color, making it difficult to

decipher. "Yes. Metallic."

"*Very* nice."

Mick jangled the room keys. "Say good-by, Adrienne. It's late."

She swiveled toward him, leveling him with a 'you're not my baby-sitter' look. Which he pointedly ignored.

Denny Ray sighed dramatically. He took her hand and dropped a warm kiss upon her knuckles. "I'll see you tomorrow afternoon."

"Of course." She withdrew her hand. "It was nice meeting you."

The feel of his lips lingered on her skin. The sensation left her feeling vaguely unsettled.

He saluted Mick. "Later, buddy."

Adrienne could almost hear Mick's teeth grind. Denny Ray slid both hands into his pockets and sauntered back toward the front of the motel, humming a simple tune she didn't bother to identify.

Mick unlocked Adrienne's door and ushered her inside. Following her in and turning the bolt, he snapped up the light switch, then tossed both room keys on the nearest table.

Adrienne spun to face him.

"Your behavior with him was despicable," she said, her tone frosty.

"The man is an ass."

"The man is a member of the Scott's Gulf Alliance."

"So what if he is?"

"He should have been treated with the same respect you gave the Dietrichs and Ronald Kershner. You know how important this deed is to Tennessee. All it would take is for Denny Ray to make a fuss about how you treated him, and the whole deal could be off."

"That's won't happen, Adrienne."

"How do you know?"

"Just call it a gut feeling."

He didn't elaborate, and she recalled how close-mouthed he could be. When he was ready to tell her more, he would.

"Why was he late for dinner?" Mick asked.

"He had a flat tire." She cocked her head. "You recognized him right away, didn't you?"

"Yes."

"How?"

"I used to live in the area. Long time ago."

"He didn't notice you at the restaurant."

"He was too busy drooling over you."

She considered him a long moment. The irritation still emanated from him. He looked grouchy. Peevish.

"I think you're jealous." The certainty of it brought an incredulous smile to her lips.

He pulled off his jacket, tossed it onto the chair. He refused to look at her. "I'm just hungry. I should have grabbed something at the restaurant."

"Oh." She'd forgotten the white sack she carried. She held it out to him. "Here you go. I bought you some supper."

He took the bag and removed the Styrofoam container from inside. He flipped the lid open, and his dark brow rose in surprise.

"I hope it's not too cold by now." She felt guilty ordering him a hamburger to go when she'd had steaming hot Cordon Bleu for dinner.

"Double patty?" he asked. His mouth, normally so hard, softened into a pleased half-smile.

Illogical pleasure swept through her. "With an extra order of bacon on top. And a side of Ranch for the fries."

"The way I like it." The huskiness of his voice skidded over her nerve endings, turning her soft inside. "You haven't forgotten, have you?"

"No."

She'd tried. God alone knew how she'd tried.

She turned away. Setting her purse and briefcase on the bed, she fumbled with her hair clip.

Yes, she'd admit that much to him. She hadn't forgotten the little things. How he preferred his cola, mixed half regular, half diet. His fetish for neatness, except when he read the newspaper and lazily scattered loose pages around him. His passion for sports, fast cars and late night television.

"Thanks for thinking of me, Morelli."

In that silent stealth of his, he'd moved up behind her. She could feel his heat, the breadth of it, against her body.

Her fingers turned into thumbs. The barrette refused to cooperate.

"Let me help." His warm breath drifted across her nape. With the barest touch of his hand against hers, the clip snapped open. "There."

For a moment, she remained where she was, absorbing his nearness and wanting to lean back into him, feel his arms encircle her waist and draw her close.

In the next, she stepped aside.

"Thank you." She forced herself to breathe, to shake her hair out over her shoulders. She couldn't let him affect her like this. "What would you like to drink with your hamburger, Mick? I could run to the store and get you a couple of beers or--or something."

Of course, he wouldn't let her out of his sight for a beer run. The idea was ridiculous. Why had she even suggested it?

Because the man turned her brain to mush. She couldn't think straight when he was around.

"Water will be fine." His voice was low. Gentle. Did he know the effect he had on her?

"I'll get it for you." Anything to stay away from him. She recalled seeing several cups wrapped in clear plastic in the bathroom, next to the coffee pot. If only the room had a microwave too. "Sit and eat before the food gets any colder."

She turned on the bathroom light.

And stared at the words scrawled on the mirror.

*Wild blue phlox splattered red*
*Forget the land deed, or you'll be dead*

Horror choked the air from her lungs. No one knew

about the flowers her mother had been picking the afternoon she died. Their species had never been noted by the police or released to the media.

No one would have known Julia Morelli wanted a bouquet of wild blue phlox to put on the picnic table that day.

No one but her killer.

Adrienne screamed.

# CHAPTER FOUR

The sandy-haired policeman, his badge identifying him as Officer Tim Radley from the Sparta Police Department, carefully dabbed the dried blood from the mirror with a moistened cotton swab. He glanced at Mick. "We don't have a crime lab here in Sparta, so we're going to send the evidence to Knoxville."

"How long before you get the results?" Mick asked grimly.

"Could be a week or so."

Impatience swept through him. The officer might as well have said a month.

He couldn't get answers soon enough about whose blood was on the mirror. Had the killer struck again? Bled his victim in a sick attempt to scare Adrienne out of her wits?

Mick slid his troubled gaze toward her. She huddled in the chair next to the bed, her knees drawn up to her chest as if she were cold, even though he'd draped his black suit coat snugly about her. Her features were drawn, haunted, and she seemed to stare at nothing. As if she lived a nightmare that wouldn't end.

He turned back to the officer. "That's too long. Put a rush on it."

"I'll do what I can." He appeared to take no offense at the command in Mick's tone. He was a rookie, late twenties maybe, and what he lacked in experience, he made up for in his willingness to help.

Of course, the launch of an investigation which most likely involved the murderer of the governor's wife helped. And having his daughter, pale and shaken, in the room only added to the urgency.

"Whoever this guy is knew what he was doing. The place is clean of prints." A second officer, Radley's partner, removed his rubber gloves and discarded them.

"I'm not surprised," Mick said. "He wouldn't be sloppy." Not someone who managed to evade arrest after all this time without leaving behind a single clue--with the exception of the bullet fired from his gun.

Radley dropped the dried cotton swab into a paper envelope. "We'll wrap things up, then. It's after midnight. You two need to get some sleep if you can."

With the key piece of evidence ready to send to the crime lab, he began cleaning the mirror of its disconcerting message. The mild scent of a bleach and water solution wafted through the bathroom. In a few moments, all traces of blood had been removed.

"I'll call you as soon as I hear anything," Officer Radley said, packing up. "A day or two at the most."

It wouldn't be soon enough. Mick wanted answers *now*, but he nodded and they exchanged phone numbers.

"You sure you don't want me to leave an unmarked car for surveillance outside?" Radley asked. His sympathetic glance touched on Adrienne. "Might make Miss Morelli feel better."

"Whoever was here won't be back, at least not tonight," Mick said. A killer who made himself known only now, after six months, wouldn't risk detection by appearing twice in a matter of hours.

"I'm inclined to agree, but I thought I'd offer for her sake. You'll stay with her, then?"

"Yes. She won't be alone tonight."

The officer nodded in approval. "I'll be in touch."

Both policemen left, and Mick locked the door after them. He turned toward Adrienne. Her head lifted, and their eyes met.

The unmistakable shimmer of tears pulled at him, and he hunkered in front of her, wanting to take her into his arms but not allowing himself the privilege. She was too vulnerable. Hell, right now, they both were.

"I can't believe he was here, Mick." Adrienne's voice was barely above a whisper. Traces of fear and horror laced her words. "In this room." She drew her body into a tighter ball, as if she tried to keep from touching anything he might have touched. "Do you think he sat in this chair?"

"No." This time, Mick did reach for her, grasping her shoulders in a firm grip. Her fear ate at him. "He wasn't here long, Adrienne. He only wanted to leave you a message. It was his perverted way of letting you know he was around."

Her eyes closed. "I don't know if I can deal with this again."

His grasp tightened. "I'll do everything I can to keep him from getting to you."

Her throat moved, her eyes opening again. "You're not invincible, Mick. He could kill me when you're standing right next to me."

He couldn't deny it, and he refused to be less than honest with her.

"The blood on the mirror was a hell of a piece of evidence," he said, using a different tactic to allay her fear. "We'll know more about him in a day or two."

"Like maybe he killed someone else besides my mother?"

His jaw tightened. "Yes."

Her head lolled back against the chair. A tight groan escaped her.

"If he did kill someone else, it would open up a whole new set of leads, wouldn't it?" he said, appealing to the sharp logic he always associated with her. "And if he didn't kill anybody, if the blood was, say, his--"

Skepticism formed in her features. "He wouldn't be so stupid as to use his own blood, Mick, would he?"

"Everybody makes mistakes. Even murderers. Come on. Up." He took her hand and pulled her from the chair. He'd had enough conversation. Enough speculation. "Get your things together," he said. "I'm taking you back to Nashville."

She jerked her hand from his. "*What?*"

"You can be in your own bed before dawn. You're safer at home."

"I can't leave."

"You're an open target here."

"People are counting on me to be in Hickoryville tomorrow. I mean, today. I'm going to be there. I have to be."

"Those same people are *not* counting on you being stalked by your mother's killer."

"I know that. But this--this psycho wants me to just walk away from two thousand acres of Scott's Gulf. He wants to win. And you want me to let him?"

She had Mick there. But his worry for her safety overrode all else. He had to admit, if he were in her position, he wouldn't want to give up, either.

He let out a long, frustrated breath.

Her chin lifted to a triumphant tilt.

Seeing it, he scowled. "You're a stubborn woman, Morelli."

She seemed to stand a little taller, her determination to secure the Scott's Gulf land deed for Daniel taking precedence over her fear of the man who only hours ago had threatened her life.

"Yes," she said quietly. "The murderer succeeded in stopping the land deal when he killed my mother, if only for a little while. I don't want him to succeed ever again."

Understanding, Mick nodded. "I know."

She drew in a breath, then let it out again. "When it comes to protecting me, we'll do things your way," she said, reminding him of his orders to her upon their arrival in Sparta. "But when it comes to accepting that beautiful wilderness for the state of Tennessee, we'll do things my way. Got it, Corrigan?"

His mouth softened at her bossiness. "Got it."

"One more thing. Not a word of any of this to my father," she said.

"He deserves to know what happened tonight."

"He'll be scared to death for me."

Daniel had given Mick strict orders to keep him informed. An ominous threat scrawled in blood on his daughter's bathroom mirror sure as hell qualified for a late night phone call.

Mick debated his reply with a thorough consideration of the woman before him. Frightened and susceptible, she inspired a fierce possessiveness in him. A very male go-through-fire-to-save-her instinct. But her decisive attitude, her level-headedness and strong will, inspired his respect. Admiration.

And desire.

How could he deny her anything?

\* \* \*

They left the Range Rover in its parking place and took another room several doors down. Despite the late hour, the motel manager had been quick to comply with Mick's request for a change of quarters. He'd been dismayed and worried at learning of Adrienne's death threat and delivered a new key within minutes. He left with repeated offers to call if they needed anything else.

Adrienne was only too glad to gather her things and pack them hastily back into her luggage. The place had been tainted by the killer's presence. The less time she spent there, the better.

After giving the new room the usual sweep, Mick hustled her in, his sharp gaze raking over the parking lot and beyond before he followed her in and closed the door with a firm latch. He turned the lock, slid the chain into place. If someone lurked in the shadows, watching their change of location, it couldn't be helped. Adrienne took comfort in the door's security, in the heavy drapes over the windows.

And Mick.

She didn't want to be alone tonight. Not with the risks of her mother's killer coming back or of him knowing she'd moved to a different place. For now, at least, she was safe. She ran a glance around the perimeter of the room, noting how little it differed from the one they'd just vacated.

That it contained only a single, king-sized bed.

"Don't worry, Adrienne. After what you've been through, I won't force you to sleep with me, too."

She stiffened. Mick's voice had an edge to it. An unexpected roughness. Did he remember their last night together, how they'd made love, again and again, in *her* king-sized bed?

One look at the fevered depths of his eyes told her he did.

"We could request another room," she said, her pulse faltering at her own memories. "One with double beds. Or-- or something."

"We were lucky to get this one. The motel's pretty much booked for the night." He gave their key an impatient toss onto the top of the nearest table. "Take the bed. I'll sleep in the chair."

She hadn't expected him to take her suggestion of finding yet another room, of course. It was after one o'clock in the morning. They'd done enough to risk the curiosity of the other motel guests as it was.

"All right, then."

She felt guilty for agreeing. The chair didn't look big enough to hold him with any degree of comfort. But she didn't have any other choice.

Sharing the bed was not an option.

She removed his suit coat from her shoulders and shivered a little at the loss of its warmth. After hanging the garment on a hanger, she slipped her shoes off, retrieved her nightgown from her suitcase and headed for the bathroom.

* * *

Mick's nerves were coiled tight with tension.

The night's events proved without question Adrienne needed constant protection. The old man, Farley, had turned out to be an unexpected threat. So did Sparta's hostile mayor, Bernard Webster.

Both men were suspect. But if the lab results proved neither of them had scrawled the deadly message on Adrienne's mirror, then who had?

Mick leaned his head back against the chair. He'd never forgive himself if something happened to her. Daniel had entrusted him with massive responsibility. What if he failed? What if everything Griffin Silverhawk had ever taught him in protecting a client still wasn't enough to keep Adrienne from getting killed?

She'd only been in Mick's protection for less than twenty-four hours. They still had another couple of days to go before he could bring her safely home. All kinds of danger could erupt before then.

And if that weren't enough, he had to get through the night with her. Tomorrow night, too.

Some things in life could be real hell.

The bathroom door opened, and his thoughts scattered. Adrienne stood in the doorway, her black dress and shoes clutched to the front of her like a shield--an attempt at modesty when he already knew the warm, silken feel of her naked body beneath his. And every delicious dip and curve.

If anything, she was more woman now than six months ago. His stare moved from the tips of her French-manicured toenails up to finely-muscled legs and gently rounded hips. She wore a short satin nightgown that shimmered fire-engine red in the light, its hem hanging at the middle of her thigh and doing little to keep his imagination from jumping into overdrive.

"Don't look at me like that, Mick," she said, the words soft and unsteady.

His gaze connected with hers. "Can't help it. I like the view."

She pressed the dress and shoes tighter against her. "I didn't bring a robe. I didn't know we'd be roomies."

She sounded so defensive and nervous, he almost felt sorry for her. But not enough to stop looking. "Funny how best laid plans go awry, isn't it?"

Her lips thinned. "I don't think this is funny at all."

One of those skimpy straps on her gown slipped off her shoulder. He followed its descent onto her arm before she yanked it up again.

His groin went tight. He crossed his leg, squaring his ankle over his knee, hiding his arousal from her. His libido raced like a teenager's.

She turned from him, throwing her dress and jacket onto its hanger without her usual neatness. Her shoes landed on the floor with twin thuds. Her bra and slip dropped into her suitcase.

She stepped to the bed, bending over to yank back the covers and gifting him with a hitch of her nightgown and a glimpse of her delectable, matching-red-panties-clad bottom.

He swallowed hard and watched her slide into bed with more haste than was necessary, settle to a sitting position, then pull the covers clear to her neck.

"This is all your fault, you know," she said, adjusting the pillows with jerky movements.

He stiffened at her sudden accusation. "Because we're here together in this room?"

"That we're both thinking about the same thing. And you're looking at me like you could strip every thread from my body. We both know this is the absolute *last* place we should be. Together in a motel room, that is."

His eye narrowed. "There's no other option for your safety and protection."

She drew her knees up to her chest. One hand clutched the covers and kept them pressed to her breasts. She drew in a shaky breath.

"You left me," she said.

The reproach in her words was like a splash of icy water.

They cooled the fire in his blood and sent his lusty thoughts spiraling back to reality.

The truth of the past. From the moment they saw each other again in her father's office, it had been between them. Unspoken, but not forgotten. Now, she laid it all on the table.

"Yes," he said. Abruptly, he stood and, turning from her, removed his holster and yanked his shirt from the waistband of his pants. "You were a client. I had no business getting involved with you."

"That's right. A client. Someone you were getting paid to pass the time with."

His fingers halted their unbuttoning. He swiveled to face her again. "I wasn't just passing time with you, Adrienne. You know that."

She flinched at the sharpness in his tone. "I don't know anything, Mick. Not then. Not now. How could I, when you didn't even give me the courtesy of a 'Gee, thanks for a fun roll in the sheets, Adrienne, but I'm leaving you, and I'm not even going to tell you good-bye'?"

He stilled at the hurt in her words. At the brutal honesty in them. "It was easier that way. For both of us."

She made a sound of disbelief. "Easier?"

He yanked the shirt off his shoulders, hurled it into his garment bag. As it always did, the pain from his decision slashed through him. "Leaving you that morning was the hardest thing I'd ever done in my life."

"Sure it was."

His gaze snapped to hers. "I'm not lying to you."

"I gave you my--I gave you a very important part of me. You just threw it back in my face." She speared slender fingers through her hair, sweeping the auburn strands from the side of her face. "God, what a stupid fool I was."

"The relationship had to end. I couldn't protect you when my mind was--" He halted. What could he say? That she kept him tied in knots from wanting her? That she screwed up his thinking? That he was so consumed by desire that being her bodyguard would only be a dangerous failure for them both?

He clenched a fist and tried again. "What you gave me that night was pretty damned special, however old-fashioned that may sound. Don't think it didn't mean something to me."

"And still you left."

"Yes," he said, between his teeth.

"I'm sorry, Corrigan, but I'm having trouble with your line of thinking." She slid deeper under the covers and stared up at the ceiling. "Well, I'm your client all over again, through no choice of my own, so you can relax. I'm not going to get involved with you because neither one of us is going to make the same mistake twice. You're going to just do your job, the way my father is paying you to do." He detected a slight hitch in her breathing. "And I'll do my job. In a few days, this whole thing will be over. You'll take me back to Nashville, and we'll never see each other again." Her head swiveled on the pillow. Her expression turned cool and detached. "Tell me that's the way it's going to be, Corrigan."

She was a problem-solver. Factual and thorough and more than a little bossy. Her brain continually formed a game plan and focused on it. Since her mother's murder, it had been her key to surviving.

It rankled Mick that he was a problem for which she needed a solution. But two could play her game, especially when she'd smoothly provided the answer to his own problem.

His mouth formed a grim, determined line.

"That's exactly the way it's going to be, Morelli."

# CHAPTER FIVE

The next morning, Adrienne gathered her makeup from the bathroom vanity, tucked the cosmetic bag into her suitcase and zipped it closed. After a final inspection, she was satisfied she'd left none of their belongings behind.

Sunshine streamed through the open door. Mick had moved the Range Rover to a parking place directly outside their room and waited for her on the sidewalk, a cell phone pressed to his ear, one foot propped on the SUV's open tailgate.

His own bag had already been stowed. She needed only to walk a few steps out and put hers next to it. Instead, Adrienne held back a few minutes to study him.

He was dressed in tight-fitting jeans and a navy blue polp that clung to his shoulders and broad back. He wore them as well as he'd worn the expensive black suit last night. But then, with a body as hard and contoured with muscle as his, anything would look good on him.

Or then again, nothing at all.

He'd barely spoken a dozen words to her throughout the morning. The thought brought a pout to her mouth and disappointment into her mood.

She didn't regret reminding him of how he left that morning all those months ago. It was an obstacle between them that needed to be removed. She made her point. He made his. She wouldn't bring it up again.

It was far better to keep their relationship businesslike and professional, she assured herself for the hundredth time that morning. Platonic. And safe.

He glanced up at her, then, and caught her looking at him. His phone conversation halted in mid-sentence, and he stared back, his black eyes drifting over her face, her hair. So intense, those eyes. She wondered what he was thinking.

He seemed to regain his train of thought with some degree of difficulty and ended the conversation soon afterward.

"Ready to go?" he asked, straightening.

"Yes. Who were you talking to?"

"Grif."

"And?"

"I asked him to check into a few things for me." Mick took her luggage, swept it up next to his, and shut the tailgate. A few strides took him to the passenger side of the SUV, and he opened the door. "Get in. It's late."

He obviously wasn't going to elaborate on his conversation with Griffin Silverhawk. She closed up their room and climbed into the SUV. He latched the door behind her, his vigilant gaze on the other motel guests bustling about, but no one paid them any mind. He settled into the driver's seat, slipped on his sunglasses, and pushed the ignition button.

"I'm sorry I overslept," Adrienne said, wanting to make amends if he was annoyed with her for sleeping later than she should. He'd already shaved and dressed before she ever got out of bed.

She declined to mention sleep had been elusive once the lights went out last night. When she wasn't thinking of her mother's killer, she was thinking of Mick. She'd been acutely aware of his presence, his breathing . . . his discomfort. It hadn't felt right to have that big bed to herself, and she'd wrestled with the temptation to rescind her demand they not sleep together. Which only sent her restless thinking into a whole new direction.

"Forget it. If I'd wanted you up earlier, I would've awakened you," he said.

"I'm sure the chair was uncomfortable. I covered you with an extra blanket during the night."

"I know you did. Thanks."

He wasn't going to make it easy for her with his clipped responses. Obviously, he was more upset with her than she thought. She lapsed into a troubled silence.

He pulled away from the motel, drove a short distance down Main Street and turned into a self-serve filling station that advertised a snack shop inside. After parking, he turned toward her. "I need to gas up before we head to Hickoryville. You want anything to eat while we're here?"

"You never finished your hamburger last night, did you?" She frowned. Only now did she think of it. He had to be starved. "We could find a restaurant somewhere, and you can have a hot breakfast."

"I want you out of here. We're behind schedule," he said.

The time didn't concern her as much as his empty stomach. Or her guilt for sleeping later than she should have. "Maybe we can grab a bite to eat at the Golden Eagle."

"They don't serve breakfast. Not even continental. I checked." He draped a muscular arm over the steering wheel. "Which brings me back to my original question. You want something to eat?"

She couldn't see his eyes through the dark lenses of his sunglasses, but the timbre of his voice had mellowed. Was there a hint of amusement in its tone? She couldn't be sure, but maybe he wasn't as miffed with her as she thought.

"Sure," she said.

"Stay here while I fill up. We'll go inside together."

She knew better than to argue; for security reasons she must remain in the vehicle. While he fueled, she retrieved the credit card from her briefcase lying on the back seat. She removed her cell phone from her purse and laid it next to his on the console.

After the tank was full, Mick walked with her into the station's snack shop. The pungent smell of gasoline and oil from the garage next door assailed her, along with the aromas of coffee and fresh popcorn from a quaint-looking machine in the corner. The little station seemed to offer something for everybody.

"Cool wheels," the teen-aged clerk said, indicating the Range Rover with a nod of his shaggy-haired head. "Don't see those 'round these parts much."

"Thank you," Adrienne said and set several bagels wrapped in wax tissue on the counter. Mick added two bottles of orange juice and a pint-sized carton of milk. The clerk couldn't have been more than sixteen. She wondered why he wasn't in school.

"Nice place you've got here," Mick said.

Adrienne handed the clerk her credit card and arched a brow at Mick. Nice? Hardly. The place needed a thorough cleaning and some serious updating.

"Thanks." The boy swiped the card through the slot on the grimy-looking cash register, then handed it back to her. Grease blackened each of his fingernails and shadowed his knuckles. "We're pretty much full service here. 'Course, we got to be in a little town like this. Folks need somewhere to go to for their car repairs, and we're it."

Adrienne signed the receipt while the clerk carefully bagged the bagels.

"You do tires, too?" Mick asked nonchalantly, twisting the cap off a bottle of juice.

"Sure do."

He took a long drink, re-capped the bottle. "Happen to know if a man named Greer brought a tire in here last night?"

The teenager appeared surprised at the question. "Denny Ray?" He shrugged. "I don't know. I didn't work last night."

"Can you check?"

"No, sir. My folks own this station, and Ma's already taken yesterday's tickets home 'cuz she keeps the books and has to do her deposit. My pa's at the dentist with a toothache, and she's gone with him, and I had to skip school to work for him this morning. Ain't nobody here but me right now."

"I see." Mick slid a twenty dollar bill toward him. "If you'd like to call your mama for me when she gets back from the dentist, I sure would appreciate it. I'll give you my cell number." The clerk's eyes widened at the money. Mick dropped another twenty on top of the first. They widened further. "And if you'd keep the information just between us, I'd appreciate that, too."

"Yes, sir!" Grinning, he snatched the money and stuffed it into his hip pocket. "Reckon that'll be easy enough to do. You got yourself a deal. Yes, sir!"

Mick smiled, jotted his cell number down on a piece of paper and slid it toward the teen-ager, then took Adrienne's arm.

"Thanks," he said.

"My name's Tommy. Just so you know who I am when I call you."

Mick's smile stayed in place. "I know."

"You do?"

"Says it right there. On your shirt."

Tommy's chin dropped to his chest; his gaze dropped to his pocket. He gave a sheepish grin. "Guess it does."

"My name's Mick."

"Mick. Yes, sir. Talk to you soon, sir. I mean, Mick."

Mick ushered Adrienne out the door. Within moments, the SUV was heading east on Highway 70.

"Okay, Corrigan." Adrienne handed him a blueberry bagel and a napkin. "You've got some explaining to do."

"That depends."

"Do you suspect Denny Ray of something?"

"While you're under my protection and until your mother's killer is found, everyone's a suspect. I've got Grif checking on him."

"You think he didn't really have a flat tire last night?"

"Just checking out his alibi."

"Well, maybe he didn't take it to be fixed in Sparta.

60

Maybe he went to some other town around here."

"Maybe." But Mick looked skeptical.

Denny Ray a murderer? Adrienne considered the possibility.

"I don't think so," she said, thinking of his charm and answering her silent question out loud. "He's a Park Ranger. Why wouldn't he want the Murdock land deed? It's his bread and butter."

Mick checked the rear view mirror and said nothing.

She opened the milk carton and took a drink sans a straw. "Farley, on the other hand, is a different story."

Mick grunted into his bagel.

"And I've already told you how angry Mayor Webster is with us," she said. "Still, there could be any one of those men in the crowd outside the Golden Eagle last night, or even in Sparta, that could have broken into my room and written that message on the mirror."

"Who's to say the murderer is a man?"

Adrienne blinked. She'd always thought of him as being male. "I find it hard to believe a woman would shoot my mother in cold blood."

Mick glanced at her. "Women kill as ruthlessly as men. All it takes is motive."

"Statistics show men kill far more often than women."

Suddenly, Mick riveted his gaze to the rearview mirror. "Damn it."

Adrienne twisted in her seat to see Farley's battered Studebaker pickup hurtling toward them. The old man drove with horrifying speed and recklessness. It seemed impossible for him to keep control of the truck at the rate he traveled, and a rear-end collision with the Range Rover appeared imminent.

She cried out in alarm, bracing herself for the impact, but only inches from their back fender, he veered into the passing lane and swerved around them, speeding ahead until he was just a spot of green on the horizon.

Adrienne pressed a hand against her thumping heart.

"He could have killed us!"

Mick nodded in grim agreement. "But that's not what he had in mind."

She turned to him in disbelief. "How can you tell?"

"He's not sticking around to finish the job. He was just being careless again. The damn fool."

"Where's a cop when you need one?" Her appetite gone, she tossed her half-eaten bagel into the bag.

"Can't believe he still has a license," Mick said, glancing at a sleek, black Lexus passing them. Two men inside studied them openly. "I'll give Officer Radley a call so he can file an incident report on the old man."

The sedan accelerated and pulled ahead. Adrienne watched, detached, her thoughts still preoccupied with Farley, who certainly deserved to lose his right to drive. It was only a matter of time before he killed himself--or someone else.

The Lexus slowed, made a hard U-turn and headed back toward them on the highway, its speed increasing as it drew closer. Moments after they passed, brakes squealed. Mick's glance shot to the rear-view mirror again. He swore.

"They're coming back." He reached over, tugged on Adrienne's seatbelt in quick assurance it was secure, then gripped the steering wheel with both hands. "We've got trouble, honey. Hang on."

For the second time in minutes, her heart lurched. The sedan was heading toward them, again at high speed. "What're they doing, Mick? Who are these guys?"

He didn't answer, his concentration riveted. The highway was deserted. Woodlands rose from both sides of the asphalt, edged by a ditch growing thick with bright-colored asters, but there was no side road on which to escape.

The Lexus drew alongside them, then abruptly veered over the lane markings toward the Range Rover. Mick braked, turned the steering wheel sharply to avoid a hit, and careened onto the shoulder of the road. Loose dirt and gravel sprayed under the tires.

He maneuvered back onto the highway at a lesser speed.

The men slowed, too, then crossed over the lane a second time. Bumpers collided with a sickening crunch. The Lexus pulled back into its own lane.

Grasping the edges of her seat, Adrienne stared at the pair. They appeared well-dressed. Middle-aged. Dangerous.

*Who were they?*

The man in the passenger seat reached inside his jacket and pulled out a revolver. The window slid down.

Her breathing quickened. In her peripheral vision, she identified another vehicle rounding the curve ahead of them.

She yelped. "Mick! Watch out for the van!"

"I see it." He swore viciously. With the Lexus and the Range Rover occupying both lanes of the highway, a collision was inevitable.

The Lexus's driver reacted quickly, swerving yet again toward Mick. Mick had no choice but to veer to the right with a suddenness that slammed Adrienne against his shoulder. The Range Rover hurtled into the ditch.

The Lexus stole Mick's place in the lane with only seconds to spare before the van passed with a blare of its horn and terrified shock on the expressions of its occupants. The SUV rocked to a bone-jarring stop.

"Get out! Now!" Mick's thumb punched the release button on her seat belt.

"My briefcase!" She couldn't leave her valuable file on the Murdock land deed.

"*Now*, Adrienne!" His long arm shot in front of her, and her door swung open. He pushed her from her seat. She responded to the urgency in his voice and scrambled out empty-handed.

Grabbing their cell phones, Mick shouldered his own door open. Adrienne barely had time to comprehend that the Lexus had disappeared over a hill before he grasped her hand and began running with her into the woods. Like him, she had no intention of sticking around to see if the men came back.

Plunging into the growth of trees took them out of the

glaring noon sun and into the protection of shadows and shade. The pungent scent of pine assailed her. A recent rain had softened the dirt beneath her feet, but the swift climb over protruding roots and rough terrain left her breathing fast from exertion.

Mick was relentless in forcing her to climb higher, leaving the Range Rover farther and farther behind. Her hand clung to his. More than once, he'd kept her from falling over rocks and dead branches strewn over the ground. Her slip-on sandals were hell for running.

Finally, he stopped behind a swarthy oak, using the trunk for cover. He removed his sunglasses and made a sharp inspection of the highway below. Adrienne swiped a palm across her damp forehead.

The road was empty. The Lexus hadn't returned. Her head swiveled uneasily toward the vast woodlands surrounding them, and her imagination kicked into overdrive.

Anyone could hide out here. The thick growth of nature could work for them--or against them. Hadn't someone lurked in the forest before shooting her mother, watching and waiting for just the right moment? And she and her father had been only few dozen yards away, oblivious to his presence.

"There they are again."

Mick's low voice catapulted her back to reality. The Lexus glided down the highway at a more conservative rate of speed. When it came upon the Range Rover, the sedan pulled over, then parked on the side of the road.

The SUV gleamed a radiant red in the sunlight. It tilted at a precarious angle in the ditch, the passenger door still open after Adrienne had bolted out. The two men approached, each carrying revolvers; their cautious gazes darted in both directions along the highway.

She stepped behind Mick, instinctively seeking the protection of his body.

"They want me, don't they?" she whispered.

"Yes."

He pulled no punches with her, but she expected nothing less. "I've never seen them before. How would they know how to find me?"

She hated the apprehension in her voice, but there was no help for it. These men planned to kill her, and most likely Mick as well. Running them off the road had failed; now, they returned to shoot in cold blood.

"They're working for someone." A muscle moved in Mick's cheek. "Someone who knew you'd be on that highway to Hickoryville."

The passenger, a man with a shaved head and pencil-thin moustache, perused the inside of the Range Rover but appeared to have no interest in her briefcase or their luggage. The second man, wearing a salmon-colored shirt, pointed to the ground, at the footprints she and Mick left behind. In unison, both turned toward the woods.

Adrienne held her breath. But the shadows and thick growth of pines, oak and maple trees worked in her and Mick's favor. Shaking their heads in evident frustration, both men got into the Lexus and drove away.

The taut line of Mick's shoulders eased. He turned toward her.

"That was close," she said, her voice unsteady.

"I know. Come here." His arms opened, and she fell into them without question. Without hesitation. Her cheek pressed against the solid warmth of his chest.

His strength soaked into her. Soothed her, deep inside. What would she have done if he hadn't been with her? How would she have evaded the Lexus's attack? Would she have been able to escape?

His chin rested on the top of her head. His hand stroked her spine. "You didn't happen to get a license number, did you?"

Dismay rolled through her. "I didn't think of it."

"Me, either. And when I did, we were too far away to read the plate."

She frowned into his shirt. "You had enough to do to

keep us from getting killed."

He grunted, his silence not quite agreeing with her.

"You have our phones." Her head lifted. "We have to call the police."

He drew back and thumbed his phone awake, then made a sound of annoyance. "No coverage up here."

She checked her phone, too, and discovered it was as useless as his. "Well, that's typical for our day, isn't it? Next time I'll--"

What was she saying? The next time someone tried to kill them by running them off the road, she'd be better prepared?

"There will be a next time," he said with quiet conviction, reading her thoughts.

A sick feeling crawled over her. He released her.

"Let me take you back to Nashville, Adrienne," he said. "Now."

"No. Mick, try to understand."

"Understand what? That someone is trying to kill you? That my list of suspects is growing by the hour? That I'm finding it harder and harder to protect you because I don't know who to protect you *from*?"

She stood very still. The truth of his words pounded into her brain.

"There's no shame or failure in going back, Adrienne. Your father wants nothing more than to keep you safe. He wants you *alive*. He'll find someone else to get that land deed."

"You know I won't consider it."

He set both hands on his hips and scowled at her.

"I appreciate all you're doing for me, Mick. Truly I do. I--I don't know what I'd do without you right now," she said stiffly.

"But you have a job to do."

His words mocked her. Her chin lifted. "And so do you."

The slight flare of his nostrils indicated her quiet taunt

hit its mark.

With a muttered curse, he took her hand and led her back to the Range Rover.

# CHAPTER SIX

Adrienne read Mick the directions Izzie and Dietrich Stockton had prepared for them. A godsend, given that the SUV's navigation system was unable to pinpoint the location of each winding mountain road leading to their cabin, set deep in the Cumberland woods.

Once they arrived, Adrienne fell in love with the place. Beautiful in its simplicity, crisply-painted in white, the little bungalow welcomed her and Mick to stay a couple of days. Vibrant green grass decorated with rhododendrons, azaleas, and the occasional ceramic lawn ornament indicated the couple took pride in their second home and worked diligently to keep it maintained.

Mick parked the Range Rover and opened Adrienne's door; she stepped out, inhaling deeply of the cool, clean air. Birds sang cheery songs in the forest. Serenity was a palpable thing.

"How nice," she breathed in appreciation, her gaze lingering on a wooden yard swing surrounded by potted petunias.

Mick's glance moved over the trees behind her and to the side of her. He turned and studied the narrow road in front of the cabin. She knew what he saw. What he worried about.

Isolation. The completeness of it.

She touched his hand. "Mick."

Dark eyes dragged toward her.

"Don't worry so much. We'll be fine here," she said

with a quiet confidence she didn't altogether feel.

His mouth hardened. "Too many places to hide out there, Adrienne. A playground for your mother's killer."

She withdrew her hand, stepped back from the frustration he kept coiled inside him. "Would it be any worse if we were in the city?"

"There'd be a hell of a lot more advantages." He paused, as if collecting all of them in his head. "Plenty of cops. 24-hour surveillance. Modern technology." He paused. "Ambulances and doctors and decent hospitals."

"Mick, you're being morbid."

"I don't want you hurt. It could happen, and if it does, help is too far away."

"Well, I don't want to *get* hurt, but all we can do is be as careful and observant as we can." An overwhelming urge to touch her lips to his in assurance welled within her before she quickly repressed it. "And you're being all that for both of us."

He seemed to accept her attempt at consolation only grudgingly. Crouching in front of the left bumper, he frowned at the damage caused by the Lexus. He rubbed a thumb along the cracked paint, then fiddled with the broken headlight. "This baby's taken a beating today."

"Better that bumper than our heads," Adrienne retorted, trying not to think of the cost to get it fixed.

"Your father will be beside himself when he finds out someone tried to run us off the road."

She grimaced. One more thing she didn't want him to know about. "Please don't say anything to him until we get home."

For the second time in as many days, she appealed to Mick to withhold information from her father when she, too, knew he insisted upon being kept informed.

Mick stood. His silence spoke volumes about his disapproval with the idea. Adrienne hated it whenever he was disapproving.

Especially of her.

Still, she remained steadfast in the request. "You're making me feel like a sneaky teen-ager. And you're crabby." She opened the Range Rover's tailgate and removed her luggage. "Let's have some lunch. You'll be a happier man for it."

Mick unlocked the door with the key Izzie had given them and followed Adrienne into the cabin, carting his own luggage. The interior was as pleasing as the outside, tastefully decorated, comfortable and homey. A bouquet of fresh flowers sat on the kitchen table. The kitchen and combined sitting area were flanked by a pair of bedrooms, one to the front of the house, the second to the back.

Mick considered the cabin's layout. "This is no better than the Golden Eagle. I'll be too far away from you at night."

She cocked her head and sighed. "Have we had this conversation before?"

"It's the truth, Adrienne."

"The cabin isn't that big. I'll be okay."

Leaving her luggage inside the front bedroom, she strode to the refrigerator and studied the contents inside. Izzie had been generous in her hospitality.

"I'll sleep on the floor outside your room," he said stubbornly, following her.

"That isn't necessary. You're a light sleeper. You'll--"

"But you're not."

She paused, her hands filled with packages of lunch meat, cheeses, and a jar of mayonnaise.

It was true. She tended to sleep dead to the world. It had been Mick's ticket to leaving her that morning. Deep in slumber and completely oblivious he was gone until it was too late.

The memory hung between them, as real today as it'd been then.

She dropped the sandwich fixings onto the counter top in an untidy heap. "See if you can find some chips or something, won't you?"

The request signaled an end to the discussion. A cowardly way of admitting she didn't want to think of sleeping arrangements, with or without him.

Definitely without him, she corrected herself with a determined set of her teeth. She absolutely could not sleep with him ever again.

For a moment, he didn't move. Afraid he'd pursue the discussion, she held her breath, but he seemed to reconsider and searched through cupboards until he located a bag of corn chips.

She opened a loaf of Izzie's homemade bread and began making sandwiches. Mick popped a couple chips into his mouth. Before long, he made a serious dent in the package's contents.

"Junk food isn't good for you," she said, glancing at him and trying not to be amused at his appetite for it.

"Can't help it. I'm hungry." He leaned a hip on the counter and watched her pile smoked turkey on the wheat bread.

"How about a beer, then?" She remembered seeing some in the 'fridge.

"Huh-uh." He crunched on more chips. "Dulls my senses."

"I see."

"A good bodyguard never drinks alcohol when he's protecting a--when he's on the job."

Knowing he'd almost said the word 'client' and that she'd objected to the use of the term yesterday, she hid a reluctant smile. "And you're a very good bodyguard, aren't you?"

"Damn right I am."

She took a lemon from the vegetable drawer in the refrigerator, sliced it and squeezed the juice into a tall glass of ice water. She handed it to him.

"Better?" she asked.

"I'd rather have the beer, but thanks." He winked and drank long and deep.

She sliced one thick sandwich and arranged it on a plate. He seemed engrossed in her preparations while she did the same with a second.

"You could be helping me, you know," she said, her voice slightly chiding.

"I like watching you. You're the picture of domesticity right now."

"Should I be offended at your chauvinism, Corrigan?"

His brows shot up in alarm. "I'm not being chauvinistic."

"Many a modern woman would think so."

"There's nothing wrong with a woman cooking for a man, is there?"

"I'm not cooking. I'm only making sandwiches. Anyone can do it. Even you." She thrust two plates at him. "Here. Put these on the table."

He complied, then returned to the counter. Adrienne handed him a long knife and slid a watermelon toward him.

"I make a pretty decent pan of lasagna," he said defensively. He pressed the blade into the rind, halved and quartered the fruit.

"With garlic bread and everything?" She feigned surprise.

"Hands down, the best."

He wielded the knife with such skill and ease, Adrienne found herself fascinated with his every movement. His presence dominated the tiny kitchen. She could hardly take her eyes off him.

He was relaxed. Comfortable. For now at least, he wasn't thinking about her mother's killer or the Murdock land deed or protecting her from harm.

She was drawn to this side of him. Drawn more than she should be. And she couldn't prevent the enticing image of him in his kitchen cooking lasagna.

She turned abruptly and busied herself looking for napkins. Thinking of him like that implied being with him in the future.

It wasn't going to happen. It couldn't. She'd vowed it a hundred times.

She vowed it again now.

They sat at the table, the platter of watermelon in the center. Mick dug into the sandwich with relish, finishing two by the time she'd finished her one. Afterward, he leaned back in his chair with a satisfied sigh, patted his lean belly and flashed her a devilishly charming grin.

"I'm not feeling crabby anymore," he said.

Her mouth curved. "Lucky for me."

"Thanks for fixing lunch. I'll return the favor sometime."

There it was again. That image of lasagna.

Of the future.

She shook her head, dispelling the thoughts. "I'm not averse to fixing a man's meal. It was something my mother did for my father every day when she was alive. Seeing her in the kitchen cooking for us is one of my dearest memories."

"In this day and age, that sounds almost old-fashioned." His voice had grown deeper. Thoughtful.

What was he thinking?

Her chin tilted a notch. "Me old-fashioned? Any more so than a man who will do anything to protect a woman when she could probably protect herself?"

"Are you saying you don't need protecting right now, Morelli?"

Quiet challenge laced the words. She rose and gathered their plates. "No, Mick. I'd be lying if I did."

He rose, too, a drinking glass in each hand. He set them next to the plates on the counter. Grasping her wrist, he pulled her around to face him.

"Keeping you safe right now has nothing to do with the business arrangement your father made with Silverhawk Investigative Services." His thumb moved over the sensitive skin of her pulse, sending it tripping into an uneven beat. "This thing has turned into a personal vendetta for me."

"Why?"

Mick's gaze lowered to her mouth. And lingered there. "Because he's put you through hell for too long. More than you deserve. He's put *me* through hell because I know what he's capable of. I want him away from you. For good."

"Last night and this morning proves he's persistent."

"And it proves we don't know who he is or when he'll show up next." His gaze lifted from her lips to meet her own.

She pulled away from his grasp. She could hardly think straight when he looked at her like that. "I've taken self-defense classes. I've spent countless hours at a shooting range learning to use a gun. I've learned how to protect myself since you left me."

He nodded slowly. She got the vague impression he'd known all that already.

"But that won't stop a bullet fired at you from in the shadows somewhere. The bastard's a coward. He doesn't play fair. He'll hit when you least expect it."

"Yes," she murmured. She'd thought the same thing many times over the past months and despised the killer all the more for it.

"So. Let's stop talking about him and do dishes, okay?" He turned on the hot water, filling the sink. "Since you made sandwiches, I'll wash."

Adrienne followed his lead in the quick change of topic. "Be still my heart. A man with dishpan hands."

He made no comment to her teasing. He bent closer to the window over the sink and stared across the back yard into the forest.

"There's Farley," he muttered, clearly stunned.

She bent over the sink, too, nudging her way against his shoulder and closer to the glass. "Where?"

"That's his pickup. See it?" He pointed.

She located the green Studebaker, barely discernible in the shade of the woodlands. The aging vehicle jostled through the maze of trees at a slow rate of speed.

"Stay here," Mick ordered.

He strode out of the kitchen.  Adrienne shut off the water and hurried after him.

"What are you going to do, Mick?" she demanded.

Opening his garment bag, he removed his shoulder holster, outfitted with his mean-looking Beretta.  He strapped them on, then took out another gun, a baby Glock, and handed it to her.  "Take this.  Use it if you have to."

Her fingers closed over the cold metal.  She swallowed hard and nodded.

"Lock the door behind me and don't let anyone in while I'm gone, do you hear me?"

She wasn't so sure she wanted him to leave her alone, even if she was armed.  "All right.  Are you taking the SUV?"

"No.  I'll be faster on foot, and he won't hear me coming.  The old man has some explaining to do."

"Then I'm coming, too."  She wanted to hear what Farley had to say as much as Mick did.  More so.

"You're staying put."

"Mick!"

"Lock the door."  Already, he had one foot on the porch.  "I'll be back as soon as I can."

And before she could call out his name, he was gone.

\* \* \*

Mick sprinted across the Stocktons' back lawn and plunged into the woodlands behind the cabin.  A complex latticework of branches high overhead snuffed the brilliance of the afternoon sun and catapulted him into a different world.  The air was cooler in the forest.  Heavier.  And hushed.  As if unwilling to betray the secrets held within its shadows.

A thick cushion of pine needles and wilting vegetation muffled his run.  He leapt over protruding tree roots, his tread swift over the dips and swells of uneven ground.  He halted at a narrow trail, marked with twin ridges of tire marks, and searched through the gray-dim light for some sign of the green Studebaker.

He found it, fifty yards ahead.  The vehicle crawled over

the curving pathway, then finally creaked to a stop. Mick withdrew the Beretta from the holster and took cover behind a towering maple. He threw a quick glance over his shoulder, gauging the distance he'd traveled from the Stocktons' cabin.

From Adrienne.

He was farther away than he expected. Hell, he couldn't even see the bungalow anymore.

The pickup door opened, and Farley got out, slamming it shut behind him. He stepped toward the back end and lowered the tailgate with a noisy screech of hinges.

Whatever he intended to do, keeping quiet was not on the agenda. With the revolver pointed upward, Mick moved closer, zigzagging from tree to tree until he had the old man in clear range. Farley leaned into the pickup bed and wrapped something in a ragged towel, then produced a long-handled spade. He moved away from the truck and began digging.

Warning bells clamored in Mick's brain. He remembered the old man's hostility and contempt toward Adrienne. What was he capable of? How much violence? How far would he go to keep her from the Murdock land deed?

And what the hell was he digging a hole for?

No time like the present to find out what Farley intended to bury, and Mick bolted toward him, knocked the sweat-stained straw hat off his head with one hand and pressed the nose of the Beretta to his temple with the other.

"Don't move, old man," he said between his teeth.

Farley started, choking a curse of surprise.

"Put that spade down," Mick snapped.

The shovel fell to the dirt with a thud.

Mick pulled the safety back. "We're going to have a little talk. I'm going to ask the questions. You're going to give the answers. You understand that?"

Farley didn't blink. "Don't know what's got your feathers in a dither, boy, but I reckon you're not givin' me a choice."

"That's right. I'm not." Mick lowered the weapon but

kept the barrel trained on him. "Turn around."

He stepped back, and Farley obeyed. Sweat plastered his thinning hair to his head. He wore the denim overalls again, just as he had last night at the Golden Eagle. But now, dirt streaked the faded material. Dirt and blood.

"What are you doing out here?" Mick's voice thrummed deadly low. Suspicion fumed inside him.

Farley stared. Confusion flitted across his features until his eyes widened in recognition.

"You're that city-slicker that was with the Morelli woman last night, ain't you?" he demanded.

"I'm Mick Corrigan. Her bodyguard."

"Bodyguard! Well, ain't that just like the government to spend our tax money on foolishment like you!"

Mick steeled his expression to hide a sudden rise of anger. He had no intention of setting the man straight by telling him the state of Tennessee was not funding his services, that they were paid for out of Adrienne's father's personal account. "Miss Morelli's mother was murdered six months ago. I'm sure you knew that."

The old eyes narrowed. "Reckon most everyone 'round these parts does."

"Now Miss Morelli's receiving death threats."

"That so?"

"Someone tried to run us off the road this morning. Just like you did, Farley."

"Me! I ain't done nothin' of the sort."

"You always drive like fire was licking your heels?"

"Ain't nothin' wrong with my drivin'!"

The man appeared so indignant, Mick's suspicions wavered. He was beginning to think Farley's anger stemmed more from pride than from anything connected with Adrienne.

But he could be wrong. For her sake, he couldn't be.

"What are you doing out here?" he said, attempting a different tactic to determine motive.

"Ain't none of your business."

"I'm making it my business."

He glared at Mick and pressed his lips together.

No one could ever claim Farley wasn't mule-headed, but Mick prided himself on being a patient man. He pointed to the shallow indentation in the ground and the spade lying next to it. "That hole isn't going to get any bigger until you tell me what you're digging it for. We'll stand here all day if you want."

Farley's lips curled back. He kicked at the dirt. "One of my little friends was killed. He deserves a fittin' burial."

The bundle wrapped in toweling in the back of the Studebaker was small--the size of an infant child. Horror coursed through Mick. He whirled, his gaze flying to the tailgate.

What--or who--had died?

"My God, Farley. You can't bury--what the hell happened?"

Somber, Farley moved toward the truck. He patted the lifeless bundle, his touch gentle and clearly grieving.

"Open it, old man," Mick rasped. "Let me see what's inside."

Farley complied, parting the edges of the toweling. Mick blinked at the furry body matted with blood. No baby, he realized, stunned, but a large opossum.

"A maid at the Golden Eagle found him in their dumpster this morning and called me to come get him," Farley said. Sadness draped his voice. "Someone wrung his neck, then slit it. Breaks my heart to see him like this. Ain't right that someone could be so cruel. Ain't right."

Mick lowered the Beretta.

"Why did the motel call you?" he asked quietly.

"'Cuz they know I'm these little critters' friend. They're my buddies."

Buddies?

Mick's glance swung toward the back end of the pickup. An assortment of animal cages were stacked inside, each one filled with opossums, their beady eyes staring back at him in harmless curiosity.

Last night, when the old pickup had jumped the curb in front of the Golden Eagle restaurant and nearly run them over, Farley had had the little creatures with him then, too, their cages wobbling from the wild ride.

Mick realized Farley's devotion to them was real, bizarre as it sounded.

He slipped the revolver back into his holster. He had to get back to Adrienne. "Come on, old man. I'll help you dig the hole. Then you'd best head on home."

# CHAPTER SEVEN

Time dragged. Adrienne's imagination entertained a litany of reasons why Mick was taking so long. She'd convinced herself Farley was giving him some serious trouble. That he was armed, and what could he be doing in the woods, anyway?

Maybe he was staking out the cabin. Staking out *her*.

Mick's orders to stay put marched through her brain, and obeying them was one of the hardest things she'd ever done. She took comfort in the baby Glock, tried to rein in her imagination and wait some more.

She'd already washed the dishes and straightened the kitchen. She called Renee, only to get voice mail. Adrienne left a message, assuring her father's secretary all was well, that they were following the itinerary they prepared, and everything remained on schedule. She ended by saying she'd call back tomorrow, after she secured the Murdock land deed. Renee would never know Mick wasn't with her but gone in a determined hunt for someone who might want her dead.

Again, Adrienne checked the window over the kitchen sink. Again, no Mick.

She unpacked her luggage, taking the front bedroom and moving Mick's things to the back one. She brushed her teeth, redid her hair, touched up her make-up. She flipped through a magazine . . ..

And Mick still wasn't back yet.

Going after him wouldn't be a bad idea, after all. He might need her help. She could take the Range Rover and save some time.

A shadow passed over the sitting room window. Adrienne stilled, her alarm building from who might be in the front yard. A muffled thump indicated whoever it was wasn't depending on the element of surprise to get to her.

Maybe Mick had returned. Finally.

She took the Glock with her, just in case, and opened the door slowly, carefully. Her jaw dropped at the sight of the man in a Tennessee Park Ranger uniform sitting on the horse on the lawn.

"Denny Ray!" she exclaimed. "What are you doing here?"

"Before I answer that, sweetie, you'd better tell me what you're going to do with that gun," he said, eying the revolver aimed at him.

"Nothing." Her arm lowered. "Just prepared."

A slow grin formed on his mouth. "You expecting the bad guys or something?"

"A girl can't be too careful, can she?"

"Where's your goon?"

"Mick isn't here. And please stop calling him that."

"So you're alone right now?" He waggled his eyebrows at her suggestively.

Really. The man was just too outrageous. A reluctant smile scooted across her lips, and her annoyance with him dissipated.

"So what brings you out here, Denny Ray?" she asked again.

He leaned forward on the saddle horn, at ease on top of the horse and looking handsome in his tan uniform and wide-brimmed felt hat. "You were supposed to meet me in Hickoryville almost two hours ago. The woodpeckers, remember?"

Her fingers flew to her mouth in dismay. "Oh, I'm sorry."

After the ordeal on the highway and the distraction of seeing Farley in the woods behind the cabin, she'd completely forgotten.

"No problem." He flashed his usual disarming smile. "We can still go to their cluster of roosting cavities. They're not far from here."

"I can't. I'm leaving to look for Mick."

The smile faded. "Where is he?"

"I'm not sure." She gestured toward the woodlands. "Back there somewhere. We saw Farley in his truck, and Mick was concerned. He went to check up on him."

Denny Ray appeared to consider that. "The old geezer's probably up to no good. Come on, sweetie. Climb up. We'll look for him together."

She considered the big horse. The close proximity to Denny Ray in the saddle. And shook her head. "I'll take the Range Rover, thanks."

Before he could talk her out of it, she hurried back into the cabin for her purse, pulled the cabin's door closed behind her and jumped into the SUV. Setting the Glock on the seat beside her, she pushed the ignition button and lowered her window.

"The Rover is too big for the trails." Denny Ray didn't try to hide his disapproval of her mode of transportation. "We'll take it as far as we can, then you'll either have to walk or ride with me."

She nodded. His warning wasn't unreasonable. "Fair enough. Lead the way."

The horse cantered off the lawn and onto the road leading away from the cabin. Adrienne divided her attention between driving and searching the trees for Farley's green pickup.

Just when it seemed they'd gone farther than should have been necessary, Denny Ray turned onto a trail barely seen from the road. The SUV rocked and bounced over the rough ground, taking all of Adrienne's concentration, and before long, she'd lost her bearings. Though the trail took them right into the woods, she didn't see another vehicle, green or otherwise.

With the thick growth of foliage, the area was never intended for four wheels. She exhaled a breath of frustration, then swerved to miss a low-lying branch. The Range Rover already bore battle scars on the front bumper; she didn't want to gouge the paint with scratches, too. Braking, she leaned out the window. "Denny Ray, I can't go any further."

His hand lifted in a gesture of understanding, and he dismounted. Adrienne got out of her vehicle, taking the keys with her.

The tree growth was so dense Farley wouldn't have been able to drive his pickup through it any more than she could drive the Range Rover. And the forest showed no signs of thinning, at least not close by.

They were nowhere near Mick and the old man. They'd driven too far.

Why had Denny Ray chosen this trail?

"We should start walking in the direction of the Stocktons' cabin," she said, refusing to admit she had no idea which direction that would be. The feeling he'd led her on a wild goose chase refused to subside. "Mick was on foot. He couldn't have gone this far and either could Farley."

Something on the ground engrossed Denny Ray. He hunkered down beside it, studying it intently. "Come here, Adrienne. Take a look at this."

It rankled how he wasn't listening to her, but maybe he'd found a footprint or other evidence of the two men's whereabouts. But, joining him, she realized what engrossed him was none of those things. Instead, a gangly bird fluttered amongst the pine needles, and he gently scooped the little creature into the palm of his hand.

"A baby raven," Adrienne said.

"He fell out of the clutch." Denny Ray rose, tilting his head back to study the branches above and around them. "I wonder where it is."

"Raven clutches are large," she said, looking, too. "We should be able to see one easily enough."

Denny Ray moved away from the trail, his gaze searching

for the nest. Casting a longing look at the vehicle she was leaving behind, Adrienne reluctantly followed him.

Ribbons of sunlight beamed through the branches and provided illumination for their hunt. They couldn't leave the raven to flounder on its own. Not returning the little bird to his mother and home would be too cruel, but the sooner they could do so, the sooner she could start looking for Mick again.

Denny Ray took his job as Park Ranger with utmost seriousness. She'd give him that much. The raven's welfare clearly concerned him, and his finger stroked the black-feathered head in a gesture of comfort.

"There's the clutch." He pointed upward toward the branches of a cypress. "I think I can reach it if I climb up. Hold him, will you?" He settled the shivering bird into her outstretched palms.

He grasped a branch and swung himself up. He possessed a great deal of athletic skill and grace, she mused. At tree-climbing, he was a natural.

"Okay. Give him to me." Denny Ray crouched on a sturdy branch and leaned toward her. Above him, the raven's mother and siblings cawed and screeched in alarm.

Reaching up on her tiptoes, Adrienne carefully slid the little black bird into Denny Ray's hands. He straightened, and with the cautious and practiced movements of a man who knew what he was doing, returned the raven to its home.

He jumped back down to the ground. "There," he said, grinning in satisfaction. "My good deed for the day."

"An even better deed would be to help me find Mick and Farley," she retorted, turning in the direction from which they came.

"Adrienne, wait." Hands on hips, Denny Ray considered the mountain's incline. "Have you considered a trail assessment process?"

She stared at him. "For people with disabilities?"

"Yes. The state of Tennessee should hire a firm that specializes in the technology needed to allow wheelchairs access over these trails without paving over the wilderness. As a matter of fact, I'd be happy to recommend just such a company."

"Denny Ray." Adrienne struggled to keep her irritation in check. "My father is an outdoors enthusiast as well as being wheelchair-bound. I can assure you, accessibility is important to him. He'll give the matter top priority as soon as we secure the land deed from Murdock."

"It's a rather simple process," Denny Ray went on. "All that'll need to be determined is the grade of the land, obstacles--"

"--trail width, surface type and cross slope. I know."

He appeared taken aback. "Very good."

"I've done my homework."

"I see that."

"I'm not having another conversation with you, Denny Ray, until we find Mick and Farley." She pivoted and sprinted back toward the trail.

"But Adrienne." He trotted after her. "What about the red-cockaded woodpeckers?"

She spun. "What about them?"

"The roosting cavities." He shook his head in exaggerated chagrin. "Don't tell me you've forgotten about the photo op. You were so excited about it."

"I don't have my camera. And frankly, Denny Ray, even if I did, I wouldn't take a picture. In fact, I could care less about those birds right now."

"Their natural habitat is longleaf pines. Easy to spot." He extended a hand, as if he intended to take her arm. "There's a stand of them not far from here. I'll show you. We don't need the camera, not really."

She jerked away before he could touch her.

He was playing for time. Trying to lead her astray, farther from the SUV. From the Stocktons' cabin.

From Mick.

He had an ulterior motive. *Why?*

"Adrienne, sweetie." His fingers closed around her arm.

"Stop calling me 'sweetie'. You're acting crazy right now, Denny Ray." She yanked from his grip.

"I'm not acting *crazy*!" Teeth bared in a furious snarl, he lunged to grab her again.

Skills from the self-defense classes she'd mastered over the past six months flowed into her brain and muscles. She leapt outward with a high kick and struck him in the temple. Hard. He grunted and crumpled to the ground.

She didn't wait to see if he was hurt--or even unconscious. She ran back toward the trail, her heart thundering, her feet moving over the ground as fast as the sandals and uneven terrain allowed her.

From somewhere in the forest, a car door slammed. Adrienne skidded to a stop.

Farley's?

A second one shut. Her gaze pierced the woodlands, finding nothing. A third door slammed. Wherever the vehicle was, it was hidden. The hair on the back of her neck rose.

Then, dried leaves rustled. Pine needles crunched. Twigs snapped, and Adrienne spun toward the sounds.

Two men stepped through the trees. One bald-headed, the other wearing a salmon-colored shirt. Recognition shot through her, a searing shock that they'd found her here, deep in the Tennessee wilderness.

She took an involuntary step backward. Their antagonism, their harsh expressions, proved intimidating. Though the afternoon was warm, each wore an expensive-looking suit. Adrienne's pulse pounded with the certainty their revolvers were hidden beneath.

A third man appeared. The other two took position on either side of him.

"Miss Morelli," Mayor Webster said and hitched up his pants. "Well, well, well."

Her head lifted. She hid her surprise and mustered all the social graces her mother had ever taught her.

"We meet again, Mayor," she said. She swept a hand

outward, indicating their surroundings. "Under rather unusual circumstances, wouldn't you say?"

"Depends on how you look at it."

"Oh?"

"Might be as good a time as any to have a little talk with you."

"I see." She let her skepticism show as her gaze swept over the other two. "And that's why you just happened to be out here? To have a little talk with me?"

The mayor appeared to consider that. A cold smile appeared. "I was taking my friends here on a little tour. And la-de-da. We find you."

"Your friends."

"They're . . . investors. They want the resort as much as I do."

Her brow arched on a new wave of skepticism. The man was lying through his teeth. A tour? Investors? Hardly. The coincidences of their appearance were too suspicious to be believable.

"You've discussed the matter often enough with my father," she said firmly. "There will be no resort."

He scowled. "You're as stubborn a woman as your mother was, aren't you?" he demanded.

She stiffened. "I'll take that as a compliment."

"It wasn't intended as one."

"The ceremony in Hickoryville is due to begin very soon," she said. "Mr. Kershner is fully prepared to transfer his company's deed over to me. Everything is already arranged."

"But you, my dear Adrienne, have the power to stop it."

His mocking use of her given name sent shivers of unease down her spine. She didn't like the familiarity with which he used it, or the drawled, calculated tone he used to say it.

"I have no such power, Mayor. And if I did, do you really think I'd use it for your benefit?"

"You should know by now I'm very determined to

persuade you."

She had to concentrate; she couldn't let the three out of her range of vision. Mayor Webster was likely behind those frightening moments on the highway when the men rammed the Range Rover. Or maybe he worked for someone that was.

Either way, he was desperate to block the Murdock deal. But he was running out of time. In a few hours, the deal would be done.

The knowledge infused her with confidence. Triumph.

"I wouldn't think a man in your position would leave bloody messages on my bathroom mirror, all in the name of 'persuasion'," she purred. "But, as you can see, the tactic didn't scare me away. Nor did your attempt to run me off the highway."

Confusion flickered in his expression. "I don't know anything about bloody messages," he snapped. "But if I thought they'd keep you from accepting those acres for the State, I'd sure as hell write more of them."

Adrienne's confidence wavered. If he wasn't the one who was behind the warning, insinuating that he was the killer, who was?

Even if Webster was telling the truth, his hostility and persistence as one of her father's enemies forced Adrienne to take him and his intentions seriously. She was only beginning to know all that he was capable of.

"Please try to understand Tennessee's reasoning for wanting the Murdock land deed," she said, hoping he didn't hear the plea in her voice.

"To preserve the wilderness," he sneered.

"Yes."

"There's plenty of mountain left for wilderness. All we want is a little patch to build a resort!"

"A 'little patch'? Two thousand acres' worth?" Adrienne couldn't stop the retort. "Think of the people who'll be affected by your business venture," she said. Many times, her father had countered with the same argument.

"They'll have to move. Their lives will be uprooted from all they've ever known."

"That's progress, isn't it?" He showed no sympathy, only a growing impatience.

"The traffic and crowds will destroy the serenity of this entire area for miles around."

"Folks'll get over it."

"But these are a gentle people." She thought of the Stocktons, of their kind and simple natures, of how the couple was born here, raised a family and would die here. They knew no other way of life than on this mountain. "You, as an elected member in this community, should know that."

"Mountain Crest Resort will provide hundreds of jobs and pour money into the surrounding economy," he said, his voice terse.

"As well as into your pockets!"

Webster's sideburns quivered; his face flamed red with indignation.

"And we haven't even talked about the wildlife," she said. Like the baby raven, trembling and afraid away from his nest. "Shall we go there, Mayor?"

"You're as thick-skulled as your daddy!"

"I'll take that as a compliment, too," Adrienne shot back.

"You leave me no choice, young lady. You won't listen to reason. There'll be consequences you'll be responsible for. You and your imperious daddy."

"Is that a threat?" She hid the challenge behind a mask of indifference, but inside she quaked with outrage.

And a very real, very burgeoning, fear.

He muttered something under his breath to the pair of men beside him. They nodded and pulled back their suit coats, revealing the weapons they carried at their waist. In unison, they stepped toward her.

"Whatever you're planning to do right now won't change anything." Did she sound like she was afraid? She forced courage and vehemence into her voice. "I swear it."

"Consequences, young lady. Consequences."

She slipped one foot out from its leather slip-on sandal, then the other.

She would show them 'consequences'.

The two men had nearly reached her. One leap forward, and she could reach them, they were so close. The blood pounded at her temples. She strove for calmness, waiting for the right moment.

Just as she was about to kick out her leg in her first self-defense maneuver, a shot rang out. *Thwap!* The bullet hit the dirt in front of her, sending leaves and pine needles flying. Adrienne cried out in surprise. Both men whirled from her with savage curses.

The bald-headed man leveled his revolver toward the trees, but another shot rang out before he could pull the trigger. Blood spurted over his hand. The weapon flew out of his grasp, and he yelped in pain.

His partner jumped back. The mayor yelled. Like a pack of dogs, the men retreated.

And Mick stepped out from around a maple tree.

# CHAPTER EIGHT

"Get behind me, Adrienne," Mick ordered, moving toward her.

Sweat plastered his shirt to his back. He was breathing hard from his run after he discovered the abandoned Range Rover. When he spotted the Lexus creeping through the trees, his panic had kicked into overdrive.

Thank God he found her in time.

Knees bent, feet bare, body angled to kick out, she was in position to defend herself against all of them. He kept his grip tight over the Beretta and edged closer. A few more steps, and then he was there. With a sweep of his arm, he pulled her safely behind him.

"What the hell is going on here?" He leveled Webster with a cold glare. "Harassing an innocent citizen, Mayor? The daughter of the governor of our illustrious state, no less."

Webster turned red at Mick's accusation. "Who in blazes are you?"

From beyond the trail, Denny Ray stumbled toward them. Pine needles and leaves clung to his clothes and hair. His hat was missing, too. He halted, his stare fixed on Mick, and scowled. "He's her bodyguard."

Webster's eye narrowed. "What happened to you?"

"Fell. Knocked myself out cold." He brushed at the front of his shirt. "Adrienne and I were searching for an endangered species of woodpeckers," he said, his hands busy, his eyes down. "Next thing I know, I'm on the ground." His gaze lifted, then. Locked onto hers. "Thanks for going for help, Adrienne."

She stiffened and made no acknowledgement. Mick realized, then, he was lying. The whole scenario didn't fit, but before Mick could confront Denny Ray, Adrienne curled her fingers around Mick's wrist.

"Let it go," she said under her breath.

Mick clenched his teeth. But said nothing.

The mayor nodded once, quickly. "We were out for a drive. Taking a tour, by God. Lucky we came upon Miss Morelli when we did. If you're needing a doctor, we can take you into town." He gestured at the bald man struggling to tie a handkerchief around his bloody hand. "Both of you."

"Where's my horse?" Denny Ray glanced around the area.

"You can come back later for him. Get in the car." Webster pivoted, then turned back to Adrienne. "Just remember what I told you, young lady," he said. "I intend to do what it takes to stop this land deal from going through."

He strode away, his cronies following. But Denny Ray held back.

"Later, Adrienne," he said and winked.

Mick frowned at the insolent promise. Denny Ray disappeared into the forest shadows, too, and before long, a motor purred to life.

Mick turned to Adrienne and ran a thorough gaze over her, finding her pale. Troubled. He resisted the urge to take her into his arms. "You okay?"

Her mouth pursed. "Yes."

"You went all the way out here to see woodpeckers with him?"

"No," she said, tucking auburn strands of hair behind her ear. "I came out here looking for you."

Whatever happened in the woods beyond the trail, Adrienne had been forced to defend herself against Denny Ray. Alone. The sting of Mick's failure to protect her burned.

He draped an arm around her shoulders and headed

toward the waiting Range Rover. "C'mon, Morelli. You've got some explaining to do."

\* \* \*

"Maybe I had him figured all wrong."

Back at the Stocktons' cabin, Adrienne plopped on the front lawn with a loud sigh.

"Denny Ray?" Mick joined her on the grass. "How?"

She lay on her back and stared into the sky. "I think he acted the way he did because he was trying to help me save face with the mayor. After I knocked him out and all."

"Or maybe he was trying to save face, too."

"Hmm." Did Denny Ray have an ulterior motive he didn't want anyone else to find out about? Or was he simply fanatical about Tennessee's endangered wildlife? "Still, I think I overreacted in the woods. I believed him when he told me about the woodpeckers. He seemed so genuine about it. At least, at first."

"He's a Forest Ranger. A member of the Scott's Gulf Alliance. Why wouldn't you believe him?"

"It's so bizarre."

"Bizarre enough that you had to go into fighting mode so he'd leave you alone."

"He was determined to keep me from looking for you. He kept making excuses. Like he was stalling for time or something."

"He set you up."

Mick was much more blunt about the niggling suspicion she was reluctant to acknowledge, even to herself.

"It's too much of a coincidence Webster and those two men happened to show up right then, isn't it?" Her head swiveled against the soft grass to consider Mick. "So how did *you* find me?"

"Through the electronic data emitted from the Range Rover. When I got back to the cabin and saw you were gone, I called Officer Radley. With his help, the navigation system's company told me where you were. At least, where the SUV was. Otherwise, I wouldn't have found you in time."

"I was glad to see you. I didn't bring the Glock with me," she admitted, rueful.

"Three men against one woman. Four, including Denny Ray. You wouldn't have had a chance with all of them."

"I was pretty good in my martial arts class, you know."

"I don't want to find out just how good you really are." He rolled from his sitting position and straddled her body on all fours. He gazed downward. His eyes, dark and worried, roamed over her face. "You scared the hell out of me when I discovered you gone. I'd given you strict orders to stay put until I got back."

The roughness in his voice betrayed his emotion.

It moved her, that emotion.

She lifted a hand to his cheek. "You were gone so long, Mick. Denny Ray only stopped by because I missed my appointment with him. And he said he'd help me find you."

Mick turned slightly, as though he craved more of her touch. He pressed a kiss into her palm.

"I'm glad you knocked him cold on his ass," he said.

"You don't think I overreacted, then?"

"No." He eased his body onto hers, bracing himself on his elbows. "Farley's not as dangerous as I thought, by the way. Eccentric, maybe. And mule-headed. But I don't think he'd hurt anyone."

Adrienne absorbed the pleasure from Mick's weight on her. His warm protection and strength.

"How do you know that?" she asked.

"I don't. Call it a gut feeling. He was burying a dead opossum. That's why he was in the woods."

"An opossum?" Adrienne stared up at him.

"He's devoted to them."

"That's weird."

"He resents the government messing in his life. He wants everyone to leave him alone." Mick's head dipped; he nuzzled the sensitive skin behind her ear. "You going to wear your red nightgown again tonight?"

Her pulse faltered at the sudden switch in his thinking; her mouth softened. "What does that have to do with Farley?"

"I've been thinking of you in it."

"You have not." She pushed against him, amused in spite of herself. "You've been thinking of Farley and his 'possums. And Denny Ray and the mayor and--"

"It's true, Adrienne." His expression unexpectedly serious, he gazed down at her. "I'm always thinking of you. Even when I don't know that I am, I am."

She pressed her fingers to his lips. She wasn't ready for this. Not when she tried so hard to forget him these past months. She wanted to keep believing she meant nothing to him. It was easier that way.

"Don't say anything more, Mick. Please."

"Maybe that's part of the problem, Morelli," he said gruffly. "I haven't said enough."

His cell phone rang. He eased off her and reached for the device clipped to his belt. Stretching full-length on his back beside her, he put the phone to his ear.

"Corrigan," he said. Someone spoke on the other end, and his attention sharpened. "Hey, Tommy. How's it going?"

The teen-ager at the Sparta gas station. Adrienne sat up and hugged her knees to her chest.

"Okay," Mick said into the phone. "That's what I needed to know." He listened for a moment. "Thanks, Tommy. Appreciate it." He ended the connection.

"Well?" Adrienne asked.

"Denny Ray never brought a tire into the Sparta gas station. Flat or otherwise."

"He could've taken it somewhere else. Spencer is close by. Or Crossville."

"Tommy says Denny Ray lives in town. Wouldn't make sense for him to take the tire anywhere else but Sparta."

"Anything's possible, Mick."

"Sounds like you're defending him."

"I'm not. But he's part of the Alliance. Izzie and Dietrich adore him. And since they've known him so much longer than I have, I have to trust their instincts."

"But not mine?"

He looked offended. Perhaps he was only jealous; after all, Denny Ray was an outrageous flirt, and Adrienne had made no effort to hide the fact that she liked him. While she hadn't forgotten his strange behavior this afternoon, nor did she understand it, she wanted to believe there was a valid reason for his actions. For now, she'd give him the benefit of the doubt.

Looking grim, Mick tapped a number into the cellular.

"Who are you calling?" Adrienne asked.

"Grif's private line. I need more information from him."

"Such as?"

"Grif. It's Mick." Mick glanced at her, dividing his attention between her and his boss. "Yeah, she's here. Everything's fine." He reached out and circled her calf with his hand. Her legs were bare beyond the hems of her capris, and his thumb stroked her skin, his grip loose, almost absent, as if he merely wanted to touch her but had no real reason to do so. "Hey, I need some information. You got some time to check out a few things for me? Good."

He looked at ease lying there, prone on the Stocktons' lawn with his ankles crossed. But his features were a mask of concentration; she could almost see his mind working in methodical precision.

"I need a license number traced. The plates are on a late model black Lexus." He gave Grif the number. "And can you do a corporate entity search for me? Get me a list of the board of directors at Murdock, Inc. The Scott's Gulf Alliance, too. Yeah, both."

Adrienne's eyebrows shot up at the request. Did he doubt the credibility of Denny Ray's involvement with the charitable group somehow?

But there was no question of it. Izzie spoke highly of him--at least in matters other than his punctuality.

Mick lowered the phone. "Did you bring a laptop with you?"

"Yes," she said. "It's in the cabin."

He spoke into the phone again. "Just email us the information." Again, his dark eyes found her, his conversation bouncing between Grif and herself. He asked for her email address, then repeated the sequence of letters she gave him to her private account, nodding as Grif apparently repeated them back to him. "That's right. Give this top priority, will you?" He fell silent, listening to whatever Grif told him. He kept his glance on her, devouring her with his eyes while he concentrated on the voice at the other end.

Finally, he nodded. "Interesting. Thanks. I'll be in touch." The conversation ended, and he re-clipped the phone to his belt.

"Now we wait," he said.

"Yes," she said, though her experience with Silverhawk Investigative Agency predicted Grif would be efficient. The wait wouldn't be long. "Did you get a close look at the Lexus in the woods?"

"Yes. After I found the SUV."

"You memorized the license plate. Good job, Corrigan."

His mouth quirked. "I screwed up once when they ran us off the highway. I wasn't going to do it again."

Though he blamed himself for the oversight, Adrienne was just as guilty. She moved to stand. "I'll get my laptop set up."

"Not so fast." He clasped her wrist and pulled her on top of him. He smiled, a sexy and provocative curve of his lips that sent her stomach into a flip. "So. Refresh my memory. What were we talking about before Tommy called?"

She tried not to smile. "My red nightgown, I believe."

"Ah. That's right. The red nightgown."

"Your libido racing, Corrigan?"

He grinned. "Faster and faster."

"That got us in trouble the last time you were my bodyguard, remember?"

Those black eyes of his glittered. "I recall you were a willing partner."

"A mistake I don't intend to make again." She tugged against his arm. "Let me go, will you?"

Abruptly, he changed their position, rolling her to her back and pressing her into the lush grass. The scent of the warm earth surrounded her.

And Mick's vibrant masculinity.

"What we shared together that night in Nashville wasn't a mistake, Adrienne. It was a beautiful experience between two people. The only mistake was that it happened when I was employed to protect you."

"There's a difference?"

"In my mind, there is."

"Funny. In mine, there isn't."

"Adrienne."

The huskiness in his voice held her complete attention. He smoothed the hair at her temples, his touch so incredibly gentle that whatever resentment she had from him leaving her six months ago didn't seem nearly as important as how he made her feel now. This minute.

"I was wrong in not telling you good-bye that morning. I should have," he murmured. "You deserved at least that."

She bit her lip. "Yes."

"But I have to say, Morelli, you scared the hell out of me."

"The fearless and go-by-the-rules bodyguard, Mick Corrigan afraid? Of me?"

"That's right. And right now I'm afraid because I'm wanting you all over again. I want you so damn bad I feel like tossing out every rule I've ever made about a client I'm protecting."

Her head turned. "Mick, don't."

"Adrienne."

He turned her back again. His head lowered. His mouth

took hers with a hot hunger that stole her breath away and sent her plummeting into a dizzying rush of sensation.

And memories. Oh, God. It was as if those months never passed between them. As if she just now experienced him for the first time. The sensations were that strong, that vivid, and no matter how many men she might kiss after Mick Corrigan, she would never forget how he kissed her now.

Her arms slid around his neck. She couldn't stop them if she tried, the need to pull him closer to her too powerful, too real. Her mouth opened, and his tongue moved in to twirl with hers, to dominate her senses. Her head angled; she thought of nothing else but to taste more of him, to relive all over again that night he made love to her.

He tugged at the black knit shell she wore, lifted it away from the waistband of her capris. His warm hand slid over her stomach, her ribs, and delved beneath her lace bra to cup a breast, his palm both rough and gentle against the rounded fullness. His thumb stroked the sensitive nub until her hips moved against his.

But suddenly, everything became *too* real. He left her breathless from the force of the memories. She wobbled on the precipice of making love to him right there on the Stocktons' front lawn.

She'd vowed once that it would never happen again. Mick would leave her in a day or two, his employment with her father ended. Adrienne refused to have the taste of his kisses or the warmth of his body on her skin when he did.

It would hurt too much.

She pushed against him with a moan of dismay. His head lifted, and she dragged in air. She shoved at his shoulders, but he remained immovable over her.

"Whatever you're thinking, Adrienne, don't," he warned.

Her gaze clashed with his. "You're not making the rules this time, Corrigan. I am."

"You're afraid of this attraction between us," he growled. "Don't be."

"I'm your client, remember? Or are you just needing a

fun way to pass the time until Grif sends you the information you need?"

Mick's jaw hardened, and he swore.

"Get off me," she said and though the words should have sounded emphatic, even angry, they came out much too panicky. She pushed again at his shoulders, and this time, he slid off her. She scrambled to her feet. Avoiding his sharp gaze, she hurried up the porch steps and grasped the doorknob.

But she didn't go inside. With the truth of her own actions weighing heavy on her conscience, she strove for the composure she would need to face him again.

Her mother would have been proud.

When Adrienne finally turned around, all her defenses back into place, her demeanor cool and in control, she found him right behind her. She tilted her head back to face him squarely.

"Perhaps I've been too harsh," she said. "You weren't the only one in my bed that night, were you?"

His eyes darkened. She sensed he'd relived their time together as often as she had. And that he hurt from it, too.

"For what it's worth, Morelli," he said, his voice low. Husky. "I haven't been with another woman since then. I didn't want--there's no appeal--" He clamped his mouth shut.

Shock rolled through her. He could've had any female he wanted. A different one for every night on the calendar. A male as healthy and virile as Mick Corrigan would be a hot item on any woman's want list.

He thought he was doing the right thing when he left her all those months ago. Yet somehow, his integrity and honor had backfired on him.

She turned away to hide her reaction and slid the key into the lock. Before pushing the door open, she swiveled back to him. She didn't question the wisdom of what she was about to admit, only that hc deserved her honesty as much as she deserved his.

"I gave you a pretty damned special part of me, Mick. No matter what happens between us after we leave these mountains, you might as well know there'll never be a man like you in my life again."

He held her glance.

"Never?" he asked softly.

She shook her head, riveted by the heat in his eyes.

"Not in my lifetime," she said and went inside.

* * *

Mick made a thorough sweep of the cabin and found it safe from an intruder. Adrienne set up her laptop on the Stocktons' kitchen table and logged into her email account. Grif had already sent several messages.

She clicked on the first one, and a list of names appeared.

"The Scott's Gulf Alliance," she said and tapped a finger on the screen. "There's Denny Ray, right under Izzie and Dietrich."

"Are the rest of the names familiar to you?"

"Yes. I recognize them from correspondence we've had from the group. Looks legit."

"But you've never met any of them personally?"

"No. Dad attended the board meetings with them. Not me." She grimaced ruefully. "I'm just the lowly daughter. He's the governor, you know."

"All right." Mick filed the names away in his memory. "Go on to the next one."

She clicked again, and the second message opened. "Murdock's board of directors."

"How about these?"

"I know some of them, but not all." She mentioned a few names on the list, among them Ronald Kershner. "My father has had the company investigated, Mick. Before my mother died. He would never have considered the state's acceptance of their land deed unless they were squeaky clean."

"Yes. I know."

"So why did you want both lists?"

"For cross reference. I want to see if a name shows up twice."

She glanced at him in surprise. "But that would be a conflict of interest."

"Exactly."

Intent on the screen, he leaned closer and took over the laptop's cursor to switch back and forth between the messages, double-checking one more time in case he missed someone. He hadn't.

He opened the final post from Grif. "He's traced the plates. The Lexus is leased to a company called 'Tyler Enterprises'."

Adrienne made a sound of derision. "Well, that makes sense. They're the ones who want to build the resort," she said. "They've made Dad's life miserable. And now they're trying to do the same thing to me. Click on the link Grif sent you."

She indicated the address of a website that clearly belonged to the corporation. Within seconds, an elaborate image appeared of a pine-covered mountain range with a bird soaring over one of the peaks.

"Mountain Crest Resorts." She frowned and studied the image hard.

"What's the matter?" Mick asked.

"Something about that logo looks familiar," she said.

"Maybe you saw it on one of their letterheads or something."

"I don't think so. As far as I know, Tyler Enterprises has never contacted my father directly. Scroll down, will you? There's more to Grif's post."

Mick did, reading as he went. "He's cut and pasted a list of Tyler Enterprise's board of directors for us." Mick studied the names. "Wait a minute." He clicked back to the previous message listing Murdock's board of directors. "Tyler, Tyler," he muttered under his breath as he scrolled down the alphabetical list of names yet again. "There it is. Eddison

Tyler."

Adrienne stared at the words. "I didn't notice it before. He's on both boards? Murdock *and* Tyler Enterprises?"

Mick whistled, long and low. "Talk about a conflict of interest, Morelli."

"But if he's owner--"

"Tyler's a common name. Could be some distant family member owns the company instead."

"It doesn't matter. If he's associated with Tyler Enterprises, who wants to build the resort, what is he doing on Murdock's board, who wants to keep Scott's Gulf pure wilderness? Doesn't make sense."

"No, it doesn't. But there's his name in black and white." Mick switched back and forth between lists. "I'll check into it."

Adrienne shook her head in bemusement. "Like I said, no one from Tyler Enterprises has contacted Dad to try to convince him to refuse the two thousand acres."

"But Mayor Webster has."

"Yes."

"We should call your father to find out what he knows about them."

She shook her head. "I'd rather not talk to him just yet. He'll only ask questions I'm not ready to give answers for. Truthful ones, anyway. Besides, Murdock is signing the deed to us in a few hours. I don't want to jinx it."

Mentally, Mick listed the scares she'd had since they left Nashville. The bloody, poetic message on the bathroom mirror. Farley. The Lexus that ran them off the road. Mayor Webster. Denny Ray's suspicious behavior.

Hell. No wonder she didn't want to talk to her father. He'd have heart failure.

Despite the late hour, they both read the Tyler Enterprises website thoroughly.

"Damn," he said after they finished. He ran a hand over his jaw.

"What's the matter?" she asked. "You look frustrated."

"I am. I was hoping we'd find Mayor Webster on one of these lists. Some sort of connection we could nail him on."

"He's made sure he couldn't be traced to them, it seems." She gasped. "Oh, my God."

At her exclamation, his gaze jumped to her. She'd grown pale.

"What is it, Adrienne?" he demanded.

"That bird." She scrolled back to the Tyler Enterprises logo. "I remember now where I saw it."

"Where?"

"On Denny Ray's watch."

# CHAPTER NINE

She had to be mistaken, Adrienne told herself yet again as she put the finishing touches on her make-up only minutes before they were to leave for Hickoryville.

There were at least a hundred different falcon designs around, especially in this part of the country where the species was revered, having recently been taken off the endangered list. Just because Denny Ray sported something similar to the logo Tyler Enterprises used didn't mean he was connected with them.

Yes, she could easily be wrong. In fact, she had to be. After all, the lighting hadn't been good outside the Golden Eagle last night. Dusk had fallen, and the glimpse of Denny Ray's gold watch had been fleeting.

She'd see him again soon. He would be in Hickoryville with the rest of the Scott's Gulf Alliance. She'd find a way to look at the watch's face again to be sure.

"If we're going to get to Hickoryville on time, we'll have to leave in the next three minutes," Mick said.

Punctual as ever, he leaned a shoulder against her bedroom door and watched her fasten a pearl earring in her lobe. Adrienne could swear the man had a built-in clock somewhere in his system that prevented him from ever being late. Or even rushed.

"I'm ready." She withdrew a strand of faux pearls from her travel jewelry case and closed the lid.

His eyes darkened appreciatively as he skimmed her sapphire blue pantsuit with its scattering of pearl beads around the neckline.

Her stomach tightened at the power of that appreciation. He made her feel beautiful without saying a word.

"You look like you could eat me alive," she said, trying to keep her tone teasing. She handed him the pearls and turned, lifting the hair from her neck.

"When you look this good, yeah, I think I could," he muttered.

"You don't look so bad yourself, you know."

"Typical bodyguard attire, that's all."

Hardly. The dark grey suit and silk tie fit as if he were born to them; they looked expensive enough to please royalty.

The man had good taste in clothes. No doubt about it. But then, he looked good in jeans and a tee shirt, too. Or in nothing at all. She almost sighed out loud.

After he fastened the clasp, the pearls rested on her collar bone, and their surface felt cool against her skin. Instead of stepping back, however, Mick's hands settled on the curve of her shoulders. His grasp tightened, as if he was reluctant to let her go. As if there was something on his mind that he needed to say.

Adrienne held her breath. A troubled light had stolen into his eyes, making them darker than usual. He hadn't been happy to learn of Denny Ray's possible connection to Tyler Enterprises, even though Adrienne had been quick to point out the evidence was circumstantial at best.

She knew what Mick wanted to say, and she refused to meet his glance in the dresser mirror. He released her; his hands curled into fists at his sides.

"If I thought I could convince you to let someone else accept the land deed in your place tonight, I'd take you back to Nashville right now," he said roughly.

"You're right. You can't convince me."

"If your mother's killer is going to strike, Adrienne, it'll be in Hickoryville. Before Murdock hands over that land deed."

She fought down a shudder. "You don't mince words, do you, Mick?"

"Not where your safety is concerned."

"We're an hour away from victory over my mother's murderer. We'll have what he wants. After all this time, do you really think I'd walk away now?"

His mouth thinned. "No."

She retrieved her sapphire blue purse from the dresser top. "Then what are we waiting for? Let's go."

*  *  *

Izzie Stockton was waiting for them. With her kind face wreathed in smiles, she rushed forward as soon as Mick put the Range Rover into 'Park'. She held Adrienne's door open before Mick could even get through his.

She took Adrienne's hand into her own. "Can you believe it, dear? It's almost time."

Adrienne smiled. The elderly woman's excitement was catching. "It doesn't seem possible, does it?"

She slipped out of the SUV. Hickoryville's only paved street had been blocked off for the evening's festivities, stealing away what few parking places were available. Cars and pickup trucks lined the road leading into town and forced Mick to do the same with theirs.

"Oh, don't you look fine!" Izzie marveled with a shake of her graying head. She stepped back to admire Adrienne's appearance. "Why, you look like a movie star, just like your mama always did."

"Do you remember her films?" Adrienne steered the conversation away from herself. She'd always been proud of the work her mother had accomplished.

"Of course I do! Julia had quite a career going for her. At least, until she ended it to take care of you."

It had been her mother's choice to retire from Hollywood at the peak of her success to devote herself to her young politician husband and baby girl. But it pleased Adrienne that her reputation lingered with her fans still today.

"And here comes your leading man." Izzie chuckled at

her own joke.

Mick wore dark sunglasses in the late evening sun. His habit, Adrienne knew, to shield his eyes as he swept them over the crowd. She knew, too, his grim expression resulted from the immensity of the job ahead of him.

The little town of Hickoryville had sprouted at the foothills of the Cumberlands. The vast expanse of mountains and the thick growth of hemlocks and spruce, pines and balsam, blanketing the slopes could easily hide a sniper.

A killer's haven.

A bodyguard's worst nightmare.

"Has everyone arrived for the signing?" he asked Izzie.

"Yes. Except Mr. Kershner. As soon as he gets here, we can get started."

"How about Denny Ray?" Adrienne couldn't help asking.

"He was one of the first to drive up. That boy has been working harder than any of us. He wants everything to be perfect for you tonight."

"I'll bet he does," Mick drawled.

Adrienne tossed him an uncertain glance. Izzie's comment threw her opinions of the Park Ranger into a tailspin. She hoped, for the woman's sake, they found a logical answer for every suspicion he raised.

Mick took her elbow, his grasp firm and blatant in its message that he intended to stay close by her side. "Shall we?"

She gave him her brightest smile. They were minutes away from securing two thousand acres of prime wilderness for Tennessee. She wanted to savor the moments. "Of course."

"There's a whole passel of people I want you to meet," Izzie said, leading them away from the haphazard line of vehicles. "By the time we get you up to that podium, your head will fair be spinning from all of them."

Adrienne studied the simple stage erected in the street. Yards of red, white and blue bunting had been draped along the edges to hide the naked lumber. Rows of chairs lined the pavement in front of them, some already occupied by those eager for the presentation to begin.

Her mother would have gloried in the opportunity to stand in front of the crowd to give a brief speech, but Adrienne had to quell her misgivings from having to do so. She'd be exposed on that stage, ripe for any shot Julia Morelli's killer might make. She'd be helpless to prevent it.

On the other side of the street, booths had been set up, adding to the carnival-like atmosphere. Long tables covered with plastic cloths provided a place for citizens to eat the food prepared and offered for sale. The aromas of authentic southern cooking hung delightfully in the air.

"Smells wonderful!" she exclaimed. Neither of them had eaten since she fixed sandwiches at the cabin that afternoon.

"Doesn't it?" Izzie said. "I hope you're hungry. There's plenty to eat tonight."

Her husband, Dietrich, joined them, accompanied by several members of the Scott's Gulf Alliance. He introduced her, and she shook their hands, smiled and said all the right things to their profuse praise and respect for her parents' work, and to a lesser degree, her own. They were a down-to-earth bunch, easy to converse with, with none of the airs that might be found in the big cities. Adrienne enjoyed putting faces to the names she'd seen only on paper.

Since she had a few minutes to spare before the presentation, they paused near a booth where two women prepared green tomatoes for frying. A large bowl of buttermilk held a heap of marinating tomato slices. Another held corn flour, salt and pepper. A pair of cast iron skillets, filled with hot oil, crowded grills brought in for the festivities.

The women dunked the slices into the flour, then placed them in the oil for frying. It'd been years since Adrienne had tasted the southern dish, and watching these women work inspired her to make some when she returned home. Her father would enjoy them.

One of the women handed her a styrofoam plate piled

high with sizzling fried tomatoes, along with plastic ware wrapped in a white paper napkin.

"Try 'em, Miss Morelli," the woman beamed, her cheeks flushed. "They're mighty good."

"I'm sure they are, but, oh, I couldn't eat all these." Helplessly, she glanced over at Mick. "You'll have some, won't you?"

Mick's gaze dragged from the crowd to touch on the tomatoes. A corner of his mouth lifted in rare amusement.

"Sure," he said.

The woman stared at him with no pretense of hiding her curiosity. Or her appreciation. Mick slid his hand to the small of Adrienne's back to urge her onward. And let it linger there after she did.

"Her bodyguard," the woman's companion said in a whisper Adrienne could hear as she walked away. "Ain't he handsome?"

"Gawd. Handsome don't cut it."

Adrienne hid her smile. The women couldn't tell her anything she didn't already know.

Izzie checked her watch. "It's almost time to get started, Dietrich," she said. "Is Ronald Kershner here yet?"

"Haven't seen him." He added his scrutiny to his wife's over the crowd. "These mountain roads can be tricky, though. Might be that he got lost."

"Oh, Lordy, let's hope not. He'll never make it if he did. Not with the night coming on."

"The directions you gave us were simple and quite clear, Dietrich," Adrienne added. "I can't imagine him confusing them."

"We'll give him a little longer." Izzie had to raise her voice over the Sparta High School band, warming up their instruments. She gaped at a group of people on the far end of the Hickoryville street and clucked in disapproval. "Well, if that don't beat all! Dietrich, is that Ira Williamson?"

Her husband squinted. "Sure is. Him and that tourist trap snake show of his."

"Hmmph!"

"He's a serpent handler?" Mick asked sharply.

"Yes," Izzie said. "Belongs to one of those fundamentalist religions. Cults is what they are. Supposed to be against the law to handle them poisonous critters to where innocent citizens could get bit, but no one enforces it." She sniffed in disapproval. "They don't want to violate his civil rights, since he claims it's his religion he's practicing."

Adrienne grimaced. She knew snake handlers were on the fringes of modern society; their peculiarity was really their own faith and belief in the Bible's teachings. But Izzie was right. Law enforcement was difficult.

Someone in the crowd stepped aside, giving her a gruesome view of a half dozen poisonous timber rattlers as they coiled and slithered around Ira Williamson's neck and body. The man must have nerves of steel. The crowd gasped in horrified fascination.

For all her love of wildlife, reptiles fell at the bottom of the list. Adrienne could hardly stand to watch. Mick tugged her away.

"He'd damn well better keep track of them," he muttered.

"They give me the heebie-jeebies." Izzie shuddered.

"Me, too." Adrienne changed the subject. "Where am I supposed to sit?"

"The head table. See it there by the stage? The one with the pretty centerpiece on it." The place was easy to spot, but Izzie led her toward to it anyway. "Some of the Murdock folks are waiting for you."

Upon joining them, Adrienne set her plate of fried tomatoes down to acknowledge Izzie's introductions. Adrienne shook the beefy hand of Charlie Larkin, one of the members of the corporation's board of directors, a giant of a man with a belly that strained his shirt buttons alarmingly. But he had a smile to match his girth, and she warmed to him right away.

"I'm pleased to meet you, Charlie," she said.

"Likewise, young lady. I had the pleasure of workin' with your mama, God rest her soul."

"Can't tell you how happy I am to see you tonight, Miss Morelli," Larry Simms, another Murdock board member, added. His build was as slight as Charlie's was wide, and he pumped her head enthusiastically. "She'd be right proud that you've finished the work she started."

"I'm sure she's smiling down on all of us right now." Adrienne's heart constricted. Her mother should be standing here, accepting the accolades she'd earned. Not Adrienne. "But, truthfully, my father is the one who deserves the credit for seeing her dream come true. It's been in her memory that he's worked hard to rekindle your company's interest in donating the tract of wilderness land to the state of Tennessee."

"Your father's a fine man."

"Thank you. I've often thought so myself." Adrienne smiled.

"Let's sit down and have us a bite to eat," Charlie said, his voice booming with joviality, his attention already on his own plate. "The ceremony can't start until Ron gets here anyway."

Indeed. Ronald Kershner held the deed to the two thousand acres and without him, there *was* no ceremony. Adrienne took the place Mick discreetly indicated, a seat opposite Charlie that would place her back to the stage and allow her a clear view of the growing crowd. Mick took a stance close by, in front of the podium, his position unobtrusive but alert, his feet spread, his hands clasped behind his back.

The Stocktons didn't join her at the table but chatted with members of the Alliance. Adrienne knew their impatience to get the evening started and understood it. She was getting impatient, too. She wanted nothing more than to hold that land deed firmly in her hand.

"Well, look who's here," Charlie said, his southern drawl thick with disgust. "Eddison Tyler."

Her curiosity caught, Adrienne's glance searched the maze of people. "Where?"

"Over there, by the band kids. He's wearing a red tie."

Her stare latched onto him. He was smaller than she expected. A wiry man who faded in a crowd. He had no 'presence' as some would say, given the wealth from his family's company, Tyler Enterprises.

Correction. His *assumed* wealth. And his assumed family. Adrienne knew nothing about the man other than he shared the same name as the powerful corporation that worked behind the scenes to undermine her parents' work.

Tyler showed no inclination to join his fellow Murdock board members at the head table. Adrienne took advantage of the time to learn a little more about him.

"You sound as if you don't like him, Charlie," Adrienne mused.

"I don't make no bones about it, young lady. Eddison and I never got along."

"Never seen a man so focused on himself," Larry said. "He's been against this project from the beginning. Made your mama mighty frustrated at times, I suspect. Though she was too gracious to show it."

Adrienne recalled the last conversation she had with her mother that horrible afternoon at the mountain chalet. Her features clouded during their discussion; her father had mentioned someone being the proverbial 'bad apple'.

Had Eddison Tyler been that apple?

"You see, Miss Morelli, each one of us on the board at Murdock owns a piece of that wilderness. Our by-laws stipulate unanimous agreement is needed on any decision made regarding that property. Tyler resisted the rest of us for a long time," Charlie said.

"What made him change his mind?" she asked.

"Your mama. She could be very persuasive when she wanted to be." Larry shrugged. "But after her death, Tyler reneged on the deal."

"So Murdock was back to square one."

"That's right. Then your daddy came into the picture. He was mighty determined to see Tennessee get that land because your mama wanted it so bad. He aimed to see that she got it posthumously."

"Mountain Crest Resorts lobbied harder than ever," Charlie said, chewing around a mouthful of chicken thigh. "We had two deals on the table. Use these two thousand acres for a resort and pump some decent money into the economy--"

"And destroy some valuable wilderness along with it," Adrienne said.

Charlie wiped his mouth on a paper napkin. "Exactly. Or we could donate it and keep it preserved for damn near forever."

"We voted the resort idea down. Tyler wasn't pleasant about it, since it was his family's project, but by then, the rest of us plumb didn't care. We threatened to have him ousted off the board if he didn't quit his whining. The whole thing had gone on long enough. We owed it to your mama's memory to finish the deal we'd promised her before she was --before she passed on."

Adrienne considered the man as he stood with the group engrossed in the snake handler. So he had a vested, familial interest in Tyler Enterprises, after all. No wonder he resisted the donation of the land.

Charlie and Larry's explanation of the inner workings of the corporation's decisions regarding Scott's Gulf fascinated Adrienne. Obviously, both men held Julia Morelli in high regard, as did the rest of Murdock's board of directors.

Eddison Tyler seemed to be the sole exception.

"Hey, boys, what's up?"

Carrying a plate of chicken, coleslaw, and corn fried in bacon grease, Denny Ray took a seat beside Charlie. He was dressed in creased slacks and a dress shirt for the evening's festivities, and Adrienne's gaze immediately sought his wrist. Unfortunately, he wasn't wearing the gold watch she noticed last night; instead, a sportier piece circled his wrist, a familiar and inexpensive name brand with a black leather watchband. No form of Tyler Enterprises logo appeared on it.

Disappointed, her gaze lifted and encountered his. He winked, as cocky and flirtatious as ever, and an unexpected fluster went through her. He was more like the Denny Ray she met yesterday at the Golden Eagle--and less like the perplexing Park Ranger he'd been this afternoon.

"Hey, how're you doin', Adrienne?" he asked, shoveling a forkful of corn into his mouth. "You're looking mighty pretty tonight."

"Thank you." A faint bruising showed on his temple from where she'd kicked him. If he could put the events of this afternoon behind them, then she supposed she could, too.

"Won't be long now, will it?"

"No. At least, it won't be if Ronald Kershner arrives in the next few minutes."

Charlie glanced at his watch and frowned. "It's not like him to be this late."

"He's staying at the Golden Eagle, isn't he?" Larry pushed his plate away. "Suppose someone should drive into Sparta and check on him?"

"Let's call the motel first." Adrienne reached inside her purse for her cell phone.

"Y'all talking about calling Mr. Kershner?" Izzie asked. She took a seat next to Adrienne and set her cell phone onto the table top. She sighed worriedly. "I just did. His room and cell phone. He didn't answer either one."

"He must be on his way, then," Larry said.

Adrienne exchanged a troubled glance with Mick. The growing concern everyone felt was a palpable thing. She was determined to learn more of the Murdock representative's whereabouts, even if she had to climb into the Range Rover and go looking for him herself.

"I'm calling the motel's office." She scrolled through her list of contacts and found the number, then put the phone to her ear. Charlie and Larry, Izzie and Denny Ray, all watched her expectantly while she waited for someone to pick up.

"Good evening, Golden Eagle," a cheerful voice greeted on the other end.

"This is Adrienne Morelli with the state of Tennessee." Rarely did Adrienne use her influence as the governor's daughter to get what she wanted. But tonight was an exception. Two thousand acres was at stake. "I'm supposed to meet with an associate who's staying at the Golden Eagle. He's not answering his phone. Do you know if he's left a message for me or anyone else?"

"No, ma'am. No messages here that I can see."

She'd given Ronald her cell phone number last night at the Golden Eagle. She knew he had it; she'd watched him jot it down in his leather-covered planner. Why hadn't he called her direct if he was going to be delayed?

Her mind struggled to find every angle. "Would you pull up his name in your computer? I'm wondering if he's checked out early."

"His name, please?"

"Ronald Kershner. K-e-r-s-h-n-e-r."

"One moment."

Soft music came on the line.

Izzie shook her head. "I'm sure he intended to spend the night at the Golden Eagle. I distinctly remember him saying he was leaving tomorrow because he planned to make a side trip into Knoxville for--"

"Miss Morelli?" Adrienne quickly yanked her attention back to the motel employee. "We're still showing him checked in."

"You do?" Adrienne bit her lip. Nothing was adding up.

"Tell you what," the affable clerk said. "Let me put you on hold again. He left his license number with us. We have a view of that section of rooms from the office. I'll just step outside to take a peek to see if his car is parked outside his door."

Once more, the canned music played in her ear.

Izzie's lined face showed her worry. "Maybe he's taken sick or something."

"Maybe." Adrienne sighed. What then?

"Could be he got held up at the clinic. Those doctors there are always so slow."

"You would've thought he'd call us, though," Charlie said.

"He's diabetic, you know. Has been for years. Maybe his blood sugar's been acting up or something," Larry said.

"Hmmm." Adrienne drummed her fingers on the table.

"Ma'am?" The clerk took her off hold. "His car is parked outside his room, but I'm not at liberty to say anything more than that."

Abruptly, the line went dead.

Adrienne gaped at the phone in her hand.

"Why, land's sakes, child. What happened?" Izzie asked.

"He hung up on me. He was being so helpful, and then he just . . . hung up."

"Well, don't that beat all."

She turned to Mick. Though he didn't speak, she read his thoughts as vividly as if he'd spoken them aloud.

Ronald Kershner left no word about his delay in joining them in Hickoryville. He was still checked in at the hotel. And his car was parked right outside his room.

Why wasn't he here?

Something was terribly wrong.

# CHAPTER TEN

The Sparta High School band played the state song, "When It's Iris Time in Tennessee," with youthful enthusiasm. The notes from the graceful waltz filled the evening air, and the crowd hummed along, the tune as familiar to them as a childhood lullaby.

But Mick shut the music out of his realm of concentration, his thoughts riveted on Adrienne's phone conversation instead. The color had drained from her cheeks; whatever the Golden Eagle's clerk told her confirmed the ugly suspicions swarming around inside Mick's head.

Ronald Kershner had every intention of being in Hickoryville tonight. His absence meant trouble.

The presentation should have started almost an hour ago. The crowd had grown increasingly restless, their attention distracted from the band's attempts to entertain them. Frowning faces stared at the head table in silent but polite demand for an explanation.

His own impatience raged. The longer Adrienne was delayed in acquiring the land deed, the higher the risk for her safety. And a stronger advantage for her mother's murderer.

He ran a sharp eye over the crowd. The killer could be any one of the blur of bodies out there. He'd be deceptive in his presence, fooling them all with enthusiasm for the acquisition of the two thousand acres of wilderness on the outside--and hating Adrienne for acquiring it on the inside.

"Well, I'm all for us climbing in our cars to have us a

look-see at what's goin' on at the Golden Eagle," Charlie said, his voice booming over the others' in their agitated discussion about what to do next. "Ron is a friend of mine. Don't mind telling you I'm worried about him."

"Lordy, all these people are waiting," Izzie fussed. "Even if you left right now, it'll be an hour at the very least before you get back here. What are we going to do in the meantime? People aren't going to wait that long. Can't say as I blame them."

"I'll make an announcement saying we've been forced to postpone the ceremony," Adrienne said. "If Ronald has fallen ill or something, everyone will understand."

"We can reschedule for the morning," Dietrich said hopefully. "Or tomorrow night, even."

"It's not that easy," Izzie said, her tone lamenting.

"It will have to be done." Adrienne's firm voice took control of the situation. "We can't have a ceremony without a land deed."

Izzie blinked back tears, and her husband patted her shoulder in sympathy. Mick regretted her disappointment. Of all of them, she'd worked the hardest in organizing the evening's celebration. Preserving this area of Scott's Gulf had been a major focus in her life.

Once again, he scanned the haphazard arrangement of vehicles on the edge of the little town and hoped Kershner would magically appear. He spied a patrolman's car driving up the road instead.

Officer Radley parked and stepped out. Mick tensed at his grim expression. The officer scanned the crowd, as if searching for someone.

Mick pulled off his sunglasses and slipped them into a pocket of his suit coat. If Radley intended to participate in the evening's festivities, he would have been here long before now.

He was here on business, Mick knew. And the news wasn't good.

"Adrienne." He kept his voice low.

Her head lifted, and he indicated the officer's arrival. She nodded in acknowledgement and slipped away from the group to approach Radley.

He met her with a curt nod. "Good evening, Miss Morelli."

"Frankly, Officer, the evening could be better," she said, her smile forced. "Why do I get the feeling you're not here to celebrate with the rest of us?"

"I thought you should know before you heard it on the news." He hesitated. "Ronald Kershner has been murdered."

"Oh, my God." She swayed and pressed trembling fingers to her mouth. Mick slipped his arm around her, holding her against him.

"One of the Golden Eagle's maids found him. He'd been shot at close range. No sign of forced entry . . . next of kin have already been notified . . .."

The patrolman's voice faded. Mick grabbed a chair and quickly eased Adrienne into it.

Raw fear bit into him. The killer had struck again to delay the transfer of the land deed. If Adrienne continued to pursue the acquisition, she would be next on the killer's hit list.

Mick had to get her back to Nashville. Now. A quick trip back to the cabin to collect their things, and she'd be safe in her bed hours before dawn. This time, he wouldn't take no for an answer.

His mind raced through the details, the phone calls he'd need to make. Her father would have to be notified immediately. Grif, too. Mick planned to insist upon 24-hour protection for Adrienne as well as her father, and--

Izzie's cry wailed over the crowd, revealing her gut-wrenching reaction to the news. Shock rolled through her husband, the other Murdock board members, the Scott's Gulf Alliance. The devastation showed in their faces.

Rumbles of distress sifted through the people as word spread of the man's brutal death. Whatever he'd done in his life, his endeavors to preserve the wilderness didn't entitle him to die for it, and Mick's gut tightened at the unfairness.

"What's goin' on here?"

Farley tromped toward them with clenched fists. He still wore the same blood-stained overalls from this afternoon, but Mick subjected him to a fierce inspection for fresher blood. After they buried the opossum in the forest, Mick had been half-way convinced of Farley's innocence, at least in running Adrienne off the road. Now, with Ronald Kershner dead, the suspicions surged forth all over again.

"Folks are sayin' someone from Murdock is dead. That right?" Farley demanded.

"Yes," Mick said. "Know anything about it?"

Farley's eyes narrowed. "You claimin' I had somethin' to do with him dyin', boy?"

"Just wondering if you know anything about it."

"Hell, no, I don't!"

"Mick." Ashen-faced, Adrienne touched his arm. "Let Officer Radley talk to him."

"Don't have nothin' to say to no cop, young lady," Farley snapped before Mick could reply. "I ain't done nothin'."

"We'll be questioning everyone involved in the land acquisition," Radley added with a stern expression. "You've been outspoken in your opinions against it, Farley. Have been for a long time."

"What's the matter? Ain't a man got a right to express his opinion no more? Why, this dadburned government--"

"Grandpa! Now, you just hush!" A middle-aged, brassy-blonde woman rushed toward them. She took Farley's hand firmly into hers. "This ain't the time to get up on your soapbox again. Land sakes!" She sighed, clearly exasperated with him. Her glance found Adrienne. "I'm so sorry he's been bothering you, Miss Morelli. Truly I am."

"He hasn't been a bother." Adrienne's mouth curved in a tight smile. "Bess, isn't it?"

"You remember me?"

"Of course. From the Sparta drugstore." Adrienne met Mick's questioning gaze. "When I had to buy lipstick."

His curt nod said he understood. An employee there, evidently. She possessed none of her grandfather's antagonism, at least, not where Adrienne was concerned.

"Come on, Grandpa. Let's go home. I guess there won't be a ceremony tonight after all," Bess said.

"No," Adrienne said sadly.

"I ain't leavin' 'til I find out what's goin' on around here." Farley resisted Bess's tug on his arm. He glared at Adrienne. "Does this mean them acres of Scott's Gulf ain't goin' to the state after all?"

"They most certainly *will* be deeded to Tennessee." She rose from her chair and met Farley eye to eye. "However, unfortunately, it won't be tonight. Out of respect for Mr. Kershner, we will postpone the signing. But those acres will be ours, Farley, even if I have to arrange a secret signing to do it."

"That so?"

"Yes!"

"Anything else you want to know, Farley?" Mick purred. It wasn't often Adrienne let her grace slip, but she stood her ground now, and Mick's hands fisted to keep from applauding.

"Reckon she told me what I wanted to know, boy."

"C'mon, Grandpa." Bess tugged again, and this time Farley didn't resist. "I'm right sorry about your friend, Miss Morelli." Bess's glance included Mick. "I sure am."

"Thank you."

After they left, Officer Radley patted her shoulder. "You'd best go on home, too," he said. "We've called in a forensics team from Knoxville to investigate. I'll keep you posted of any developments in the case."

"Please do," she said. "But there's a lot of work to do here. I want to help."

"Nonsense," Izzie said, dabbing at her eyes with tissue. "There's plenty of people around to pitch in. Things always come down faster than they go up."

"That's right," Dietrich added, his arm firmly around her shoulders. "Denny Ray's got things going already."

"That boy is good at organizing when he puts his head to it." Izzie nodded, more like herself now that the shock of Kershner's death had settled in.

It seemed to be true, Mick mused. Denny Ray had taken charge of the town's clean up. The high school band was busy packing instruments into their cases; women folded bunting and discarded decorations; men dismantled tables and chairs. The booths had closed up, food put away. Even the snake handler was gone. Denny Ray was in the middle of it all, working as hard as any of them.

"All right, then." Adrienne embraced Izzie and Dietrich with a promise she'd call soon, and the elderly couple left. Charlie and Larry, both grief-stricken at the loss of their peer, did the same.

Mick took Adrienne's elbow. "I'm getting you out of here."

"Wait," Officer Radley said. "I almost forgot to tell you we got the results in."

Mick's attention sharpened. "From the blood on Adrienne's bathroom mirror?"

"That's right. It was blood all right. But not human."

He frowned. "What then?"

"Opossum."

"Farley?" Adrienne asked, eyes wide.

"No," Mick said firmly. "He wouldn't have used their blood to write the poem. He loves them too much."

"I agree. Everyone 'round these parts knows that." The young police officer lifted his hat and scratched his head. "I'm told one of the critters was found buried in the Golden Eagle's dumpster with its throat slit. Could be whoever wrote that message wanted to swing suspicion onto the old man. He gets confused sometimes. And his obsession with them is bizarre."

"He's not the killer." Mick recalled the contents of the

poem, the cleverness of the words. Farley's back-mountain way of talking didn't fit.

Officer Radley shook his head with a heavy sigh. "Then who is?"

"Damned if I know," Mick growled. "I just hope the law around here finds out. And quick."

"We're doing all we can."

Mick set his teeth against the trite response. His impatience rejected the truth in it. "I'm taking Adrienne back home. You have my cell phone number. Call me as soon as you hear anything."

"I will."

"You ready, Adrienne?" he asked.

"My purse. Let me get it," she said.

The head table was the only one still standing. Her sapphire blue bag sat on top and contrasted sharply with the white plastic tablecloth. Next to it, someone had thoughtfully left her plate of fried green tomatoes, had even gone so far as to cover it with an inverted one, using it as a lid. A paper napkin had been draped on top.

She swept up her purse with one hand; with the other, she took the plate. The napkin fluttered off, and she froze.

"Oh, no. Oh, God, no."

Mick strode to her side in an instant. "What is it?"

Her throat worked, but she couldn't speak. She thrust the container toward him.

He stared at the message scrawled into the Styrofoam.

*Save the wilderness. Lose your life.*
*And dead you'll be like Daniel's wife.*

Julia Morelli's murderer was here. In Hickoryville. He'd been close enough to Adrienne to touch her.

To kill her.

Mick swore.

\* \* \*

Mick pushed the SUV to the limits of safety as he raced along the winding mountain road that took them from Hickoryville back to the Stocktons' cabin. Adrienne gripped the edges of her seat, more from numbed reaction to the haunting message than from Mick's driving.

She'd been spared. For a reason she couldn't understand, the killer struck at Ronald Kershner instead of her.

Anguish welled inside her. He didn't deserve to die. He'd only been doing his job. As public relations rep for Murdock, it was his duty to attend the Hickoryville ceremony. He'd had no part in the decision made by the board of directors. The signing of the land deed would only have been a formality.

Clearly, the murder was a warning to Adrienne and her father. Now, the killer would know the acquisition was delayed. He was victorious in winning more time to convince them to give it up.

And what could be more convincing than the threat of death?

She stifled a moan. When would it all end? How many more lives would be lost before the two thousand acres belonged to the state of Tennessee?

Was that beautiful land worth it?

Adrienne's head spun from the stinging questions. She drew in a long breath and shook off her confusion. Her fear. To give up now would let the killer win, she told herself fiercely. Julia Morelli paid the ultimate price for her dream. Adrienne vowed neither she nor her father would pay in the same way.

She'd have to outsmart the killer. It was as simple as cinching the deal behind closed doors, with no publicity, she decided. In Nashville, if necessary, at the Capitol Building.

But she'd have to work fast. Before the killer could strike again.

Suddenly, she couldn't wait to get home. Mick couldn't drive quickly enough.

They approached the final curve leading toward the Stocktons' cabin. He slowed and turned off the Range Rover's headlights, throwing them under a blanket of darkness. There were no street lights on the mountain, not this far from the highway, and only a faint sliver of moon provided any illumination.

The eeriness chilled her. He drove in more by feel than sight.

"If he's waiting for us, I want the element of surprise," he said, his voice low.

With the haste she was feeling now, she would've driven in like a gazelle with bells on. "You think of everything, don't you, Corrigan?"

He glanced at her. "Where you're concerned, yes."

He slipped the vehicle into 'Park'. The yard looked black as a Tennessee coal mine. She could barely discern the shape of the trees.

"I'll go in first." He reached into the glove compartment and found a flashlight. "After I check the place out, I'll bring you in, you'll get your things and we'll get the hell out of here. Understand?"

She nodded. His urgency was a volatile thing.

"Duck down in the seat so no one can see you," he said. His hand rested on the door handle. "I'll lock you in."

"Mick." A sudden fear shot through her. She didn't want to sit in the Range Rover alone, and she didn't want him to go into the cabin alone, either. "I'll come with you."

He hesitated, as if he was just as reluctant to leave her. "It's an easy guess your mother's murderer knows you're staying here. If he starts shooting from inside the cabin, I don't want you hit. You're safer in the car."

Ronald Kershner had been shot at close range. Her mother, from a distance. If the killer wanted Adrienne dead in the next few minutes, he'd find a way to do it, no matter how far away he was.

If nothing else, the night would be on her side as much as his. She'd make a difficult target sitting out of view inside a dark vehicle.

"All right, Mick. Just be careful." She slid lower into the seat.

A corner of his mouth lifted. "'Careful' is my middle name, honey."

Gripping the Beretta, he left the SUV and sprinted up the porch steps, pausing only a moment before he opened the door and slipped inside. Her heart pounded harder when she couldn't see him anymore; she quelled her imagination of all that could go wrong in the dark. Time passed with agonizing slowness, but at last, the Range Rover's locks popped up, and he was there, holding the door open for her. He grasped her arm; together, they ran into the cabin.

"Work fast," he ordered. Guided by the flashlight, she headed for her bedroom. He headed for his. "We're on the road in five minutes."

Adrienne flipped on the overhead light and spied the rumpled bed, the clothes and bath towel strewn on top. Had she really been that messy? It wasn't like her, but she'd been nervous about speaking to the crowd in Hickoryville. Obviously, she spent extra time on her appearance and less on cleaning up after herself.

She tossed her purse onto the bed and strode toward the small closet where she kept her carry-all, briefcase and single piece of luggage. A slight rustling sound stopped her in mid-stride. Her brain flashed an image of a window easing open, as if someone was outside, on the porch, trying to break in. Her gaze flew toward the only window in the room.

The starched cotton curtains hadn't moved. The casement was closed, locked securely, like it had always been.

Damn it. The night's events hurtled her imagination into overdrive, but she couldn't help moving a little faster toward the closet door to get her carry-all. She bent to retrieve it from the floor, and the rustling noise came again, louder this time. Distinct and persistent.

She froze.

The clothes on the bed moved. Just the slightest shifting, *slithering*, across the bedspread. Her heart began a slow, drumming pound.

A rattlesnake's triangular-shaped head appeared beneath

the edge of the bath towel. Its tongue flitted in and out, searching her presence. More and more of its gray and black-flecked body appeared as it slid and coiled over the mattress, down the side, then under the box spring to escape into the darkness under the bed.

Adrienne was too stunned to cry out. A chilling rattle hissed from the closet. She jerked back, her horrified stare riveted to her carry-all, to a second snake curled inside with its beady eyes watching her.

She screamed and leapt back. Terror overrode every rule she'd ever heard about reacting to a snake, but she'd almost picked up that bag. With the snake inside . . . oh, God, oh, God . . ..

Footsteps thundered across the floor. Mick bolted in her bedroom, and she whirled toward him, but another snake coiled out of a partially open dresser drawer, and she halted with a cry.

Mick breathed a curse from the doorway. "They're everywhere."

His arm hooked around her shoulders and dragged her backward against him, his determination to yank her out of the room overriding her inability to get out on her own. She sucked in air, fighting down a debilitating fear.

"He was here, Mick. He was here." Her fingers dug into his forearm and clung.

"I know, honey. I'm getting you out. We're going someplace where he won't find you."

She whimpered her despair. No matter what Mick said, whatever he promised, the killer would find her. He knew where she was.

He always knew.

He was only biding his time. Toying with her. Scaring her.

Mick pulled her into the living room and snapped on the overhead light. He released his death grip on her and steadied her in the corner near the door. He pushed the baby Glock into her palm.

"I'm going to get a few things." He clasped her chin, forced her to look at him. "Stay right here. They won't hurt you if you leave them alone. But if one gets too close, shoot it."

She nodded and gripped the pistol with both hands, her arms extended with the barrel pointed toward the floor. He stepped away from her and into the hall, to the closet between the bedrooms.

"Hurry, Mick." She pressed back against the wall. Her wild gaze clawed the carpet, the furniture. Her skin crawled in dread of the venomous reptiles. "Just hurry. The place is infested."

Another snake, no, two more, hissed and slithered beneath the couch. Another sidewinded its way into the kitchen and behind the refrigerator. They sought the darkness, a place to hide. Adrienne numbly recalled rattlesnakes only struck out when threatened.

But oh, God, there were so many, so many . . ..

"Let's go." Mick appeared next to her, his arms full of blankets. He grabbed her wrist, flung open the door and ran with her into the darkness outside.

The SUV's locks popped up. He threw the blankets into the back seat. After fumbling with the handle, Adrienne managed to get the passenger door open. She leapt inside and drew her knees up tight against her chest. She couldn't stop shaking.

The motor purred to life. Mick shoved the gearshift into 'Drive', and with dirt and gravel spinning beneath the tires, they tore out of the Stocktons' driveway and raced into the Tennessee night.

\* \* \*

*It was all he could do to keep from laughing out loud.*

*Corrigan and Adrienne ran away like scared mice, and all because of a few, well-planted rattlers.*

*He had Ira Williamson to thank for the cold-blooded beauties. His little sideshow in Hickoryville provided the perfect opportunity to give Daniel Morelli's daughter a message she wouldn't soon forget.*

*Stubborn bitch.*

*How many times was he going to have to tell her?*

*When would she finally start to listen?*

*He was proud of the poems he'd written. Clever ditties, if he didn't say so himself.*

*But they weren't working. Not like he thought they would.*

*Time to get serious. Really serious.*

*The next time he saw Adrienne Morelli, she would listen to every word he had to say.*

# CHAPTER ELEVEN

They hadn't driven very far before the realization slammed into Mick.

They could be tracked.

He glared down at the button on the high-tech dash, the one belonging to the vehicle's global positioning system, and slammed on the brakes, right there in the middle of the road.

"What are you doing?" Adrienne gasped.

"We have to get out." He cut the engine. "Now."

"Get out?" She twisted in the seat, her gaze stabbing the black ribbon of road behind them. "Is someone after us?"

"Not yet." He reached toward the back seat and snatched the flashlight.

"Damn it, Mick, there's no way I'm getting out of--"

"This system"--he tapped the screen on the dashboard-- "emits electronic data, and our location can be detected, remember? I used it to find you when Denny Ray took you into the forest this afternoon. The killer could do the same thing."

A breath rushed out of her lungs. "So what are we going to do?"

He eyed her elegant pantsuit, the heels on her silver pumps. "Run for it."

She blinked.

"Get out," he said again and reached beneath the dash to pull the lever to the hood.

"Okay. Okay." She unbuckled her seat belt. "We'd better disconnect the battery, then. The tracking service won't function without it."

"I'm a step ahead of you, Morelli." He exited the SUV, lifted the hood and shined the flashlight over the engine system. While he disengaged the cables, she grabbed the blankets from the back seat.

He took one from her, tucked it under his arm, and pulled her with him from the road. He turned on the flashlight; the beam could be a dead giveaway of their location, but to traipse up the mountain without it would be foolish. They needed to see to escape whoever was after Adrienne, and there wasn't enough moonlight to be of any help.

And with the shoes she was wearing, she didn't need a turned ankle, either.

"Where are we going?" she asked.

"A place where we can hide out for awhile." His hand dwarfed hers. Her grasp was tight. Trusting.

She dodged a branch. "How far away?"

"Not sure."

"Within running distance?"

"I doubt it."

"Oh, great."

"I haven't been there in a long time. My bearings are a little rusty right now. Watch out for those rocks."

She leapt over them. "This is a big mountain, Corrigan. It's dark. And your bearings are rusty?"

"They'll come back to me."

"We could run until we drop and still not know where we are."

"I'm not that lost."

She slowed to a stop, her chest heaving from the uphill exertions. "We have to call somebody. The police or--or something."

He watched her, her closeness allowing him to see her fear, so strong he could almost taste it. "We'll call for help when we're safe enough to wait for it. Right now, we have to keep moving."

For a long moment, she didn't say anything, as if she needed some time to convince herself of his logic. To believe in it. Finally, she nodded, drew in a breath and blew it out again. "Okay. I can run as long as we need to. I'm not going to make it easy for him to find us."

"Neither of us are."

They took off again, but the uneven terrain and her dress heels kept them from the speed they could've maintained if they were both wearing Nikes in broad daylight. Adrienne had trained her body for endurance most of her life, Mick knew, and she matched him mile for mile up the mountain. Eventually, however, even he had to admit they'd run far enough.

They needed a Plan B.

The hill abruptly leveled into a clearing. Winded, they stumbled to a stop and fell into each other. Mick caught her in a one-armed embrace, leaning into her as much as she leaned into him. The bulk of the blankets they carried prevented them from full-body contact, but Adrienne managed to turn into him enough to rest her forehead against his chest.

"Have you ever had a client who was as much trouble as I am?" she asked between breaths.

He couldn't help a rueful grin. "Never."

"I'm sorry to put you through all this. It goes beyond the job description."

"Am I complaining?" He let the bundle under his arm drop to the ground, turned off the flashlight and wrapped the other arm around her. He settled his chin on the top of her head. "Let's see. The title of my final report to Silverhawk Investigative Services will be: 'Client, Adrienne Morelli. Number one Pain in the Ass.'"

Her head lifted, and though her mouth pursed in a pout, he could see her reluctant amusement, too. "Mick, stop. That's not funny."

The canopy of branches blocked out the stingy moon and shrouded them with a deep, velvet darkness.

Somewhere, a bird fluttered its wings, the only sound to break the stark, cavernous silence except their own hushed voices.

They were safe here. He wanted to assure her of that. Still, the peace was deceiving. Fleeting. They couldn't linger long.

"Where's your sense of humor, Morelli?" he asked. He lowered his head, dallying longer than he should, and brushed the tip of her nose with his own.

"It seems I've lost it somewhere between a threatening poem and a cabin full of venomous snakes."

"That'll do it, I guess."

"Works for me."

Despite her flippant response, he heard the worry in her tone, and it became imperative that she believe in his protection. He wasn't going to let her get hurt. He wouldn't fail.

He would die first.

He angled his head, closed his mouth over her lips and absorbed their trembling. He sought to soothe her with the kiss, but an unexpected fire erupted inside him, and his arms tightened around her, bringing her closer to his chest.

She sank into him, one arm sliding around his neck, as if she craved the soothing. Her head angled, too, seeking more of him, but just when Mick's mind emptied of all but the feel of her, she stiffened and pushed against him, bringing thoughts of their circumstances rushing back again.

"Oh, no, you don't, Corrigan," she said, her voice shaky. "Kiss me like that, and you mess up my head. I have to be able to think straight."

"Maybe we both needed that kiss." He regarded her. "You feel better for it?"

She tucked her hair behind her ear. Swallowed. "Yes."

He sensed her reluctance to make the admission. And took satisfaction from it. She didn't want to acknowledge the effect he had on her, he suspected, even to herself. "Then it was worth the time we took to share it."

He stepped back, all business again, and picked up the blanket he'd dropped. He straightened and discovered her attention riveted on something behind him.

"There's a light over there," she said. "Someone's yard, I think."

A rough-hewn shack was nestled in a shallow valley carved into the mountain. A single yard light, strung on a pole at the back of the structure, bathed the area with dim illumination.

The shack's windows were dark. Either the place was empty or its occupants had retired for the night.

Mick's glance scoured the place--he noted the absence of animals, the clutter strewn on the ground--and settled on an old pickup.

Bingo.

"Ever hot-wire a truck before?" he asked.

Her eyes widened. "You can't be serious."

"Watch me." He turned on the flashlight again, took her hand and led her down the hill.

"But we'd be stealing."

"Borrowing. We'll give it back."

"I'm representing the state of Tennessee, Mick. In my position--Dad will never condone us doing this."

"He'd do the same thing if he was stuck on a mountain at midnight trying to get away from someone determined to kill him."

Their steps quickened once they descended the hill; they kept their entry into the yard cautious, stealthy. Mick's muscles coiled as they drew closer to the pickup. A dog sensing their presence could start barking any minute or, worse, attack.

"Maybe they have cats," Adrienne whispered, on the same line of thinking he was.

Luck was evidently on their side. A dog would've picked up on them by now. Mick dropped the blanket into the truck bed and opened the dented, rusting door. The hinges creaked and groaned, and he winced, darting a quick glance to the shack. Thankfully, no lights came on, and he squatted to run the flashlight's beam under the steering column.

"Help me push the truck out of the yard," he ordered in a low voice. "That pole light makes us an easy target." Leaning inside the cab, he checked to make sure the gears were set at 'Neutral.'

She quickly deposited her blanket on top of his. She opened her door inch by inch, avoiding the screech of hinges as much as she could. She glanced over at him with a whispered 'okay'.

They leaned their bodies into the push. With their combined muscle, the tires began to turn. The yard's slight decline worked to their advantage, and the truck rolled fairly quickly, forcing Mick and Adrienne into a sprint to keep up. He reached in, grasped the steering wheel, and made the turn from the premises onto a dirt road which, he presumed, would wind about the mountain and eventually lead to the highway.

Once the ground leveled out again, the old truck slowed to a stop.

"Climb in," Mick said. "It'll just take a minute or two to wire this baby to life. Hold the flashlight for me, will you?"

The truck's bench seat had long since seen better days, and foam shown through in places where the vinyl had cracked and torn, the edges curled and stiff. Trash littered the floorboard; dust and grime layered themselves wherever they could reach, and Adrienne grimaced in distaste.

"This thing is *filthy*," she said, settling in carefully. She took the flashlight and shined it beneath the steering column for him, but just as he reached under, she made a sound of protest. "Mick. You'll get your jacket dirty."

He paused, conceding she was right. "You're fussing like a wife, Morelli. You know that?"

She pointedly ignored him while he shrugged out of it and handed it to her. "Must be a woman thing. You paid a fortune for that suit. A shame to ruin it."

He loosened his tie and rolled up his shirt sleeves, baring

his forearms, and declined to inform her he rather liked her fussing over him. "Must be a guy thing not to think of that."

"Typical, isn't it?" she retorted.

He grinned and set to work. Soon, the old truck sputtered and spit and rumbled, and he eased out from under the column. Just as he was about to climb behind the wheel, he noticed what lay in the back end with their blankets.

Empty animal cages.

Damn.

He stepped back and took another look at the truck body. Once inside the truck's cab, he pulled the door closed, being careful not to slam it. "You're not going to believe this."

"What?"

"We just stole Farley's pickup."

Her jaw dropped. "Farley? Oh, no. He'll be *livid.*"

"Can't be helped. We didn't recognize it in the dark."

"And if we had?"

He tossed her a reckless grin. "We would've taken it anyway."

The old Studebaker grumbled down the rough road, as cantankerous as its owner. Mick dared to put the headlights on low beam. They could travel faster with them than without them.

"You're right. We needed the wheels tonight. He didn't," she said, talking herself out of their crime.

"We'll bring the truck back tomorrow. I promise."

"He'll hate me more than ever," she moaned. "First, he thinks I'm taking away his precious wilderness. Then I help steal his only means of transportation. How's that for making a good impression on someone who hates government intervention?"

"He'll get over it."

She sighed. "So where are we going?"

"There's a house up on the mountain a ways," he said. The time had come to confront things too long buried in his past. "We'll spend the night there if we have to."

"Friends of yours?"

"No. The place is vacant."

She frowned. "Are you sure we can just show up?"

"Positive."

She eyed him with grave doubt. "Okay, Corrigan. If you say so."

The road, hardly more than a rutted trail, wound through the backwoods like a corkscrew with seemingly no logic or direction. Mick delved deep into his memories for anything that looked familiar, but it'd been years since he was this deep into the forest, and in the dark, every tree looked alike.

Of course, Farley's truck didn't have any of the bells and whistles of the Range Rover, no computerized display of their location or the distance they'd gone. Not even an old-fashioned compass stuck to the windshield.

But Mick was getting close. He could feel it.

The woods opened up, and a creek glistened in the headlights. A crude wooden sign leaned precariously on the water's edge, and he drew the truck as close as he could.

Adrienne shined the flashlight on the words. "Catoosa Creek."

*Just follow the Catoosa, son, and you'll find your way home.*

The soft drawl of his mother's voice slid into his mind. He hadn't thought of the creek in years, but as a young boy, the backwoods in this part of the mountain had too often been his escape, allowing him to be gone for hours, hiding from his father's drunken rages, leaving his mother alone to defend herself.

Like a surgeon clamping off a vessel draining of valuable life blood, Mick shut down the memories. The guilt would kill him if he didn't.

It was how he survived all these years. Shutting down the guilt.

Only desperation forced him to go back now. Desperation and a maddened killer stalking Adrienne.

"You okay, Mick?"

She reached out and touched his arm. Mick realized he'd been sitting frozen, staring at the creek's weathered sign, gripped by the icy fingers of his past.

He roused himself. Forced a smile.

"Sure, honey. You know what?" With a grinding of gears, he urged the old truck forward again. "I'm not lost anymore."

"Ah-ha. So you admit it."

He scrambled to correct himself. "Lost is the wrong word. 'Looking for bearings' is better."

"Hmmm." She eyed him knowingly. "And I'll bet you never ask for directions, either."

"A guy thing again?"

She smiled. "You got it, Corrigan."

He loved this lighter side of her. If their banter helped ease the fear of her mother's killer for even a little while, he'd banter the whole night long.

Hell. If only it were that easy.

* * *

The little house was hardly more than a shack, smaller than Farley's, weatherbeaten, and so full of bad vibes Mick had to swallow hard to beat them down.

He ran his gaze over the yard, the run-down coop where his mother once kept a few scrawny chickens, the clothesline with its sagging wires.

And the wood shed.

It haunted him the most, that shed.

"Did you used to live here, Mick?" Adrienne asked quietly.

His head swiveled toward her. Her perception startled him. "Yes. Unfortunately."

She studied the grounds, too. "Are you embarrassed by it?"

The feelings that surfaced in him about his childhood home had nothing to do with the unsightliness. Only the memories were ugly.

"No," he said.

What would she know about such things? She had parents who adored her since the moment she took her first breath. She was born with the proverbial silver spoon; her growing up years couldn't have been happier.

He opened the truck door abruptly and brought an end to her questions. In the dim overhead light, he saw her puzzlement, but she dropped the subject and got out, too.

She swept a slow glance around her, as if trying to see as much as she could in what little moonlight they had. "I'd bet this place is gorgeous during the day. All these trees. I can smell the pines, can't you? The peace."

The loneliness. The solitary confinement any kid would feel who wasn't allowed to play with other kids his own age.

He grunted. "A handyman comes out to check on things occasionally. Looks like he hasn't mowed for awhile. I'll have to give him a call."

She turned back to him, her expression suddenly serious. "Speaking of calling, we should let someone know where we are."

Strangely enough, for all his ill will toward the place, he felt safe now. Much safer than he ever did when he lived here.

He found the cocoon of darkness comforting. He didn't turn on the flashlight, not yet, but strode toward the house slowly, taking it all in, letting the years fall away. The porch and stairs seemed narrower than he remembered, but Mick conceded his perspective had changed. Things would look a hell of a lot different to a boy than they would a man.

He eased down on the top step, and Adrienne sat beside him.

"Who are you going to call first?" she asked, propping her elbows on her knees, her chin in her palms.

He tapped his phone awake and scrolled through his contacts. "Grif. I want your father to hear about Kershner's murder from him. And I want Grif to assure him we're safe."

She sighed. "Poor Dad. He'll be devastated about this whole mess."

The screen kept circling for service.

"We're out of range," he muttered.

"Sparta's closer, and we didn't have trouble at the cabin today," she protested, studying the screen, too.

"We're too far into the mountain." Annoyed, he shut the phone off to save the battery and clipped the phone back on his belt.

"We're stranded out here, then."

He heard the apprehension in her tone. "Is that so bad?"

"Feels strange not being able to communicate with anyone."

"Technology has spoiled us, Morelli. Wasn't so long ago folks out here didn't even have running water."

"I know," she said, her tone pensive. "So now what?"

Heat coiled through him at the prospect of spending the night with her. Of keeping her warm in the dark. "We try to get some sleep."

She straightened. "Good thinking on those blankets, Corrigan."

"Gets cold at night. And the house has never been wired for electricity. There's plenty of wood around here. We can start a fire, at least."

Her mouth pursed. "That's something, anyway."

He took her hand and pulled her up with him. "No one knows we're out here, Adrienne. We're completely safe. This place has been vacant so long, I doubt anyone even remembers it's here," he said. "Okay?"

She hesitated. "Okay."

Though Mick believed his own words, he'd know by morning if they were true.

\* \* \*

*He glared at the abandoned Range Rover.*
*A clever trick to throw him off the hunt?*
*Corrigan's bodyguard act had to stop.*
*Time was running out.*
*He had to make Adrienne listen.*

*But, first, he had to find her.*

*His gaze slid up the hill, then down the empty highway. He seethed with fury. With blistering frustration.*

*Corrigan could've taken her into the woods. Or they could be on their way back to Nashville. They could be anywhere in this godforsaken part of the country.*

*He stormed toward the waiting black Lexus, got in and slammed the door. In the next moment, he was gone, squealing tires down the highway, leaving the Range Rover just as he'd found it.*

# CHAPTER TWELVE

Adrienne sat cross-legged on the blanket in front of the fireplace. Heat from the flames bathed her face and warmed her skin. A golden glow danced around the lone room.

That's all there was. One room to the entire house.

Hard to believe Mick had lived here as a little boy. The house, if one would call it that, was a crude structure, containing only a living area. It didn't even have a kitchen. Or a bathroom. And where had he slept?

What few windows there were had long since been boarded up. Except for a thick layer of dust and cobwebs in every corner, however, it was clean enough. The place was devoid of furniture and conveniences except for an ancient iron stove at the back of the room. Had his mother really cooked on the thing?

"Pretty depressing, isn't it?" Mick asked.

He straightened from stoking the fire. He'd freed his tie from its knot, and the ends hung carelessly down the front of his shirt. He looked relaxed, but tiny furrows in his forehead suggested the memories of his childhood home had not been pleasant.

"It's not something I would have expected," she said carefully. "But a family doesn't need a lot of possessions to be happy."

He made a rough sound of derision and dropped the second blanket beside her. He stretched out on his back over hers, using the balled-up blanket as a pillow.

"Were you?" she asked, growing intensely curious about

his past. "Happy, I mean."

"No."

Her heart squeezed at the pain in his swift, curt response.

"It took me a long time before I even understood the meaning of 'happy'," he added. "Years, as a matter of fact."

She reached out, brushed a lock of hair from his forehead. "Want to talk about it, Corrigan?"

His expression shuttered. He stared past her into the fire. "Why would you want to know about my sordid past, Adrienne? You wouldn't relate."

Her mouth softened into a smile. She wouldn't let his defensiveness put her off. "What else do I have to do but listen? We have no television, radio, or Internet. No telephone. No laptop. Not even my briefcase to occupy us."

His glance, hot and unfathomable, lingered over her. "Need an idea for something we could do?"

A sexy sultriness had slipped into his voice, and her pulse leapt, but she managed to ignore the provocative challenge. At least, on the outside. "Talk to me."

He was quiet so long she thought he would deny her. Finally, with a heavy, burdened sigh, he rolled over onto his side and propped his head up in his hand. He took her fingers into his. His touch was gentle. Pensive.

"I was my parents' only child. The marriage was rocky, and with me in the picture, things only got worse. My father couldn't hold a job, not that he tried very hard. The drinking took over his life and made my mother's miserable."

"There would've been community services available for her," Adrienne said quietly. "Alcoholics Anonymous and the like. Did she ever attend a meeting?"

"Even if she knew about it, he never would've let her off the mountain to go. He ruled her life and mine."

"He sounds awful." The words were out before she could stop them. "I'm sorry, Mick. That wasn't kind."

He dropped a kiss to her knuckle, telling her with the gesture he took no offense. "He *was* awful. You don't know the half of it."

"I'm not sure I want to know."

He studied her in that unfathomable way of his, the depths of his eyes hiding his thoughts--and the realities of his past. "Comfortable?"

He tugged on her hand, urging her to lie down next to him. He rearranged the blanket-pillow, giving her half. She settled in and conceded the position was more relaxing.

Cozy comfortable.

And much too intimate.

He remained on his side. His hand rested on her stomach; a fingertip absently stroked one of the faux pearl beads on her jacket.

"Keep talking," she urged gently, needing to concentrate on something besides that lean, masculine hand and all it could do to her while she laid next to him like this.

"He drank away what little money they had," Mick went on. "And when it was gone, he took his anger out on her." A muscle in his jaw moved. "She was just a little thing. There were times I was scared he'd kill her."

"Oh, Mick." Adrienne ached for the little boy he once was, for the terrors he must've endured.

"When it suited him, he came after me. Sometimes, I'd taunt him. Dare him to hit me instead. I was built like him, not her, so I was stronger, at least toward the end."

"Did you ever tell anyone? A teacher? A family member?"

His mouth tightened. "No. My mother was a proud woman. Unfortunately, I'd inherited her Silverhawk pride. Deep down, we both hoped he'd change one day, like magic, and we'd be a happy family." He grunted. "Of course, he never did."

"Surely Griffin would've helped you if he'd known."

"Looking back, it was stupid of me not to tell him. I should have. Maybe she'd be alive today." He sighed, a deep, from the cavern-of-his-chest sigh that revealed years of regret.

"But didn't he ever visit you? Or you'd go to visit him?"

"She would never allow him to see us, not with the ugly state of her marriage. Our living conditions would've shocked him; he never would've stood for it. She always made up excuses to keep us apart. A damned shame, too. He was her only brother."

"Didn't Griffin suspect something was wrong?"

"I'm sure he did as time went on. One day, my father found out Grif had started sending her money and that she'd been hiding it so he couldn't buy whiskey," Mick said. "All hell broke loose. He roughed her up pretty good. I was hurting, too, when he finished with me, but I managed to run to one of the neighbors for help. Hell, I was only fourteen, and up to then, I always thought I could take care of her. Protect her from the bastard. But that day, I was sure Mom was going to die. They called the sheriff, who took him to jail and her to the hospital." Pain smoldered in his grim features. "I couldn't have failed her more. I shouldn't have let things get out of hand like that for her."

Adrienne realized she'd been holding her breath. "What happened then?"

"Grif stepped in. Took me to live with him so that Social Services wouldn't put me in foster care. Mom was in pretty bad shape and was laid up in the hospital for a while. Dad eventually got out of jail and left. Last we heard, he took to riding the rails and eventually got killed. Pinned between two cars or something. Don't know for sure. And I don't particularly care."

"Oh, Mick. I'm sorry."

"Don't be. I never shed a tear over him. I doubt my mother did, either."

Adrienne guessed she did. Tears of what might have been. Surely, she loved the man once.

"Grif enrolled me in a good school in Memphis. I was getting along so well that Mom refused to let me come back to the mountain. She wanted me to have a better life with him than she could've given me. She never really healed from her injuries, or maybe she died from a broken heart. I'll never know. But after her death, I inherited this little piece of mountain. I haven't been back until now. Tonight."

Moisture formed beneath Adrienne's lashes. She reached out, cupped his cheek. "That's quite a story, Corrigan. My heart is breaking that you were unhappy for so long."

He turned slightly, rubbed his jaw into her palm, as if he craved her touch and treasured it.

"Want to know when I finally learned the true meaning of the word 'happy'?" he murmured.

"When?" she whispered.

"When I made love to you six months ago."

Whatever she'd expected him to say, it wasn't that. Her eyes widened a little. Swirls of heat formed deep inside her.

"Want to know when I learned about 'unhappy' all over again?" This time, he didn't wait for her respond. "When I left you the next morning. I've regretted a lot of things in my life, Adrienne. And that ranks damn near at the top of the list."

He sat up abruptly. She sat up, too, and from behind him, wrapped her arms around the breadth of his strong shoulders. She rested her cheek against his back.

Yes, she had hurt when he left her. And she lived a mountain full of unhappiness right along with him.

But she understood him better now. His childhood had shaped him to be the man he was today. Despite a past that could've caught him in a vicious circle of poverty and abuse, he emerged a man with a strict code of honor. He'd righted his life and succeeded at it. He was, she suspected, determined to be as opposite his father as he could possibly be.

"Emotions ran high back then, Mick. For both of us. I didn't do anything with you that I didn't want to."

"You were an emotional wreck. I took advantage of you."

"No." Her head lifted, and she tugged him around to face her. "I was an adult. I knew exactly what I was doing when I climbed into that bed with you."

"I was stronger than you. I knew better."

"Like your father?" she demanded. "Do you see yourself as 'overpowering' me in a forbidden way, like he did to your mother?"

He jerked back. "Don't compare me to him."

"That's why you became a bodyguard, isn't it?" she said, driving her point home. "To protect those who can't protect themselves. I'd bet the farm your clients are always female."

His nostrils flared. He gripped her arms and pushed her back onto the blanket. He loomed above her, his expression fierce. Defiant.

"Is that so wrong, Morelli? To guard someone who doesn't have the training or the skills that I do? You know what it's like to be afraid. Really afraid. Well, damn it, so do I. I know it can cripple mentally. The brain shuts out logic and common sense, to the point where someone else has to do the thinking. Someone on the outside who doesn't have as much at stake."

"That's what Griffin did for you," Adrienne said. "He guarded you against people who could hurt you. He made decisions for your welfare that neither you nor your mother could make on your own. And only then could you survive. Without him, you never would've had the success you have now."

"You think I don't know that?" Mick said roughly.

"You're the best bodyguard a girl could have, Corrigan." Adrienne touched a fingertip to the firm line of his lower lip, traced its fullness, one side then the other. "The absolute best."

Some of the fierceness left him. His grip on her loosened. "Guess I have to be good at something, don't I?"

"It would destroy you if you weren't, I think."

He drew her fingertip into his mouth, nibbled gently. "There's something else I can be good at it, you know."

Her heart did a funny flip. His name escaped her on a soft breath. She knew what he was thinking. What he wanted.

What they both wanted.

He sucked on her finger, the deliciously warm moistness in his mouth an arousing aphrodisiac. He'd taught her about sex between a man and a woman, that heady feeling of being held in masculine arms and experiencing a soul-destroying pleasure unlike anything else two human beings could enjoy.

But it'd been her mother's killer who taught her that life was short. That it could be stolen away without warning. Or fairness. And that if she didn't make love to Mick tonight, she might never have another chance again.

She wanted another night in his arms like they had in Nashville. So many times since then, she'd missed him. Ached for him. Never mind that he left her early the morning afterward; she knew now he had his reasons. The code of honor he valued so much allowed him no other recourse.

"You're my client, Adrienne," he said huskily, picking up the trail of her thoughts. "I don't want to make the same mistake I did back then."

"I'm not feeling like the product of a business arrangement my father made with your uncle, Mick. Being with you, just the two of us in front of the fire, alone in this part of the mountain, well, I feel like your--"

She halted, searching for the right word.

He chuckled and lowered his head, nuzzled the soft hair at her temple. "My woman?"

She might as well admit it. Promiscuity had never been her forte. "Yes. However archaic that might sound."

"I like the way it sounds."

She slipped her arms around his neck. He eased downward, his body warm and heavy over hers. She savored him. "I don't want to think about a deranged killer out there. Make me forget about him, Mick."

His mouth took hers with a hungry groan. His head slanted, allowing him to claim her more fully, succumbing to her plea to escape the harsh realities of tomorrow or even the next minutes and hours. The fierceness of the kiss suggested his own need to forget what might have been, what might never be. He plunged into the sweetness of 'now', taking her with him for the ride.

He kept the contact of their lips firm, demanding, dominating her with his growing need. She opened for him, meeting his tongue when it delved inside, seeking hers. The taste of him filled her senses, intoxicated her with his maleness, proclaimed that for now, at least, he was all hers.

A soft sound of excited pleasure slipped from her throat at the prospect of what they could, and would, experience together. He had taught her as much those months ago, and her nerve endings tingled in anticipation.

His mouth dragged over her chin, opened and sucked gently.

"I shouldn't be making love to you," he said huskily even as he moved to the curve of her neck, his teeth biting gently on her skin along the way. "I'm your bodyguard. I have to concentrate--"

"So concentrate on me instead, Mick. Us. For a little while, that's all."

She was shameless with him. But the truth of his words only added to the excitement. The threat of danger was great. Her mother's killer would be hunting them even now, and any falter of their concentration could be deadly.

They were stealing time for stealing pleasure. But she wanted him. Wanted him more than she'd ever wanted or needed a man before. It had always been this way. With him, she felt safe. One hundred percent protected.

And deliciously female.

A slow, devastating grin formed, that rare but reckless curving of his lips which had the ability to send her pulse tripping into overdrive.

"Oh, I'm concentrating all right, Morelli," he drawled. His warm breath fluttered in her ear, and he nipped at her lobe. "I can barely think of anything else but touching and feeling every inch of you."

She laughed softly. He was usually so reserved, so serious. A bodyguard first and foremost. It wasn't often he gave the world a glimpse of the inner man, his true self.

Tonight, he did just that with her, and her heart opened wider to him. She was perilously close to falling in love with him.

Maybe she already had.

Her fingers found the narrow strip of leather holding his hair in its queue. He had beautiful hair, thick and heavy, the deep blue-black of his heritage. She freed its weight and ran her fingers through the strands, spreading them over his shoulders.

She curled her fist into its length and kissed him again. The fervent possession of his mouth rocked her to the core and left her shaking with a spiraling feminine need. Through the sensations whirling inside her, she became aware of his hand moving over her belly, parting the buttons of her jacket. He spread the garment wide, and fire-warmed air met her skin. His fingers skimmed over her ribcage and then to her back, releasing the clasp to her bra. Her breasts spilled from the lacy undergarment, and he filled his palm with a swollen mound.

"Beautiful," he breathed huskily. "Every part of you is so beautiful."

She almost disagreed with him, like she always did when someone complimented her. She had nothing of her mother's attractiveness, so striking and profound and memorable that it was only natural for people to compare them, daughter to mother.

Yet Mick made her feel truly beautiful, and she reveled in it. All the years of feeling a little too inferior melted away. It wasn't important anymore, not when he looked at her with such hot desire, his wanting a tangible thing between them. He was not a man of loose words. He told her she was beautiful, he meant it, and she believed him.

His thumb swept over her sensitive nipple. Heat flooded through her as he prolonged the seduction, until her hips began to move, seeking the fulfillment he promised.

His head lowered, and he took the nipple into his mouth, sucked strong and long until she arched against him, wanting to push him away and hold him to her, all at the same time.

She clawed and tugged at his shirt until the buttons gave way. She had to feel his chest against hers, that delicious melding of skin. His swollen sex pressed against her thigh, assuring her he wanted her just as much.

She felt no shyness with him. No inhibition. Her breathing quickened into pants, her need for him growing frenzied with each stroke of his tongue on her.

He shifted a little, murmuring her name, his own need. He suckled the other side while his hand found the zipper at the front of her slacks, and in a heartbeat, they were off and tossed aside.

She was naked beneath him. She demanded the same from him, and he assisted her in undressing him, and soon his clothing tangled with hers on the floor.

Firelight poured over every corded muscle, the sinew and coiled strength proclaiming his absolute maleness. His skin gleamed bronze; her hands splayed across all that muscle, stroked and discovered and wanted more.

He moved over her, his mouth hungry on hers again. Her every sense, every instinct, every acute nerve ending, was honed perfectly into him, and she knew the instant he hesitated.

"Hurry, Mick," she panted, not questioning his reason for doing it, not when her need for him overrode all else. She wanted him inside her, deep and fast and furious. She had to end this sweet ache that was fast building to a crescendo. Her arms curled around him, urging him between her thighs.

"I don't have protection, Adrienne." As if in a moment of clarity, he growled the words, his restraint perilous. He seemed on the edge of release himself as his teeth grazed her jawline in frustration. "Damn it, we can't go any further."

Would it be so terrible to risk the creation of his child? To be the mother of it? She knew her body; the chances were low, but if she would be wrong, and she did conceive after all, what a precious gift his baby-child would be.

Precious and pure.

Her hands slid down his back to cup his hips and settle them perfectly over own, showing him without question she knew exactly what she was doing. His head lifted, and raw emotion burned in the obsidian depths of his eyes. He understood, and he gave, and he filled her being, made her whole again, as he'd done that night so many months ago.

She moaned his name and took him in deep, each thrust leaving her gasping from the tightening coil of sensation inside her. Her back arched, she clung to him, meeting him thrust for thrust, until the coil reached its peak and burst. She cried out as the climax rolled in hot, glittering waves through her.

His body quickened its rhythm, his buttocks clenched; with one final thrust, he groaned his own release and shuddered long and hard into her.

Spent, he sank down on top of her, and she curled her arms around his back. A sheen of perspiration covered their bodies. Adrienne couldn't remember feeling so warm, so sated.

So complete.

She held him with his body sprawled in a blatant, masculine claim over hers for a long, long time. Finally, he stirred, and it was all she could do to open her eyes.

She met his lazy, satisfied smile.

"You look good wearing nothing but your pearls, Morelli."

She'd forgotten she still wore them. Husky laughter curled from her throat, and she snuggled into him.

"You're looking pretty good yourself, Corrigan."

An understatement, if she ever made one. Bare skin was flattering on him.

"I have to get dressed," he said.

"Sleep naked with me."

"I can't." Despite his words, he made no effort to reach

for his clothes. Instead, his hand stroked her spine in languid strokes. "You've distracted me enough. I'd be at a serious disadvantage if trouble caught us by surprise."

Trouble.

Her mother's killer. And Ronald Kershner's.

The words were like a bucket of ice water on her heated skin, and she drew back.

"Yes," she said, understanding.

Finally, he moved off her and reached for his pants. "You'd better get dressed, too, honey. I want you ready to run on a moment's notice if we have to."

"Of course." She understood that, too.

The mood was gone. Shattered into a million pieces.

It saddened her. Mick, her lover, had transformed back into Mick, her bodyguard. Adrienne sat up to put on her pantsuit once again, and she mourned the loss of the perfect, blissful world they'd escaped into for a little while.

And re-entered the frightening, real one.

# CHAPTER THIRTEEN

A chill had crept into the room. Mick withdrew his arm from around Adrienne's waist and slipped out from beneath their blanket. The crisp air nipped at him, and he pulled the covering higher over her, taking care not to disturb her. She slept deeply, and he saw no need to wake her.

Yet.

She'd fallen asleep surprisingly fast after they got dressed, but he stayed awake most of the night. He was used to putting a client's comfort first. It was all part of the territory. He could survive on little sleep when a client's safety warranted it. And Adrienne's safety did.

His muscles were stiff from the hours spent on a hard floor. Moving to the fireplace loosened them, and once he stoked the fire into blazing flames again, the heat finished the job. He was fully awake now. Alert. Ready to go. He'd let the room warm up, then wake Adrienne.

He glanced at his watch. Past dawn already. He strode toward the front door and unlocked it, frowning at the rusted latch. It was a wonder the thing held, as old as it was. The lock wouldn't have been much protection against someone trying to barrel their way inside, but at least it was something.

He opened the door wide enough to slip through and paused on the front step. The morning air carried a bite, and the brilliance of the sun was startling after the cabin's dimness. He pulled his hair back into its queue. While he buttoned his shirt and tucked the hem into his slacks, he scanned the wilderness surrounding the shack's overgrown yard.

A symphony of morning songs filled the forest. He strapped on his shoulder holster and took it all in. The cheerful notes of a Carolina wren. A robin and an eastern towhee. Somewhere, unseen but persistent, a wild turkey warbled his own refrain, off-key but enthusiastic.

A busy place, the forest. Alive. Beautiful.

The thought left Mick pensive. He'd never considered his former home to be beautiful before. His troubled childhood had closed his eyes to the allure; the ugly memories had murdered and buried it.

But here it all was, vibrant and pristine, as alive today as it'd been for centuries.

He had never appreciated the beauty. Something inside him squeezed, a very real regret of all he'd lost.

Or had he?

He'd ignored this part of the mountain for so long because it cost too much to come back. To remember. He stayed away because the wounds would always be fresh. Hurting. And raw.

Had his return last night with Adrienne been a dose of strong medicine? The first step he must take to begin the healing?

A slender ribbon of water, a run-off of the Catoosa, meandered through the trees. Movement at the creek's edge jerked Mick's thoughts back to the present and the reason he was here with Adrienne.

He strained to see what was out there. The movement came again, and he realized it was only a beaver, hard at work building a haphazard-looking dam.

Harmless, but it reminded him of the risks they took by staying here longer than necessary. He stepped back inside, closed the door securely and crossed the room to Adrienne, still sleeping in front of the fire.

He hunkered down beside her. Firelight glinted off her hair and painted the strands with rich, red-gold highlights. The crescents of her lashes rested on her cheeks, flushed pink from the fire's heat.

He'd fallen in love with her.

The certainty of it rocked through him. Steadied him. Made him all the more determined, if that were possible, to shield her from the violence and hate of someone so determined to kill her.

Because she was his. And he would do anything in his power to keep her from getting hurt.

Anything.

* * *

*Well, well, well.*

*There they were, down in the hollow.*

*It'd been a wild guess Corrigan would take Adrienne to his family's boarded-up shack to hide out for awhile.*

*But it'd been the right one.*

*Smoke curled from the chimney. Parked behind the place sat Farley's old Studebaker. Corrigan must've stolen it for a quick getaway after leaving his beautiful red Range Rover behind.*

*Must've felt a little desperate last night to take that ol' bucket of bolts, eh?*

*Good. Very good.*

*Corrigan's shack had been vacant so long, most everyone had forgotten about it.*

*He had, too.*

*But it took him hours of traipsing around this damn mountain in the cold and dark until the guess came to him.*

*Too much time had been lost.*

*Adrienne should have been dead by now.*

*Now that it was daylight, Corrigan wouldn't be hanging around long.*

*He'd have to work fast.*

* * *

Mick shook Adrienne's shoulder gently. "Hey, sleepyhead. Wake up."

She roused with a start. "What is it?"

"Late, that's all. We have to get moving."

She sat up, speared her fingers through her hair, and

stretched her back. "How late?"

"Almost eight."

She frowned. "You shouldn't have let me sleep so long."

She swept aside the blanket and stood up. Except for her shoes, she was fully dressed. The sapphire blue pantsuit showed the strain of being slept in, and she brushed at the wrinkles with little success. Finally, she gave up. "Don't suppose you have any coffee around here, do you?"

"What's the matter, honey?" he crooned and took her into his arms. She snuggled into him. "Didn't get enough sleep?"

"Mmm. I found something more exciting to do." She tilted her head back and batted her eyelashes, flirting outrageously. "You kept us safe last night. Guess you could have slept naked with me after all."

"Hindsight," he grunted. "I'll make it up to you."

"Sounds like you want to make love to me again." Lifting up on tiptoe, she pleasured him with a lazy kiss. "When?"

He hesitated. Reality bulldozed its way between them. "As soon as I can."

"Not tonight?" She drew back. Her sobering expression revealed her realization that the morning was going to be different than their night. "What happens next, Mick? After we leave here?"

"I'm taking you to a safe house."

"Are you kidding me?" Her shocked gasp showed her fierce disagreement. She jerked out of his embrace. "I won't go."

"It's for your own good."

"I want the land deed, Mick. I can't get it if you hide me away. As soon as I get back to Nashville--"

"There's not going to be a signing until your stalker is found, Adrienne," he bit out.

"That's not your decision to make. It's mine. I'll call my father when we can get those damn cell phones to work."

"Whoever your mother's killer was, he knew her plan from the beginning. An inside man, Adrienne. He knew every step the state was taking to get the land deed. He probably knew them just as soon as she did." Mick halted to let the words sink in. "It's the same thing with you. The person who wants you dead is someone you know. You probably even like him. He's one of your *friends*. At the very least, he's the killer's informant."

She paled. She took another step back, her arms huddled tight about her.

"Why did you make love to me, Mick? So I would be putty in your arms and agree to everything you told me to do today?"

He stiffened at the accusation. "You're not playing fair, Adrienne."

"Why didn't you tell me you intended to send me to a safe house *before* we had sex?"

"So now it's having 'sex' and not 'making love'?"

"A technicality."

He muttered an oath of frustration. "I love you, Adrienne. I want you *alive*."

"If you love me, then let me have that land deed. I'm so close!"

"So is he. *And we don't even know who he is!*" Mick shot back. "Besides, you're not close. It'll be hours before we get back to Nashville. Days could pass before you make other arrangements with Murdock."

"I won't let it go that long."

"Your father's probably frantic," he said, forcing calm logic into his voice. "Grif, too. Someone would've found the Range Rover by now. The police will be combing the entire mountain looking for us."

"We'll discuss this further in Nashville." She slipped on her shoes. "I just need a few minutes to--what did you do for a bathroom when you lived here?"

"There's an outhouse in the back. I have no idea what shape it's in. I'll go with you."

"You will not." She headed toward the door. "Female privacy, if you don't mind."

He set his teeth but decided not to push the issue. "If you want to use the water pump to wash up, the handle's probably rusted, and you'll have trouble lifting it, so--"

"I'll manage."

"I'll bank the fire and be out there in a minute," he called after her.

She slammed the door. Hard.

Unease sifted through him. He didn't like not being able to see her, but conceded her need to be alone for a few minutes was understandable. He put on his suit coat and set to work folding blankets and dousing the flames in the block.

\* \* \*

A safe house?

This time, Mick had gone too far.

Did he really expect her to agree? Just hang out somewhere while the rest of the world passed her by? After all their hard work to secure the two thousand acres for Tennessee?

Absolutely not.

She wouldn't give the killer the satisfaction. It was what he wanted--to have her out of the picture so Tyler Enterprises could start its lobbying for an exclusive resort all over again.

And what if Murdock got cold feet and withdrew their offer permanently? Two people had died because of this project. No one in good conscience would want to risk a third death.

Adrienne couldn't blame them. All the more reason to work quickly. And she couldn't do that if she were hidden away like dirt under a rug, all under the pretense of being protected.

She halted at the decaying outhouse and eyed it with grave reservation. The poor thing leaned to one side, too tired to stand on its own. And who knew what critters made their home inside?

Repulsed, she shivered. She didn't have to use the outhouse anyway. She could wait until Mick took her to a public restroom somewhere on the way back home.

She'd love to wash her face, though. Rinse her teeth. Freshen up a little.

And cool down.

The water pump was an ancient-looking piece of plumbing, to say the least. She tried to lift the handle, but it wouldn't budge.

She stepped back and set her hands on her hips. The way her morning was going, she wouldn't be surprised if the well beneath it had dried up, too, but she wasn't about to ask Mick for help to know for sure.

Sunlight winked on the narrow band of water flowing just beyond a stand of assorted deciduous trees. The Catoosa, she remembered from last night. Glistening like mammoth yards of pure silk. Plenty of water there to wash up in, and she'd be within sight of the shack. When Mick was finished with the fire, he'd see her, no problem.

She strode toward the water. Mick wouldn't approve of her straying away from him, even for a few dozen yards, but she'd be finished and waiting for him by the time he even learned what she'd done.

\* \* \*

*He almost didn't see her coming.*

*Stepping quickly behind the thick trunk of an oak tree allowed him to watch her walk right past. Close enough he could jump out and grab her.*

*If he wanted.*

*But not yet. No, no, no.*

*First, he would make her listen. If she refused, then she would pay the price.*

*With her life.*

*Corrigan wasn't with her. Must still be inside that rundown shack. But he'd come soon. He wouldn't leave her alone long.*

*Turning, he lifted a hand in a silent signal to the others.*

*They knew what to do. He'd instructed them, step by step, over and over again.*

*They freed him for the best part. They would take care of Corrigan.*

*And he would take care of Adrienne.*

*Smiling a little smile, he stepped out from behind the oak tree and quietly followed her down to the water.*

* * *

Mick strode out of the shack, his arms full with the folded blankets. Other than the smoldering ashes in the fireplace, there was no other evidence he'd spent the night here with Adrienne.

He dumped the blankets in the back end of the Studebaker, then fished the shack's door key out of his pocket. After locking up behind them, he returned the key to its hiding place beneath a large rock near the porch, more for the handyman's convenience than any real security. Not that there was anything inside to take, but it made Mick feel better knowing the place wasn't an open invitation to vagrants, two-legged or otherwise.

He headed toward the outhouse, saw no sign of Adrienne, and figured she must still be inside, although, given the condition of the structure, that surprised him. Along the way, he noticed the ground around the water pump was dry, and if the rusted handle was any indication, she wouldn't have been able to use it anyway.

He reached the outhouse and rapped on the door. "Adrienne?"

She didn't answer.

Alarm flickered through him. The privy leaned precariously, and the frame had long ago sprung. The weather-beaten door was jammed shut.

She couldn't have gotten in if she tried.

He whirled, his gaze clawing the empty yard behind the house. He sprinted toward Farley's pickup, and she wasn't there, either. A quick run toward the front of the house showed nothing.

He resisted the urge to yell for her. If she'd been taken,

if *he* got to her, then Mick opted for the element of surprise.

He clamped down the fear that threatened to overpower him, the sickening sense of failure that insisted he should never have let her out of his sight. He went for his Beretta and turned toward the wilderness.

She was out there somewhere, and God help him, he hoped she was still alive.

\* \* \*

The view was breathtaking.

Adrienne stood at the edge of the Catoosa Creek and took it all in. The clean, invigorating scent of pine, the towering oaks and maples, the sweet bird songs that tweaked her heartstrings.

Tennessee, one hundred percent.

The shallow water babbled crystal clear to its banks, and she crouched to dip her hands into the gentle flow. Cold, too. Inviting.

She splashed some onto her face. The icy briskness cleared her mind, revitalized her for the upcoming battle with Mick.

The very idea of a safe house fired up the blood in her veins all over again. During the ride back to Nashville, he'd be relentless in pursuing the issue. Determined to prove to her he was right. His complete and absolute dedication to protecting her made him oblivious to her take--and solution-- to the problem.

Really, the man was too full of himself.

*I love you, Adrienne. I want you alive.*

The avowal dropped into her thoughts with an abruptness that left her heart forgetting to beat for long moments. Mick wasn't a man to say those words unless he meant every one.

He would only leave her, though, when this was all over. She'd foolishly thought he was in love with her the night she gave him her virginity. He up and left afterward, and it nearly destroyed her.

*He would leave her again.*

163

Wouldn't he?

Suddenly, she wasn't so sure. She'd seen the way his eyes darkened to midnight whenever he looked at her, how those smoldering glances lingered on her longer than they should. His touch was gentle, his kisses soul-destroying. And he'd made love to her last night with the unleashed desire of a man who cared deeply for his woman.

A distorted, shadowy reflection appeared on the surface of the water. Mick's footsteps behind her sent a pebble skittering toward the creek, where it landed in the water with a tiny plop.

She felt guilty for taking longer than she intended to freshen up, especially when he was anxious to leave. And maybe, she owed him an apology for being so emphatic against the safe house idea. He was only looking out for her safety, after all. She straightened and turned toward him.

"Mick, I've been thinking--" She froze. Her eyes widened. "Denny Ray!"

* * *

Mick spied the black Lexus first, before he saw Denny Ray. He kept to the shadows of the hickory tree, his back pressed against the trunk. There was no reason, no logical, simple, damned *reason*, for Denny Ray to be here, skulking in the backwoods with a gun in his hand.

Unless he intended to kill Adrienne.

Everything made sense now, and Mick's blood ran cold from the horror of it. Being a member of the Scott's Gulf Alliance made Denny Ray privy to information about the two thousand acres of wilderness and the state's acquisition of them before the news broke to the general public.

Or Tyler Enterprises.

Double-dealing for a profit, the bastard. As a Park Ranger, he had the perfect cover. The blood money from the mountain resort, his greed, meant more to him than fine, decent people like Julia Morelli and Izzie and Dietrich, all of whom trusted him.

Adrienne trusted him, too. She wouldn't think not to

until it was too late . . ..

Denny Ray was almost there, creeping steadily toward her while she was bent over the water. She didn't know he was behind her, not yet. Mick stepped from the tree, his finger on the Beretta's trigger. He took aim, every muscle coiled, every breath slow and measured in his throat. His mouth opened to warn her, to order her to stay down, but too late, he sensed the presence of someone behind him.

In automatic reflex, he spun around. Recognition slammed into him, but before he could snarl a single, vehement word, his attacker's arm swung down, and the butt of his revolver struck Mick's temple.

Brilliant stars of pain flashed before his eyes, and he crumpled to the dirt.

# CHAPTER FOURTEEN

Adrienne stared at Denny Ray. No longer was he the flirtatious, flashily-dressed womanizer she was accustomed to seeing. Though he still wore the dress shirt and creased slacks from last night's festivities in Hickoryville, they were disheveled, his hair was tousled, his cheeks unshaven.

The cockiness was gone. Instead, tense and on edge, danger emanated from him like heat off asphalt, a tightly coiled antagonism he could barely hold in restraint. The clarity of it shocked her, and she took an involuntary step backward. Had he been up all night, searching the mountain, concerned for her and Mick's welfare? Had that concern twisted into angry relief?

Only then, did she see the gun in his hand, and she knew.

Dear God. She *knew*.

"It was you all along, wasn't it?" she said hoarsely. Her gaze lifted from the revolver. Pure, unadulterated rage slammed through her. *"You killed my mother!"*

Hate exploded inside her, driving her to hurt him for all the pain he'd caused her, her father, everyone. She lunged toward him with her fists swinging, but he was too quick, jumping back before she could strike a blow. He aimed his weapon at her chest.

"Don't provoke me to kill you, too, sweetie." He held the weapon carelessly, as if its ability to take out a life so easily meant nothing to him. "You haven't been listening to me."

She willed control over the hate. Managed it with every fiber of her being. Overcame it to think, to be prepared.

"I sent you notes," he went on conversationally. "They said what I meant, and still you didn't listen."

"The poems? You're right, Denny Ray. The message was clear. But it doesn't matter. You're too late."

"No," he snarled. "Nothing's been signed."

"The decision has already been made by Murdock Corporation. You *know* that. The signing is only a formality."

"There's still time to make him listen, too."

"Who?" Adrienne's brain raced to follow Denny Ray's bizarre logic. "My father?"

"If his little girl is killed, then he'll listen for sure, won't he?"

Little girl. How often had her father called her that over the years? Or her mother?

A thousand times. Long after she'd grown into a woman, and Adrienne's eyes smarted with sudden emotion.

"You're coming with me," Denny Ray said. "We're going to call him and tell him to give up those two thousand acres. And he'll listen because he'll know he's next if he doesn't. Isn't that right, sweetie?"

She had to stay calm. Focused. Controlled. She couldn't let fear and hate cloud her thinking.

"We'll schedule another meeting with him and the Murdock board of directors," she said carefully. "You can attend. He'll listen to anything you have to say. We all will." Another piece of the mystery puzzle dropped into place. "You're working with Tyler Enterprises, aren't you?"

His lip curled back. "Mountain Crest Resorts will bring more money to this mountain than you can fathom, Adrienne."

"We'll reach a compromise," she said, hating the desperation that had crept into her voice. "We'll be fair to you."

"You're lying!" he barked, contemptuous. "You'll say

anything to get what you want. You've always been daddy's good little girl, haven't you?"

The revolver waved alarmingly, and she took a quick step back. The heels of her shoes slid into the wet, rocky soil lining the bank of the Catoosa. Water seeped into the leather, chilling her toes.

Her mind raced to Mick. He would've come after her by now. Something had happened, something terrible, to keep him from protecting her. A sob welled into her throat.

She was on her own. She'd have to defend herself against Denny Ray.

Or die trying.

\* \* \*

Mick staggered between consciousness and the dark, clawing pull of oblivion. He fought to pull himself through the fog, to stay awake. To be aware. He had to help Adrienne, but his eyes wouldn't open, wouldn't focus. He had all he could to do keep from falling over the jagged edge into blackness.

Someone yanked on his arms, his legs. Sounds, too. He struggled to concentrate on them. Men grunting and swearing. Two dragged him into the forest, another hissed orders. Mick could smell the pines, feel the sharp sting of the needles against his skin and clothes.

Someone slapped a long piece of duct tape across his mouth. He lay still, not fighting them. Not yet. If they knew he wasn't out cold, they'd kill him to make sure he was. One of them tied his ankles and wrists behind his back with rope, jerking him carelessly, painfully, as if he were already dead.

And then they were gone.

Adrienne. They were going after her. Denny Ray's accomplices. Three of them.

Mick moaned in desperation; he fought the blackness, battled it with all he had left.

Rushing footsteps pounded the ground.

"Snap out of it, boy." Someone slapped at his cheek, over and over. "Can't figure out what the mayor was doin' cuffin' you like this. By Gawd, that's the government for you."

The old man's gruff voice penetrated Mick's oblivion. Farley. Farley was here. Mick clawed his way up, up. Some of the darkness slipped, faded to gray.

"Give me some of that, Bess," Farley snapped.

Water splashed into Mick's face, jerked him closer to the light. He coughed; his head rolled back and forth like a wet dog's.

"Be careful with him, Grandpa. Land sakes, you'll drown him!"

Mick forced his eyes open. The figure swam before him, but gradually the haze receded, and his vision cleared. He never thought he'd be this glad to see the old coot again.

"Untie me." Behind the duct tape, the words came out indiscernible, but Farley seemed to know what he wanted. The old man worked a fingernail under a corner.

"Got yourself in a heap of trouble, didn't you, boy?" he muttered, giving the tape a swift yank.

Mick grimaced at the sting, tested his jaw and managed to talk.

"They came looking for me. Us, I mean. Adrienne." He tried to sit up, but the ties hindered him.

"They're down by the creek with her. Easy, now. Just give me a minute to untie you, y'hear?"

Bess pitched in to help, and the ropes fell free. Mick scrambled to his feet, swayed, and steadied himself.

"They the ones that murdered Miss Morelli's ma?" Bess asked anxiously.

"I'm figuring so," Mick said. Where was the Beretta? He found it in the weeds where they'd kicked it out of the way. Mick relished the cold feel of the gun in his hands.

Farley took up his shotgun. "Reckon you could use some help, boy. Just tell me what the plan is."

Denny Ray held Adrienne prisoner by the creek. Mayor Webster stood to one side, flanked by the two henchmen who tried to run the Range Rover off the highway.

Mick turned to Farley. "There is no plan for you. I'm going in alone." He gestured sharply to Bess and her Chevy pickup. "Go for help. Take your grandfather with you."

"Like hell!" Farley sputtered.

"Ssh, Grandpa!" Bess hissed, taking his arm. "You're going to give us away. We have to get him and Miss Morelli some help, like he says. Come *on*."

Mick didn't stick around to argue with Farley. He bolted into the woods, zig-zagging between the trees to keep from being detected, his step light but sure over the debris strewn across the forest floor.

He took cover behind a hickory tree and debated firing off a couple of rounds to give the impression the men were surrounded, then discarded the idea. Adrienne could get hit in a crossfire.

Bottom line was he had to get between Denny Ray and Adrienne. No other way to protect her but with the cover of his own body.

Denny Ray called all the shots in this game, but Mick had an ace or two up his sleeve. He tucked the Beretta into his back waistband, beneath the cover of his suit coat, put his hands in the air and started walking toward them.

* * *

Denny Ray was like a wild man, crazed from greed.

"Why do you want the resort?" Adrienne asked. The air in her lungs squeezed so hard, her chest hurt. She had to keep him talking, buy herself some time. "Is it just the money? Or is there another reason you'll kill me to keep the deal from going through?"

"Because he wants to get off the mountain like I did, Adrienne. Don't you, Denny Ray?" Mick asked.

Adrienne gasped at the sound of his voice. He strolled out of the woods, as casually as if he were walking in the park.

But if she was surprised to see him, Denny Ray was doubly so.

"You were supposed to tie him up!" he roared to Mayor

Webster.

Startled panic flickered across the man's fleshy face. "He was tied, Denny Ray. I did it myself." He jabbed a glance into the woods, as if he tried to determine how Mick managed it, then snapped an order to the two henchmen. "Get him! He had help gettin' out of those ropes!"

"No!" Denny Ray yelled.

The three men froze.

"I'll take him, too." A shadowy morning beard gave Denny Ray a ruthless look. A slow smile formed on his lips. "Yes, yes. The two of them." The smile vanished, and he jerked his weapon at Mick. "Stand over there with her."

"Sure. Whatever you say, Denny Ray." Mick agreed easily. Too easily. "You okay, honey?" he soothed, walking right up to her.

Her gaze riveted on him. She didn't know what he was up to, but he seemed oblivious to the weapon pointed at his back.

He mouthed the words 'Take my gun'.

And comprehension dawned.

"Oh, God, Mick!" Faking a sob, she crumpled against him. His arms enfolded her in a quick embrace; her hands moved quickly beneath his suit coat, finding the Beretta and somehow managing to hide it beneath her blue jacket.

"Get away from her, Corrigan!" Denny Ray yelled.

Mick released her, his hands reaching for clouds again. Adrienne scrubbed at tears that were never there and crossed her arms tightly.

"Don't try that again!" Denny Ray warned.

"She's scared, Denny Ray. She's entitled to a little reassurance," Mick said.

"The hell she is! Stand over here"--the gun waved wildly again--"where I can see you better."

"Denny Ray, we got to get out of here. Now!" the mayor said, shifting nervously. "You hear me, boy?"

Denny Ray ignored him. So did Mick. He kept himself in front of Adrienne, guarding her even under capture. A very real sob welled in her throat.

"So do tell, Denny Ray," Mick drawled. "Your old man still holed up in the sanitarium? Heard he went crazy a while back."

The color drained from Denny Ray's cheeks, then bloomed into a vicious red. "Leave him out of this, Corrigan!"

"Takes a hell of a lot of money to live the lifestyle you've taken a liking to. Takes even more to hide the old man away in that private institution in Nashville, drugged up on the latest medicines. Can't do both on a Park Ranger's salary, can you?"

"Shut up!"

"Am I right, Denny Ray? Bet it cost you plenty to pay off the sanitarium's director to keep it hush-hush, didn't it? You didn't want folks around here to know your daddy went crazy. They might think the same thing about you some day."

"Shut up, I said!"

"You faked his death. Paid Sparta's one and only mortician a hefty sum to stage the burial."

The revolver shook alarmingly. "How did you find out?"

"Silverhawk Investigative Services is damned good at what they do. You can run, but you can't hide, Denny Ray. There's always a trail to follow."

"He was no better than your pa," Denny Ray spat. "And you ain't no better than me, Corrigan. But you act like you are." He sneered in derision. "Living in the big city and working for that hotshot detective agency. Got yourself a damned fine education, too, didn't you?" His contemptuous glance slid over Adrienne before jumping back to Mick. "I'm guessin' you even got a piece of the governor's pretty daughter. One of the advantages of being her bodyguard, wasn't it?"

A muscle moved in Mick's cheek. "She's done nothing to you. And neither did her mother."

"Well, you didn't deserve none of it 'cuz you ain't no better'n me, y'hear?" he yelled, as if Mick had never spoken. "We wuz both born on this mountain. Just 'cuz you got off and I didn't, you ain't no better."

Stunned to hear him slip into the backwoods tongue of his childhood, Adrienne gaped at him. No one moved. Or breathed.

"Yeah, Pa's in the looney bin. Go ahead and say it. *Looney bin*! But at least he wasn't no drunk like your pa was. And your Cherokee squaw-mama just wasn't woman enough, was she? Folks knew how he was always beatin' on her. Why, she--"

Mick roared and lunged for him. Denny Ray pivoted and tried to side-step him, but Mick slammed his shoulder into Denny Ray's chest, sending him hurtling toward the creek. Denny Ray scrambled to keep his footing, and Mick followed him in with a tackle that landed them both in the water. They splashed and fought like trout on hooks.

Adrienne whipped out the Beretta. Grasping it with both hands, she swung toward the blur of moving men, to the henchmen who leveled their guns at Mick, to the mayor yelling at them to shoot.

Mick didn't have a chance against any of them. Denny Ray took all his concentration, his fight to survive. He couldn't defend himself against the three men who would kill him in Denny Ray's place.

Suddenly, the roles had reversed. Adrienne no longer needed protecting. Instead, her bodyguard did, and the months of personal training, her determination to protect herself after her mother's murder, kicked in.

"Call them off, Mayor," she shouted. Feet spread, arms extended, finger on the trigger, she aimed the Beretta on Webster. "Or I'll shoot you dead in the heart."

His nostrils flared in barely-contained rage. "Now, you listen here, girl. That resort belongs on this mountain! It's for everyone's good, and it's high-time you let your daddy know it!"

"This discussion is closed." Behind her, Mick and Denny Ray still struggled in the creek. In the end, one of them would win, and she couldn't take a chance that it'd be her mother's killer. She snapped a harsh glance at the two henchmen. "Put your guns down. Easy. All of you. One by one."

"I think the better order would be, Miss Morelli, that you put down *yours*."

Cold metal pushed against her temple. Adrienne stilled at the lethal sound of Eddison Tyler's voice behind her. His gun cocked close to her ear.

She should have known he'd be here, hidden with the black Lexus in the trees. It was his resort that was at stake. Of all of them, it would be him who'd want Adrienne convinced to his way of thinking.

He left her no choice but to drop the Beretta. She couldn't defend Mick any more. She couldn't defend them both against so many armed men.

Heart pounding, she lowered the Beretta but didn't let go, vaguely aware the creek waters had fallen silent, that Mick had pulled Denny Ray unconscious out of the water, that only Mick's taut, labored breathing broke the stunned silence.

"Hold it right there, rich boy," Farley ordered, stepping out of the woods. "Unless you want a bellyful of buck shot."

Tyler sucked in a startled oath. He was a small man, wiry and not much heavier than Adrienne. She reacted to his break in concentration, slammed her arm upward and knocked his weapon from his hand. A solid punch to the jaw toppled him to the ground with a moan.

Mayor Webster's revolver whipped toward her. Mick yelled and dove for her, but Adrienne whirled faster, and in split-second speed, she aimed and squeezed the trigger. Webster's gun flew, and he cried out, his arm bloodied and useless.

The two henchmen tossed their weapons and raised their hands. Behind them, Sparta's entire police force fanned out, led by Officer Radley. Griffin Silverhawk, too. And her father, pushed in his wheelchair by a worried-looking Bess.

"We're safe now, honey." Mick's strong arms circled her. He held her hard, his mouth in her hair, murmuring her name over and over.

Her eyes closed in relief. Cold, muddied creek water soaked from his clothing into hers. The sapphire blue pantsuit would be ruined, but she didn't care.

It was over. And she had won.

Julia Morelli's dream would finally come true.

# CHAPTER FIFTEEN

The shocking news alleging Denny Ray as Julia Morelli's murderer rocked the entire mountain. The Stocktons' cabin served as headquarters for the press, law enforcement officers, the Scott's Gulf Alliance and a horde of curiosity-seekers, keeping the ever-gracious Izzie busy plying them all with coffee, lemonade and homemade chocolate-chip cookies.

Of course, the little cabin had been cleared of every rattlesnake. Adrienne refused to set foot inside until a half dozen Park Rangers assured her they were gone. Even then, Mick had to hold her hand and inspect every inch of the place with her so she could see for herself and be convinced.

Afterward, she gloried in a long, hot shower. All that was missing was Mick showering with her. If they'd been alone, he would have, she knew. The stark longing in his eyes as she closed the bathroom door behind her confirmed it.

While the water sluiced over her body, uncertainty buffeted her mind. What would happen next between them? His contract with her father had ended. She had no need of his protection, no more fears to confront. He'd go back to Memphis; she to Nashville. He had commitments there. Other clients to protect. She had her work with the state of Tennessee. Would he disappear from her life once again, like he'd done six months ago?

Having no answers, she dried her hair, then dressed in jeans and a clinging turquoise tank top before returning to the living room. The unexpected arrival of the CEO of Murdock Corporation swept aside thoughts of her future with Mick and allowed her to focus on the present.

She was delighted to see him. A dear man, the CEO. And determined to give away the two thousand acres of wilderness. He saw to it that the signing was done right there on Izzie's kitchen table. A humble beginning to a new chapter in the wilderness' preservation. And a final closing to a tragic one to procure it.

Izzie and Dietrich beamed with pride. Applause rose up amongst those members of the Alliance fortunate enough to witness the deal. Photographers' cameras flashed; reporters scribbled furiously on pads or wielded recorders. Her father signed the deed with pride and flourish in his wife's place. It was only right that he did. Even better, Adrienne was spared speaking in front of the microphone that had always intimidated her.

During the impromptu ceremony, Mick stayed in the background, at the edge of the crowd overflowing the cabin, his stance watchful, as always. It was his way, she knew. Guard and protect unobtrusively. A little boy's devotion to his mother had provided a man with an honorable life's work. It was who he was.

Finally, the crowd thinned, and Adrienne sought out her father, sitting in his wheelchair beneath a shady elm tree. She hadn't seen him alone before now, and she took advantage of it.

A smile creased his face at her approach. "Well, finally, a few minutes to talk to my little girl."

She smiled at the endearment. After her harrowing experience this morning, the words were musical. "Only a few?"

She sat in a folding chair next to him, and he took her hand into his. "We can visit more on the way home. I want to know everything that's happened since you left my office two days ago."

She hesitated. "What about Mick?"

"When we received word from Officer Radley that Ronald Kershner had been murdered, Grif chartered a private plane out of Memphis and met me in Nashville. We rented a car and drove out here. Mick will drive it back with Grif. You and I will take the Range Rover."

"I see." She battled her disappointment.

Her father smiled. "Why do I get the feeling I'm not your first choice in traveling companions?"

"Oh, it's not that at all," she hastened to say, then shrugged ruefully. "Well, maybe it is."

"He's a fine man, Adrienne. I would never have put you in his care if I didn't think so."

"Yes," she whispered.

Mick was the best there was. No other man would compare to him. Ever.

"They don't make husband material like that very often." Her father cleared his throat loudly and squinted into the sky.

A startled laugh escaped her. "Are you trying to tell me something?"

"I think you already know."

She didn't even try to deny it. Her heart swelled. "Yes. Yes, I do."

He gave her fingers a gentle squeeze. "Losing your mother has taught me how precious life is. I've also learned there are some things worth going after no matter the price."

"Would there be a price for Mick?" she wondered.

"Only you can answer that, honey." He tugged her closer for a kiss on her cheek. "He's over there, talking with Farley. We don't have to leave just yet. Say what you have to before we do."

"Thanks, Dad. I love you."

Izzie appeared with a pitcher of lemonade to refill his cup, and Adrienne left him to her chatting. Farley sat behind the wheel of the Studebaker. He watched as Adrienne drew nearer, his grizzled features no longer suspicious.

She extended her hand. "I haven't had a chance to thank you for your help, Farley," she smiled. "Your timing couldn't have been better."

"Lucky for us, he doesn't listen to orders," Mick added, one foot propped on the floorboard.  At her questioning glance, he grinned.  "I'd sent him off with Bess to get help.  He didn't do it."

"Didn't need to," Farley said gruffly, taking her hand in a firm grip through the open window.  "Bess saw your uncle and the cops comin' down the road.  She took off to warn 'em 'bout what was happenin'.  I stayed behind to keep an eye on things."

"How did you find us anyway?" Mick asked.

"Tire tracks, boy.  When you stole my truck.  The dirt at my place was soft enough, all I had to do was follow where you went.  Easy to do."  He eyed Mick shrewdly.  "Didn't know you was Dermot Corrigan's boy."

Mick frowned.  "You knew him?"

"Heard of him."

Thankfully, Farley said nothing more.  The understanding in his expression revealed gossip had always traveled fast on the mountain.  Mick's turbulent childhood hadn't been a secret.

Adrienne decided to change the subject.  "We apologize for stealing your truck, Farley.  Under the circumstances, we were desperate."

"Never mind 'bout that.  You two done what you had to.  Reckon I would've done the same."

"Would you?"

"Damn right."  He shifted, and the seat springs creaked.  "Guess it don't matter none, anyway, not after all you did for us folks on the mountain.  What with you losin' your ma and all, just 'cuz she wanted to save the wilderness."

"Does that mean you approve now?"

"It still means I don't trust the government!" he shot back, on the defensive as always.  "But I guess I understand what y'all was trying to do."

"Think about it from the state's perspective, Farley," Mick added.  "Tennessee is proud of the wilderness.  They're not going to take it away from you."

"That's right," Adrienne said quietly. "Your life isn't going to change now that the state owns the land. Not one bit."

"You mean I can still keep my 'possums?'"

"Of course, you can. Every one of them," she assured him.

"Hmmph!"

But Adrienne saw the relief in his grizzled face.

"Come on, Grandpa!" Bess yelled to him from her own pickup. "Time for us to go home."

"Thank you, Bess," Adrienne called. "For everything."

"Don't you go thanking me, Miss Morelli. This mountain ain't had nothing as good as what you've just given us for a long time."

"The next time you're in Nashville, call me. We'll do lunch." Adrienne waved.

Bess' jaw dropped. She leaned out the window toward Farley. "Did you hear that, Grandpa? Miss Morelli just invited me to *lunch*! Can you believe it?"

Farley revved up the truck. "I believe it!"

He gifted Adrienne with a broad wink. He gunned the engine, and the Studebaker tore off, taking some of the Stocktons' lawn with it. Adrienne held her breath until both trucks disappeared from sight.

"Nice people," she said, blowing it out again.

"Very." Mick draped an arm around her shoulders. "After living in the city so long, I've forgotten how down to earth folks out here can be."

Adrienne glanced at him after hearing the pensiveness in his tone. "You sound like you miss it."

"I do."

He led her toward the back of the cabin. Rose bushes grew abundantly in a garden Dietrich had fashioned, and Mick bent over to pluck a pink one, its petals only beginning to open.

He handed it to Adrienne. "Careful of the thorns."

She inhaled the fragrance and vowed to keep the rose as a reminder of today. Would it be their last one together?

"It's lovely," she said softly.

Mick hooked both thumbs into his pockets. He stared into the trees.

"Grif has talked about opening an office in Nashville," he said finally.

She cocked her head. "Really?"

"I could move there. Head it up, you know."

Her pulse tripped. "I see."

"It'd be an easy drive out here, too. A few hours is all. I could fix up the old place real nice. Have a home in the mountains again."

She swallowed. She was afraid to hope. "It's beautiful country. Perfect to build a new house."

"We'd leave the wilderness pretty much untouched, though. That's all part of the appeal. The wilderness."

"Of course." Smiling a little, she considered him. "'We', Mick?"

He swore and turned to her. He bundled her tight against him, crushing the rose between their chests. "Damn it, Adrienne. I don't want to see you with a gun in your hand ever again. Maybe you don't have a killer stalking you anymore, but there's plenty of things that can go wrong, and you need me to think about those things, so that--"

"So why don't you just ask me to marry you, you big lug, and then you can protect me the rest of my life?"

He drew back. She'd never seen him looking so unsure of himself. "Will you marry me, Adrienne?"

She cupped his face tenderly between her hands. "I told my father a few days ago that I didn't need a bodyguard anymore. I was wrong, Mick. I do need one. I need you."

He covered her mouth for the kiss she fervently gave. Her heart swelled near to breaking for this man who would never leave her again.

"You didn't answer my question, Morelli," he said huskily. She feigned forgetfulness. "What question was that?"

He growled and nipped at her neck.

She suffused into happy giggles and snuggled into him. "Yes, of course, I'll marry you."

And the state of Tennessee would soon have one more thing to celebrate.

*THE END*

Dear Reader,

If you know me or have read my books, you'll know *Her Mother's Killer* is a new genre for me. While I'll always love my cowboys and the Old West, writing a contemporary romantic suspense was a refreshing change. I enjoyed putting Mick and Adrienne in almost constant peril, and as for the romance, well, how could I not? For this Nebraska girl, learning about the state of Tennessee and its beautiful Cumberland Mountains was a bonus. I didn't have the pleasure of experiencing the wilderness firsthand, but I have a new addition to my bucket list!

I hope you've enjoyed *Her Mother's Killer*. To learn more about me and my books, please visit my website:

www.pamcrooks.com

Pam
PO Box 540122
Omaha, NE  68154

Best Fried Green Tomatoes

4 tomatoes
2 eggs
½ cup milk
1 cup flour
½ cup cornmeal
½ cup bread crumbs
2 tsp coarse kosher salt
¼ tsp ground black pepper
4 cups vegetable oil for frying

Directions

Slice tomatoes 1/2 inch thick. Discard the ends.

Whisk eggs and milk together in a medium-size bowl. Scoop flour onto a plate. Mix cornmeal, bread crumbs and salt and pepper on another plate. Dip tomatoes into flour to coat. Then dip the tomatoes into milk and egg mixture. Dredge in breadcrumbs to completely coat.

In a large skillet, pour vegetable oil (enough so that there is 1/2 inch of oil in the pan) and heat over a medium heat. Place tomatoes into the frying pan in batches of 4 or 5, depending on the size of your skillet. Do not crowd the tomatoes, they should not touch each other. When the tomatoes are browned, flip and fry them on the other side. Drain them on paper towels.

(www.allrecipes.com)

## Excerpt

The Secret Six
Historical Suspense Series Set in Prohibition-Era Chicago
**The Spyglass Project**
By Frankie Astuto
Available January, 2013

Prologue

*Wittenberg, Germany*
*July, 1918*

There was only one good thing that came from being a prisoner of war in this stinking piece of hell.

We were still together.

I wouldn't have survived this stinking piece of hell if it wasn't for the six men huddled in the dirt with me. Or maybe they wouldn't have survived without me. But even before we were thrown into the most heinous camp in Germany, we'd learned to trust each other with our loyalty and our lives.

"Go on and take the damned peach, Major." Captain Drew Hammond kept his voice low so the other prisoners wouldn't hear. Since our arrival nearly five months ago, we'd learned what a man would do when he was desperate for something to eat. And a fresh peach was worth killing for. "You'll need it more than we will."

Like me, Drew had lost the bulk that once gave him the strength of two men. His dingy green woolen uniform was in tatters, and his feet were bare of stockings and leather boots. He extended his arm, offering the fruit, bought and paid for with his last cigarette in a deal made with an enterprising German guard.

I knew he spoke of our plan to escape. A decision I'd spearhead if and when the time came, but one that would require a stamina none of us possessed.

I ignored his offer and finished sharpening a strip of tin

against a rock, testing the edge against the pad of my grimy thumb. I'd fashioned the metal from a can pilfered from a pile of trash near the guards' camp. A far cry from the U.S. Army bowie knife I once owned--and now in the possession of some bastard Kraut--but the blade would cut well enough.

"We wouldn't be here today if we didn't take care of one another." I infused a quiet firmness into my voice for the benefit of my captain as well as the others. The seven of us, more like brothers than fellow soldiers. "Isn't that right, Drew?"

A moment passed. "Yes, sir."

His somber tone convinced me the peach would be good for morale. I took the fruit and carefully set it on another piece of tin, its warped shape large enough to use as a plate. Aware my actions held the keen attention of the other six, that their mouths were watering as pathetically as my own, I pushed the blade into the juicy flesh and removed one slim wedge.

We stared at the glistening shape.

And for a moment, no one said anything.

Until Kane Purcell rubbed his bearded chin.

"Not rotten," he muttered.

I continued my careful cutting, one wedge after another. "No."

Not this time.

Not that it would've mattered.

Jarrett LaCroix skimmed a cautious glance over the prison grounds, clearly concerned our bounty would only bring trouble from the thousands of desperate men penned up on ten and a half acres inside the barbed wires.

But the rampant misery kept our activity unnoticed, and soon, seven matching wedges rested on the tin. I held the plate toward Rico Mendoza and Lee Pennington, the youngest of our group. "Take one."

Rico's hair was overgrown and tangled, his lips blistered from the sun. He feigned a grimace. "My belly's burning, Major. I can't eat or else I'll lose what little I've got in me."

He turned away toward the shade of our crude wooden hut and crawled in.

"I can't, either." Lee went in after him. "Never could abide peaches. Always preferred apples myself."

"I'm too tired to eat anything. Think I'll take a nap." Kane joined them.

And so did Jarrett. "Afraid I'm more partial to an onion, Major."

I glowered at the whole scheming bunch. "You'll help me eat these, or I'll shove a slice down each of your damn throats. You need the nourishment as much as I do."

Suddenly, beside me, Grant Halverson stiffened. "Guard coming. North gate. Forty paces."

Our glances shot to the lone Kraut striding purposely toward us. A kid barely into his twenties and likely illiterate, but with an arrogance and hate for the American doughboys that left us all suffering. I swore under my breath and flipped the peaches into the dirt, covering them quickly with the tin plate.

By the time I looked again, the guard was almost upon us. He halted, so close I smelled the perspiration on his skin.

"You Major Michael Malone?" he demanded in a thick German accent.

No reason I could think of why he'd need to know. Or why he'd taken the time to find out. Tense, I nodded once. "First Infantry Division, American Expeditionary Forces."

I made sure there was pride in my voice, but the guard's face contorted, showing tobacco-stained teeth. Before I could see it coming, the damned Kraut slammed the toe of his boot into my ribs, putting all his weight into the blow.

I hurtled into the dirt, gritted my teeth against the pain, and roiled with the hate and frustration from my inability to hit back.

"Just curious," he said.

He was gone by the time I could find the strength to right myself again.

"Major!" Kane and Jarrett, Rico and Lee, scrambled out

of the hut, all talking at once. "Jesus, you okay?"

"Never been better," I said and tried to breathe.

"What the *hell* was that all about?" Drew ground out.

I didn't answer, but I cursed the circumstances that made us prisoners of the enemy. Unarmed, starving, hurting. Soon dead if I, as their leader, didn't do something about it.

Grant stared down at the dirt and uttered a soft exclamation. "Looks like he brought you a present."

My glance dropped, too. A stubby twig lay on the ground, right next to the piece of tin hiding our peach.

A twig that hadn't been there before. Rolled tight around it, a strip of paper. I breathed a stunned oath.

A message. From who? Who would've dared to contact me like this, using a German guard to smuggle the message in?

I forgot the fire in my ribs. Forgot my hate, my determination to escape.

I reached for the stick and unrolled the message. Recognition of the scrawled handwriting rocked through me.

My kid brother's.

Sweet Jesus Christ.

Benjamin was here? In Germany?

The possibility--the evident truth of it--thundered inside me.

"What's it say?" Drew asked, hushed.

I read the note. Then I read it again.

"Benjamin--he wants to rendezvous. Tonight." My gaze lifted toward the prison hospital, situated on the southeast side of the camp, and to the pine woods beyond. "Near the South Gate at midnight."

"Midnight." Grant's skepticism dripped. "Just like that."

"Does he think it'd be that easy?" Jarrett demanded.

"Pardon me for saying so, Major." Kane frowned. "But you said yourself that he--."

"I know what I said."

I hadn't seen Benjamin in more than two years. Not

since the night our father had been killed in a violent explosion along Jersey City's waterfront, along the Atlantic coast. A succession of barges and freight cars loaded with munitions and supplies for the Allies, all of it blown up in a sabotage scheme that rocked the harbors and soon after compelled the United States to join the war against the Central Powers.

My father had been on duty that night, a policeman in charge of guarding the pier. In his agonized last words to me, he revealed how he'd seen my brother's face in the glow of the fires. His certainty of Benjamin's betrayal.

A traitor to his country.

"Could be a set-up, Michael."

I resisted Drew's warning. Even now, I didn't want to believe what my brother might've done. Never once did I stop praying my father had been wrong.

"Maybe," I said.

But I had to risk the meeting. I had to look in Benjamin's eyes, see the expression on his face. I had to find the truth about what really happened the night the Malone family was knocked to its knees.

I lifted the tin plate and rescued the seven peach slices from the dirt.

"Whatever you're thinking, I'm going with you," Drew said in a low growl. He reached for a wedge and roughly wiped it clean. "Just so you don't go getting killed all by yourself."

I ignored my captain's grim prediction. I reached for a wedge, too, took a small bite and savored the juicy taste, knowing its nourishment would give me the strength for what laid ahead.

\* \* \*

We waited until the hours crawled into darkness and the prison camp fell into its evening routine. Until the master of the bloodhounds had roused his dogs from their kennels and taken them on his rounds. Until the groaning prisoners fell into a miserable, listless sleep.

Only then did Drew and I steal noiselessly toward the South Gate. Once inside the wire fence which surrounded the hospital, we headed toward the narrow stream running through the grounds, the lower part of which was used as a primitive lavatory, as disgusting as it was daunting.

We paused to reconnoiter. The summer's heat had turned the polluted water vile. A Kraut guard always watched this part of the creek, shadowed heavily by the pine woods towering over it, and my gaze clawed the dense, moonless night. I saw nothing, heard nothing, *felt* nothing.

But a mute gesture from Drew indicated a dark lump leaning against a pine tree farther up, with the unmistakable shape of a rifle beside it. Most likely, the water's stench had driven the guard a dozen yards upstream. His shape wasn't moving.

I waited to make sure it wouldn't. Finally, convinced the Kraut wasn't aware of our presence, I exchanged a terse nod with Drew, took a breath and stepped into the slimy ooze.

I steeled myself against the revolting sensation against my bare feet. I eased lower, onto my side, tensing against the soft splashing sound my body made. I kept my face out of the water, always careful to keep the guard in sight. Grasping roots and limbs along the side of the stream, I pulled myself forward, my mind focused on a certain gap between the barbed wires and the bottom of the creek. An opening just large enough for a man to slip through. When I reached it, I passed under the fence... and was outside the prison camp.

I kept moving. I strained to hear some sign Drew was behind me, but it was nearly impossible with my pulse pounding against my temple; I could hardly breathe from the fear he'd get caught because of me. And shot. Both of us, like animals.

Then, movement near the outside of the fence, and Drew's head came up. I couldn't get distracted by relief. Any moment, the guard could hear us, see us. Seconds ticked into minutes. Yard by yard, I tugged myself through the putrid water, farther away from the prison. Closer to Benjamin.

In the silence, soft rippling sounds indicated Drew still followed. I fought exhaustion. I'd lost much of my strength during our imprisonment, and yet the need to bolt out of the water, clamor over the bank and run like hell nearly overpowered me.

I clung to control. The control that kept me alive these past months and helped me fight the need to hurry now. The dogs wouldn't pick up our scent if we stayed in the water. We had to keep on just as we were. Sacrifice time for the safety of our lives, and to fail, when we were so close....

The rendezvous point appeared. A break in the woods, an opening between the pines, and God save us both, we'd made it.

Breathing hard, I heaved myself up over the tree roots and onto the high bank. Drew collapsed next to me.

"How far you figure we're downstream?" he rasped.

"Half mile, maybe." My panting response came out in a whisper; my glance pierced the darkness for signs of anyone following. Finding none, I allowed myself precious moments of rest. I thought of the five men left behind, that if this rendezvous succeeded, that it wasn't a set-up after all, they'd all be in this very spot tomorrow night. Free. Just like we'd planned.

The muted blowing of a horse shut down my thoughts. I sat bolt upright, bracing myself to be shot, my ears expecting the dreaded baying of the bloodhounds as the killer beasts charged toward us....

Three horses emerged from the woods. In no hurry. The blackened shapes of men in dark hoods filled the saddles, their silence, their stealth ominous, and suddenly, time fell away to that awful night back on the Jersey shore--.

My heart drummed inside my chest. Something inside me, something sick and terrible, told me my father hadn't been mistaken.

The men pulled up. I cursed the night and my inability to see faces. Mostly, I hated being vulnerable and defenseless.

"You look like a damned scarecrow, Michael."

My gaze swung to the man on the left. The hood muffled the voice, but my mind raced to identify it, to delve past the sarcasm and thinly-veiled surprise to detect anything familiar.

"Yeah, well, I left my best suit behind," I drawled.

I could feel their stares. I knew how I looked with my ragged uniform dripping and clinging to my body, how my shoulders had turned bony, my beard tangled, my long hair caked to my head. How I must smell, too, and Drew being no different.

But sudden impatience snapped through me. There was no time to think of their opinions--or care about them. I dragged my gaze over each man.

Only to return once again to the one on the left.

The way he sat in the saddle, one slim hand over the other on the pommel. His shoulders slightly hunched. I could just about taste the tension shimmering from him.

"Take the hood off, Benjamin," I said.

His horse shifted, flicking its tail. No one moved. No one spoke.

*Please God, please God, please God. Don't let it be Benjamin.*

Then, slowly, the thin hand grabbed hold of the mask and pulled.

Pain cut right through me, and the months fell away. Two years' worth of time, throwing me backward to my dying father's side, our huddled bodies illuminated by the fires, the air around us reverberating with the explosions that wouldn't end....

To the words my father had rasped in my ear.

*Benjie. I saw him, Michael. I saw him....*

Incrimination of his youngest son.

Searing hurt cut through me. Blazing fury.

I would never forgive my brother. Not then. Not now.

"You're a damn fool, Benjamin," one of them said in a rough whisper.

My gaze swung to the man in the middle. He spoke with

an accent. European, but only slightly.

Benjamin's head swiveled. "He would never have agreed otherwise."

"Maybe he still won't."

"Let me handle him--"

*"Don't say my name!"* The snarled command shattered the night's silence.

Benjamin flinched. "I'll handle him," he said through gritted teeth. "Like we decided."

My tension eased. So. They wanted something from me. What, I couldn't imagine, but a feeling of control, of relative calm, settled over me.

"Go on, then," the third man said finally, his muted voice more refined. "We've got you covered." He lifted the blackened shape of a revolver and pointed it toward my chest. "Just in case he tries anything stupid."

Benjamin's head turned back toward me. "He won't."

"He's an American patriot, isn't he?"

A moment passed. "Maybe that'll change."

I narrowed an eye. What the hell was *that* supposed to mean?

"It will. If he wants to stay alive."

The European's rough whisper knocked the tension right back into me. I hadn't forgotten how easily our voices would carry. Or the precious minutes ticking. Nor could I ignore the skill of the bloodhounds, even this far from the prison.

"Get off the horse, Benjamin," I ordered softly. "I don't like being talked down to."

Benjamin lifted his revolver; until now, I hadn't known he was carrying. The fact that he was festered.

"We've got a proposition for you, big brother," he said. "We went through a lot of trouble to track you down. I'd like to think you'll listen to what we have to say."

"That would depend, wouldn't it?"

"The major wants you out of the saddle, Benjamin." For the first time Drew spoke up, and the low timber of his voice carried a vein of command worthy of his rank. "I suggest you listen to him."

Benjamin leveled him with cool regard. "Captain Drew Hammond, aren't you?"

"That's right."

"They say you two are real tight."

I thought of the other five, still back at the prison camp. All of us, tight as bullets in a gun chamber.

"You got that right, too," Drew said.

Benjamin finally dismounted, then, and stood with feet spread, his revolver steady-aimed at me. "I know all about you, Michael."

It took all my willpower not to exchange an uneasy glance with Drew. "You should." My mouth formed a sardonic quirk. "We're brothers, remember?"

"They call you 'Polecat'," he said, ignoring the reminder. "And the captain here, he's 'Gator'."

Jesus.

The code names we swore to protect. "We know who you are," Benjamin continued. "We know you work in secret for the Army. The Secret Seven, spying against the Germans." He paused. "Rebels like me."

I was grateful for the night, that it hid my stunned surprise, the sickening realization our covert unit assigned to collect intelligence for the War Department had been uncovered by these conspirators.

"You like living in that hell back there, Michael? Because if you don't, you don't have to go back. You can escape with us now. Tonight. You'll be a free man."

"Escape with you." The outrageousness of the suggestion rocked through me.

"Fight for Germany with us," Benjamin said. A pleading quality had slipped into his voice. "Help us win the war."

"You're asking me to be a damned traitor," I hissed.

"I'm asking you to save yourself."

My hands itched to grab my brother by the throat and shake some sense into him. Hard. What had gone wrong in his life that he'd turn against his homeland and take sides with murdering cowards?

*And he wanted me to be just like him?*

"Your precious government doesn't care about either of you." Again, the European-accented voice taunted us from beneath the hood. The revolver swung lazily back and forth, shifting its aim between Drew and me. "They forgot about you. They're just going to let all you doughboys rot in the camp." He sounded amused. "Did you ever think about that, Michael?"

I had to admit it had crossed my mind plenty of times. Honest and upright American soldiers like myself captured, humiliated, then left to suffer and languish under the Kraut soldiers' cruelty.

An eternity of suffering.

Senseless dying.

The price of war men like me had to pay.

"You're good at what you do, Michael. Word is you're the best there is." Benjamin spoke again.

I clenched my teeth. I refused to deny it, yet my mind screamed *how do you know about me*?

"Just say the word, and we'll make sure your name is taken off the prison roll call list. The captain's, too. Both of you will just... disappear."

Once more, I thought of the other five, waiting anxiously in the hut. Grant, Kane and Jarrett. Rico and Lee. What would they think if Drew and I abandoned them? Just jumped to the enemy's side to save ourselves?

I'd die first. Drew would, too. Both of us, prepared to give our last breath for the country we loved.

"And if we refuse?" I asked, not bothering to hide my mockery.

A pistol cocked. The European's, clearly the gang's leader. "We can't let you tell your friends about our little proposition, can we?"

"Michael." Benjamin sounded desperate. "You'll be *free*. We'll be together again, us two."

I slid my gaze back to my kid brother. The moon shone

through the thinning clouds and revealed the toll the war had taken on him. The skin stretched taut over his cheekbones. The harsh jut to his jaw. The mouth that formed an unyielding line.

Benjamin had grown hard. Harder than his twenty-four years should allow. I *felt* the callousness more than I could see it. How many lives had he taken in cold-blood? Innocent people like our father?

"If Dad was here, he'd be real disappointed in you, Benjie," I said slowly.

His body flinched, as if I'd caught him by the collar and forced him up straight. His lips curled, and he lifted his revolver.

"Go on," I taunted. "Kill me. Like you killed him."

"I never killed him, damn you!"

"You were there, setting the fires. He saw you, Benjamin. He saw you working for the enemy!"

"He--"

"Shut up!" the European hissed. "The dogs are coming!"

"How did they reward you?" Nerveless against the warning, the certainty of detection and flogging with the rubber whip that would no doubt kill me this time, I persisted, my contempt, my *pain*, driving me to learn the despicable truth. "Was it worth it, Benjamin? The money they paid you for the things you could *buy*?"

"You'd never understand." He shook with the hate that blistered me, clear to my bones. Why hadn't I known? How could I not have seen how much Benjamin despised me before now? This awful moment? "You're too damned full of patriotism and all that God Bless America shit, aren't you? Well, I'm good at what I do, too. Y'know that? I'm just as good as you are! Hell, I'm *better*!"

I shook my head, reeling from the hate. From the burning pain. "Benjie." I swallowed. "Benjie, listen to me."

"Major." Unease threaded Drew's voice. "The dogs."

I heard the baying, then. The pounding of powerful legs

racing toward us. A frenzied pack of men and horses and dogs, all blood-thirsty savages that would inevitably tear us apart.

Soon.

In seconds.

Benjamin's head swung; his glance raked the darkness beyond the pines. My muscles coiled, my body bracing to leap forward and grab him, the need in me desperate to do something, anything, to save my brother from what was to come.

The European leveled his revolver. Not at me, but at Benjamin, who didn't know, who didn't see, and my mouth opened to warn him, warn him, warn him--.

But the words didn't come. Dear God, not soon enough, not fast enough, before a sharp *pop* ripped through the night. His body jerked and hurtled to the ground.

Again, the revolver moved, this time toward me. White hot rage erupted inside me. Blazing, furious hate.

But Drew threw himself against me. The air whooshed from my lungs, and I felt myself falling, splashing, *drowning*....

Chapter 1

*Chicago, 1926*

"One step in front of the other, boyo." Drew kept firm hold on Michael's waist and managed to keep him upright. "Into the elevator. There you go."

It'd been a long, staggering walk from his automobile parked at the curb into the five-story apartment building where the only friend he called his best lived. But it'd been an even longer drive from the local precinct where Michael had been held for possession of illegal liquor and public drunkenness.

Again.

It happened every year on July 20th, the anniversary of Benjamin's murder. The day that could've resulted in their own deaths if Drew hadn't succeeded in saving their lives first.

He knew all about Michael's need to drown the pain.

He understood.

"Quit treatin' me like a damned two-year-old in knickers." Scowling, Michael weaved forward to push the button that would take him home. He missed. "I can walk jus' fine, y'know."

Drew punched the number 5 for him.

"Sure you can," he said amiably.

A little graft helped convince the cop who arrested Michael to look the other way and not ask questions. Luckily, the officer had served in the World War and had less respect for the Volstead Act and more for a man who had once given his best for his country.

Drew cursed the circumstances that hurtled Michael's life into a downward spiral. Since neither of them could turn back time and make things right for him, learning the truth about Benjamin's motive--and who he'd been involved with-- was their only option.

Hell, it was their obsession.

"You feelin' sorry for me again?" Michael demanded, peering at him through bleary eyes.

"Not at all," Drew lied.

"I'm all right." He shifted against the side of the elevator, keeping himself from leaning too far sideways. "I'm jus' fucking fine."

"I can see that."

Michael frowned. "It's a bad day, that's all."

Drew nodded, frowning, too. "A very bad day."

The elevator clanged to a stop, and Michael braced his feet against the motion. His glance locked with Drew's, resurrecting the bond, the brotherhood, between them. It pulled at Drew, deep inside.

"Thanks," Michael muttered. "For gettin' me out of jail."

"You'd do the same for me, boyo."

"I would." Rousing himself, Michael straightened. "My floor. I can take it from here."

"I'll walk you in."

The scowl returned. "You're not my mother, damn it."

The doors opened. Drew slipped a firm arm around Michael's waist and took the brunt of his weight again. "I'm going to take that as a compliment. I happen to like your mother."

"Yeah, well, she's always been a sucker for a smooth-talkin' son-of-a-bitch."

Drew chuckled. Michael gave him a drunken grin and made a wobbly turn toward the left.

Drew tugged him to the right. "Your apartment's this way. Give me your key."

"I'd a-figured it out." Michael groped for the key in his pocket, then plunked it into Drew's outstretched palm.

"Eventually, I suppose." Drew unlocked the door and guided him inside to the couch; Michael collapsed, one foot on the floor, one leg outstretched on the cushions.

"I'm going to make coffee." Drew headed to the small

kitchen. "When you're sobered up, we have to talk."

"'Bout what?"

"I've got a good lead on something."

"Yeah, yeah, jus' like the rest of 'em."

The caustic comment stung. There'd been a hundred leads to follow throughout the past eight years, and they'd worked their asses off on each one, only to be bitterly disappointed when none of them panned out.

But Drew had a gut feeling this one would.

"A singing society," he said. "German. I'm pretty sure it's a front for a Nazi organization that's taking hold in the country."

He filled the percolator with water, added coffee to the basket and turned the pot on. He noted how clean Michael kept the place, like an old lady with a fetish for being orderly and meticulous. A throwback from their time in the POW camp where Drew himself had nightmares from the filth, the fear he'd never be clean again.

Thank God those days were over.

All that was left was revenge.

"In fact, I'm going to check one out tonight." He glanced out the kitchen window. Almost dark. He didn't have much time. "I'd like you to go with me, okay?"

He opened the refrigerator and pulled out ham, cheese, and mayonnaise, then went on the hunt for a knife, finding one right where it should be. He glanced over his shoulder and frowned at the silence coming from the living room.

"Michael? You listening?"

He couldn't discern the noise Michael made but took it for what it was. A response. Drew worked a little faster, spreading the bread and heaping ham on one slice.

"I'm writing an article for *Spyglass* about this particular singing society," he went on, thinking of how he'd start with a roster of its members. "Vivian set me up with a rookie reporter to help. Her assistant. A little Italian doll."

Her dark-eyed image loomed in his thoughts, and he paused in his sandwich-making. He'd only just met her, but he was already half in love with her. She was so damned innocent. He wondered how someone so pure could exist in an often ugly world. How could she survive, especially as an investigative reporter?

He intended to teach her how. Lucky for him, patience was one of his best virtues, and beautiful women one of his favorite pastimes.

Drew added cheese to the sandwich and sliced the whole thing in half. He opened a cupboard, withdrew a plate and a coffee mug, filled both and strode back to the living room.

He halted in mid-stride. Except for his jaw which had lagged open, emitting noisy snores, Michael hadn't moved.

Drew muttered an oath of disappointment. So much for joining him in his investigation tonight....

But he supposed it couldn't be helped. It was July 20th, after all. The eighth anniversary of Benjamin Malone's death. Drew couldn't blame Michael for getting himself juiced. If Benjamin had been his kid brother, Drew would've gotten juiced, too.

He set the sandwich and coffee on Michael's desk. Finding paper, he penciled a quick note, letting Michael know they had much to talk about and that Drew would call him, first thing in the morning.

Then Drew covered him with one of his mother's knitted afghans and left, quietly pulling the door shut behind him.

\* \* \*

Claus Nussbaum closed his eyes and reveled in the beauty of the male voices surrounding him. The melodious words of the old German folk song lifted him, carried him away to a place he couldn't yet be, and filled him with the sweet ache of longing for what his life had once been.

*Ich denke was ich will und was mich beglücket....* Yes, he mused, his mind smoothly translating the words. He *did* think what he wanted, what made him happy. *Doch alles in der Still', und wie es sich schicket....* But always discreetly, and as it was suitable.

It was how he survived.  By being discreet and suitable.

Brilliantly clever.

His mood darkened from the reminder of the secrets he must keep, and he opened his eyes.  The time to reveal himself and all he had done had not yet come.  But it would one day.

When his beloved Germany defeated the infidels.

When Nazism reigned supreme in the world.

Here in the home of his friend, the leader of their singing society, he lingered in his chair, the one he routinely took in the back row so no one could stare at him--or guess who he really was.

He took comfort in the talented voices.  They belonged to men who believed as he did, and their resonance filled the corners of the room.  So strong and rich, the voices.  So powerful.  Just like the words they proclaimed.

Too soon, the song ended, signaling the close of the society's weekly meeting.  In camaraderie, the men would drink the dark beer he provided as a simple sign of his gratitude.  They wouldn't care the beer was illegal or that each of them had broken the American law which made alcohol forbidden.

Such stupidity, this country.

Prohibition made the United States look like a fool to the rest of the world.  The politicians never dreamed how impossible it would be to enforce the law--or the amazing profits to be made from breaking it.

Profits he intended to use to his advantage.

The rustle of music books being closed and handed back to their leader roused him from his thoughts.  Fritz Gissibl approached the back row with his eyes cast downward, discreet as always, giving no indication the two of them had grown up together in their beloved Germany.  No one knew their fathers had been employed as master butchers in the small city where they lived, that they were friends from birth and remained bound together by the ideals they fiercely shared.

Claus handed him the music book. Within its pages, he'd hidden a plain white envelope, thick from cash. Fritz appeared to test its weight, discreetly, of course, and a small smile of approval touched his lips.

Pleased, too, Claus stood. He pushed his Fedora onto his head and clasped Fritz's hand.

"*Einigkeit makt stark*," Fritz said, as he would to every member of the society preparing to leave for the evening.

"'In oneness, there is strength'." Claus quietly repeated their society's slogan. Everyone in this room knew it was so, yet the words couldn't be said often enough.

Claus strode through the nondescript kitchen and out the back door, latching it quietly behind him. As always, it was safer to leave this way. He'd parked his new Cadillac a couple of blocks away to avoid arousing suspicion from such a fine-looking machine. He needed to clear his thoughts; a walk in the crisp night air would settle his mood.

He rounded the corner of the house toward the back alley. The dark shape of a man standing in the neighboring yard stopped him cold.

Nearly hidden in the shadows of overgrown lilac bushes, the stranger centered binoculars over Fritz's window and studied the men inside, undeterred by the cheap curtains that blurred their faces and bodies. A light breeze blew through the partially open window, fluttering the hems and allowing the talented voices to escape.

Horror kept Claus from moving, from breathing. He hadn't expected anyone to find him like this. No warning, no clue, not a single hint that his true identity had been discovered.

He forced himself to breathe. To think. He'd been so careful, so clever, for so long....

Until he realized he hadn't made a mistake.

He never made mistakes.

This man, this *spy*, was working for the American government who employed agents to thirst for the blood of men like him. *That* was why the stranger was here, standing in the dark, dressed in his suit and hiding near the bushes with binoculars. To spy on him and the others who sympathized with the Nazi cause.

Fury seethed inside Claus. The Americans and their powerful government didn't accept why he had to do what he was doing. They didn't understand the beauty of the German songs. The Americans didn't believe in the songs' purpose or why they must be sung. Instead, the government was too quick to judge, too certain to hate. To punish.

Claus pushed his jacket aside and curled his fingers around the knife sheathed in leather at his waist. The blade was of the finest steel, the most efficient of the set his father had once used in his butcher shop.

Claus's feet began to move; the grass muffled the swiftness of his steps. Blinded by his binoculars, the spy never saw him, never heard him approach.

Until it was too late.

The binoculars jerked downward, and the spy twisted his body in defense, but faster, Claus plunged his knife into the man's belly, then quickly slashed the blade across his neck. The spy's body buckled, soundless but for the gargling of blood in his throat.

Along with the knives and their ability to slaughter, Claus inherited strong arms from his father. Easily, he pulled the motionless body into the bushes and hid its bulk at their roots, allowing the fragrant scent of lilacs to dull the smell of death.

Chapter 2

*The Next Morning*

Dave Elmhurst poked his head out of his office. "Hey, Michael! You got Mr. Mangiameli's Lizzy done yet?"

A dull ache persisted inside my temples. I was suffering from my indiscretion last night and had no patience with my boss rushing me. His obsession to give Mangiameli precedence over the rest of the shop's customers annoyed the hell out of me, and I refused to work faster for either of them.

I hated this time of year. The memories of Benjamin's betrayal still made me bleed, and I hated my inability to overcome the pain he'd inflicted on me.

Sometimes, the hate stirred the caged monster within me, the man I'd once been but would never be again, and I'd have to take refuge in a bottle of Bacardi rum in more quantities than I should. My drinking forced me to break the law, something I never used to do, and I hated that, too.

"Michael!" Dave yelled.

"No," I grated. "It's not done yet."

"Well, hurry it up. Mr. Mangiameli's going to show up any time now. He ain't going to like having to wait."

Scowling, a hose streaming water in one hand, a sponge in the other, I leaned under the hood of the Fordor Model T and scrubbed at some grime on the motor. I never bragged to be perfect, but even with the morning tremblies, I was the best mechanic Dave had, and everyone who came to Elmhurst Auto Repair knew it.

Still, I couldn't ignore who Aldo Mangiameli was and the respect Dave gave him. After several months of unexplained vandalism to customers' cars, Mangiameli had offered Dave 'protection'. For a weekly fee, of course. Dave had gladly paid, and the vandalism stopped.

As much as I disapproved of Mangiameli's garage racket,

it was his carelessness in not keeping his new Fordor running like it should that annoyed me the most. He owned the nicest model Ford Motor Company rolled off the assembly line this year. A sporty four-door painted an eye-catching Windsor Maroon, with electric ignition and balloon tires. Now that I'd finished modifying the left rear axle with a special Ruckstell housing containing two extra gears, Mangiameli had more speed on smooth roads and more power on rough ones, and in that, at least, I took satisfaction.

I leaned in deeper to sponge away the last of the water and linseed oil soap which had pooled on the motor, then squatted in front of the automobile to wipe down the headlights. I worked quickly, until a pair of spit-shine leather shoes appeared from beneath the chassis. My glance skimmed up smartly-creased slacks. I expected to see Mangiameli, ready to claim his newly-modified machine.

I never expected to see Commander Philip Van Fleet.

All my muscles coiled into place. Slowly, I rose. He'd been my superior officer during the World War, the man behind the Secret Seven. Heavy-browed, his hair receding but still dark and thick, he possessed sharp ice-blue eyes that could filet alive the fiercest of enemies or leave an honest man trembling.

Once, I'd trusted him, like a son who trusted his father.

Not anymore.

"Hello, Michael."

Water splattered from the hose onto the concrete floor. Ugly memories circled inside my brain, bringing back the pain, the *anger*, from Van Fleet's lies. I'd never forget how he'd manipulated his power to deny me what I needed most.

The truth.

"I heard you were a mechanic now," Van Fleet said, his cool gaze direct. "A damned good one, too."

Of course, the commander would know that about me. He'd know everything he wanted to know. It was his job, after all, to keep track of people. To learn about them. Even destroy them, if he had to.

Like he once destroyed me.

"Thank you." I managed to push past my bitterness and find a shred of civility. "Sir."

Water seeped into the soles of my work shoes. I didn't move, the irony of polite conversation clashing with the anger simmering in my veins. Van Fleet didn't deserve the respect I gave him. Odd how after three bitter years there was any respect left inside me at all. That it surfaced now only reminded me how much the commander once meant to me.

Which put me at a disadvantage.

I hated being at a disadvantage.

"So this is one of those new colors everyone's talking about these days." Commander Van Fleet's glance dropped to the Model T, but his expression remained impassive, as if he didn't give a rat's ass what kind of vehicle I'd been working on. Or what color. "Never seen one that wasn't painted black before. This maroon--."

"Why are you here, Commander?" I demanded sharply.

Van Fleet's mouth tightened. His glance lifted, and I saw the pain, then, raw and aching in his eyes.

"Drew's dead," he said.

My world shifted. "*What?*"

"Murdered last night. His body was found a couple of hours ago... throat slit... stashed under bushes...."

The thundering in my head drowned out the words and turned them incomprehensible. I couldn't think, couldn't feel past the chill that wracked my body.

*Drew? Murdered?*

The monster broke free from its cage, and a deep and raging fury spiraled through me. I dropped the hose and lunged for Van Fleet, grabbed him by the shirt front and shook him hard.

"I don't know what game you're playing with me, *sir*, but I swear I'll kill you for it," I snarled.

His nostrils flared. "It's the truth."

"I was with him last night," I hissed. "He was fine. Fine!"

"After that, Michael!" Teeth bared, Van Fleet's hands shot up between us and shoved me against the chest. I lost my grip on the shirt and stumbled backward. "It happened after that. Damn it, I saw him, too."

I stared at the commander's ragged features and read his anguish, his unmistakable grief.

"He--." My throat worked. My brain filled with a haze of memories. Drew at the jail. Drew driving me home. Drew getting me into the elevator, the apartment....

But after that, nothing. Damn it, *nothing*, until I dragged myself awake this morning.

"I know he was working with you," Van Fleet said, calmer. "He was helping you find the truth about Benjamin."

Drew couldn't be dead.

*He couldn't, he couldn't.*

I wrestled the monster back into its cage. I forced myself to breathe, to think. To understand.

"He was an honorable man. A soldier of the highest degree," Van Fleet went on. "We were privileged to know him."

*Privileged?* It was more than that. Drew was the only man I called friend. He'd saved my life eight miserable years ago. He knew the pain, the agony of unanswered questions which had haunted me ever since.

Drew understood the shame, too.

"Who did it?" I rumbled. "Who's responsible?"

"We don't know yet."

"The police?"

"Are corrupt imbeciles. They can't be trusted. If they have any evidence, they're not talking, unless they're paid for their trouble." Van Fleet's expression hardened. "Drew was with the Military Intelligence Officers Reserve Corps. Therefore, I've ordered the investigation into his death to be a military matter."

My eye narrowed. "Meaning?"

"We'll conduct our own." Van Fleet's icy gaze never wavered. "And I'm asking you to head it up."

My pulse tripped. Just as quickly as the anticipation flared, I banked it, curling my lip in derision. "So you can lie to me again? Kick me off the case? Again?"

He stiffened. "Any decision made by me three years ago resulted in unfortunate differences of our perspectives. I'm not proud of what I had to do, but I had my reasons for doing them."

"Jesus." I couldn't hold back my disgust.

"As for pulling you off of Benjamin's case, I had no other choice."

"The hell you didn't."

"Congress refused to provide the necessary appropriations to maintain Army staff. Intelligence in peacetime was and still is considered second-class and all but unnecessary. You were too high-ranking, Michael. Too experienced to keep on the government's payroll." He paused. "The War Department didn't need you anymore."

Even now, after three years, the words still hurt. "You of anyone knew how much I needed to find out why Benjamin betrayed his country. We all needed to know who he was working for."

"I was following orders handed down to me by the Secretary of War and General Pershing himself. If I could've prevented losing you, I would have. You were, and always have been, one of my best." His shoulders snapped back. His chin kicked up. "And that, Michael, is the end of the discussion."

I clenched my teeth. My time in the military forced me to recognize how it was necessary for Commander Van Fleet to retain his authority and the dignity of his position, neither of which excused the lies he'd made to suit his own purposes with no regard for mine.

That Van Fleet admitted regret for his actions was a rare concession, however. As pitiable as it was, the man's praise was salve on my wounds.

"You're a soldier, Michael. Not a grease-monkey." Van Fleet's condescending gaze flitted over me, from my oil-stained shoes to the grime smearing my coveralls. "I've scheduled a meeting this afternoon for 1:00. I expect you to be there."

He spun on his heel and strode out of the shop.

Everything within me rose up to refuse. Old resentments which insisted I wasn't obligated to obey him anymore, that through no fault of my own I'd been demoted to the ranks of an average laborer. I'd never forgive the commander for what he did. Why should I do *anything* he ordered me to do?

An automobile pulled up in front of the garage, and Aldo Mangiameli got out. He opened the passenger door, offered his hand to a beautiful blond woman and assisted her out, too.

Van Fleet's command, the meeting he'd scheduled, pounded in my head. Troubled, I turned away. I regarded the gleaming maroon Model T I'd been servicing all morning, then dropped the hood into place and tossed the dirty sponge into a bucket.

Drew was dead, and I didn't know what the hell I was going to do about it.

* * *

At 1:00 sharp, I parked my 1926 sage green Chevrolet Superior roadster on the Jackson Street side of the Chicago Federal Building and shut off the ignition. But I didn't get out.

Not yet.

Maybe I wouldn't at all.

I reached inside my suit coat for my favorite brand of courage and tossed back a swallow. The Cuban rum's familiar heat slid down my throat and into my belly, numbing my reluctance.

I returned the brass flask to my suit pocket and slid a discreet glance through the car's window to make sure no cops were around. A little graft usually solved the problem if there was, but today I had neither the time nor the patience to deal with some zealous officer spouting off the legalities of the Volstead Act.

Breaking the law, even one as ridiculous as Prohibition, wasn't a habit I was particularly proud of. But sometimes a man needed some liquid reinforcement to do what he was sure was going to be a big mistake.

Coming here promised to be that. One of the biggest mistakes I'd made in a long time. This morning at the repair shop, knowing Van Fleet wanted me to lead the investigation into Drew's murder, had turned tempting. Rewarding, even. Now that I'd scrubbed the grease from my fingernails and pulled my best suit out of the closet, well, hell, I'd begun to have some serious doubts.

I had some investigating to do, all right, but it wasn't into Drew's murder. It was *Benjamin's.* Drew would expect me to carry on the work we'd started together. He'd insist I continue my mission to find the truth. He knew, had always known, that I would never rest until the men responsible were brought to justice.

Drew wouldn't want the distraction of his own murder to keep me from solving Benjamin's.

Still... Commander Van Fleet was right to refuse to let the police investigate, and I owed it to Drew to at least hear the man out.

I glanced at my watch. Ten minutes past. I got out of my machine, locked it, and headed toward the Federal Building, acutely aware of how surreal it felt to be walking down Jackson Street like this when I hadn't been near the place since Van Fleet fired me three years ago.

His longtime secretary was waiting for me. Eunice Sanborn held open the door before I could latch onto the handle.

"Hi," I said, surprised.

String-bean slim and unfailingly conscientious, she hadn't changed in the three years since I'd last seen her. Same wavy brown hair, same pale skin, same lipstick in a shade of pink so subtle, most people wouldn't know she wore it. I guessed she even kept the same red pencil she'd always had tucked behind her ear, within quick reach if she needed it.

"It's good to see you again." If she was annoyed with my tardiness, she was too discreet to show it. If she really was glad to see me after so long, she was too discreet to show that, too. The door whooshed closed behind us. "Follow me, please."

An apology for being late hovered on my lips, but my curiosity from seeing her overrode it. What information was I missing? I'd been to the commander's office a hundred times. Not once had I needed anyone to show me the way.

"Everyone's arrived." Eunice-the-Efficient walked briskly toward the elevator, the hemmed edge of her prim navy blue skirt batting against her calves. "The meeting will begin as soon as you join them."

Everyone?

Them?

Unease filtered through me. I'd assumed the commander had wanted to talk only with me, a preliminary meeting to discuss the investigation into Drew's death.

Obviously, I'd assumed wrong.

I stepped into the elevator behind her. We both reached toward the numbered buttons on the panel, me for '8', the one that would take us up to the commander's office, but Eunice, a blink of time faster, pushed the 'B' button that would take us downstairs.

I frowned. "The basement?"

"Yes, sir. I've been instructed to escort you to a special meeting room down there."

Her evasiveness increased my unease. "Define 'special'."

She pursed her pale mouth. "*Secret* special."

"Damn." There was a meeting room hidden in the basement? "I had no idea."

"Of course you didn't." She peered up at me through her lashes. For the first time, I noticed she'd been crying. Her grief, I knew, from losing Drew. "It's secret."

Tension zinged through me. Whatever lay ahead, whatever this meeting was about and with whom, went beyond the scope of Drew's murder investigation. Again, I wondered what information the commander was keeping from me.

The car hummed downward and slid to a stop. The doors opened, and Eunice hurried out, leading me down a maze of narrow hallways with drab gray walls and plain linoleum floors until finally, we reached the far end of a corridor.

Eunice halted in front of a closed door and glanced up at me. With a key poised over the lock, her expression turned hesitant, as if she wondered if I was ready for what waited on the other side.

I removed my Fedora, straightened my tie and squared my shoulders. Hell, I was ready. So ready that if Eunice didn't open the fucking door, I'd barge through it without her.

She turned the key. I grasped the knob and walked in. My glance took in the small room: the United States flag in the corner, the portrait of President Calvin Coolidge on the wall, the clean, polished look to the place, right up to the brightness of the lights in the ceiling.

But it was the five men seated around the conference table that knocked the breath right out of me.

My men.

Or at least they used to be.

Before I left them after the World War ended, driven by my obsession to find Benjamin's killers. A split the others neither wanted nor accepted, but I'd refused to listen. Broken, angry, fragile, I'd left them all, eight long years ago.

And now, sweet Jesus, they were here.

Grant Halverson, Rico Mendoza, Jarrett LaCroix, Kane Purcell and Lee Pennington. No longer in their Army uniforms, their bodies weakened from the horrors of the Wittenberg camp, but tall and strong again, like I was, and dressed in white shirts and dark suits. In unison, they pushed back their chairs, stood at attention and saluted.

"Major." Their voices spoke at once.

Instantly, my throat clogged. No. Those days were gone. I wasn't their leader anymore. The unit and its purpose were over, ended by the World War and destroyed by its cruelties. The ugliness of Benjamin's betrayal and death, most of all.

Emotion swirled in my chest, in my brain, and robbed me of the ability to speak.

"It's been too long, sir." Grant moved forward and extended his hand. "Just wish Drew could be here with us."

In my lifetime, I'd never forget them. We'd been through hell together. We'd survived. We'd trusted and endured. Each because of the other.

"Me, too," I managed.

The emotion shifted, then, and burst free. I grabbed Grant in a quick hug, then went for the others, shaking their hands, clapping their shoulders. Time fell away, taking the pain, the uncertainties, with it, offering a certain comfort that I wasn't alone in losing Drew. They'd lost him, too.

Someone cleared his throat. Loudly.

"Gentlemen. Your attention please."

We swung toward Commander Van Fleet at the front of the room. A rare softening of his lips revealed his pleasure from seeing us together again, the men he'd trained as the Army's finest.

"Please sit down," he said. "Eunice?"

She appeared with a wheeled cart carrying a pot of coffee and an array of white stoneware cups. In moments, we were seated and served.

Van Fleet remained standing. Beside him, three chairs remained empty, yet a steaming cup had been placed at each.

"Thank you all for coming on short notice." The commander's glance touched on each of us. "You know I wouldn't have called you here if I didn't have good reason." He straightened. "Before I continue, however, there are a few gentlemen I want you to meet."

Eunice quietly opened a door I hadn't even noticed was there. Three powerful men strode through.

Beside me, Grant muttered an incredulous curse. In the next moment, six chairs clattered backward, and we rose.

"Good afternoon, gentlemen." Dwight Davis, Secretary of War, shook our hands. After him, Jacob Schurman, the American Ambassador to Germany, did the same. Van Fleet introduced the third man as George E. Q. Johnson, an Iowa-born lawyer recently appointed as U.S. District Attorney for the Northern District in Illinois.

I knew who these men were and what they did for their country. I'd read about them in the newspapers. I understood how their power reached all the way to the President of the United States.

That they were here, in this secret meeting room, with me and my five former compatriots was beyond fathoming. Their purpose, whatever it was, troubled me.

But one thing I knew for sure.

We stood on the brink of profundity. In moments, our lives were going to change.

Somehow.

We sat. Tightness etched the commander's mouth, indicating he knew our wariness and understood it. Yet it was Eunice, sitting unobtrusively in a chair with a notebook and her red pencil that he turned toward first.

"You won't be recording the minutes for us, Eunice," he said. "This meeting will be conducted without a single word written of what was said."

A brief flutter of her lashes revealed her surprise, but she quickly recovered.

"Yes, sir." She stood, taking her writing materials with her and quietly left, locking the door behind her.

The commander regarded us steadily. "I'll preface this meeting by saying that losing Drew Hammond is a blow to all of us. His cold-blooded murder cannot and will not be tolerated."

Emotion stung the back of my throat. Grant's hand fisted.

"I can't stress enough the need for secrecy from all of

you," the commander continued. "What we are about to impart is not to be shared outside the walls of this room. Understood?"

"Yes, sir," we said, our voices somber.

"If anyone is unable to accept the terms of these circumstances, then you're free to leave. Now. No questions asked."

No one moved.

No one spoke.

"Your complete dedication to this mission is crucial to the welfare of our country. If any of you are incapable or unwilling to give yourself, then--."

"Why don't you just say what you want from us, Commander?" I said.

He pinned me with a hard gaze, as if he could look deep into my soul and read the fear that had begun to take root. My reluctance, too, to commit to anything that would take me from the one mission Drew and I were determined to accomplish.

Finding out who Benjamin had been working for. And why.

"Then I'll turn this meeting over to the Ambassador," the commander said evenly.

I inclined my head coolly. "Thank you, sir."

Schurman leaned forward and clasped his hands on the table top. "Intelligence reports disclose that a large amount of money has been flowing into Germany. These reports have been verified by the Treasury Department, and initial indications are the funds originate in the United States."

Secretary Davis nodded. "In addition, propaganda reveals the leader of the Nazi Party, Adolph Hitler, is growing increasingly vocal against the Jews." He handed each of us a photo showing a stern-looking young man with cold eyes and a toothbrush moustache. "Sales of books on his ideology are soaring. His writings and speeches declare what he believes are the Jews' infidelities that will destroy Germany and take over the world, and therefore the Jews must be stopped." He shook his head, clearly thinking the man's opinions were alarming. "We've also learned from our informants that he's stockpiling munitions and improving the country's infrastructure."

I recalled how the war had weakened Germany. I'd seen firsthand how its citizens had suffered. "And you think they're paying for these improvements and munitions with the money being funneled in from the States?"

The Secretary nodded. "Yes. Hitler and the Nazi party are obsessive in their goal of establishing a large German empire in Europe. They intend to succeed with the establishment of a master race and broad territorial expansion. Hitler is working toward rearming Germany to achieve these goals. To do so requires massive amounts of money, and with all factors combined, it's not unreasonable for the War Department to fear a second world war could be impending if these fortunes are not stopped."

"Jesus," I breathed.

"Equally disturbing, this information stirs our suspicion that an organized group within our own borders has a strong allegiance with Germany and is sending these monies to further Hitler's means."

"Which left us no choice but to confer with President Coolidge. He believes, as we do, that preemptive action must be taken," said the ambassador.

"Which is where you six come in," said Commander Van Fleet.

My pulse began to pound. A slow, steady hammering against my temples. A premonition, a *knowing*, of what was coming next.

I didn't have to look at the others to know how intently they listened. That each of them, like myself, hardly moved, hardly breathed.

Profundity, at its keenest.

"We have a proposition for you," the U. S. Attorney said.

"A unique opportunity, so to speak," Schurman added.

"Never before dared by the military," Davis said.

Commander Van Fleet leaned forward. "During the World War, you all were part of an elite squad from the First Infantry Division. You were highly-trained in the latest methods known to us. Your skill and courage were crucial to the American Expeditionary Forces, even while you were captured and held as prisoners of war."

No, I wanted to scream. We'd *failed* in Wittenberg. Benjamin had been killed. His two accomplices, enemies of America, had escaped. They'd ridden away, their identities intact, their scheme unbroken. They were free, even now, to commit who knew how many crimes, and where was the success in that?

"After the war ended, you returned home to serve in various capacities within the government." His glance touched briefly on me, the only one who'd been discarded, like a piece of rotten fish. "Your sense of patriotism and devotion to your country remains unquestioned." Ambassador Schurman didn't try to hide his admiration.

"Therefore, we'd like to bring you together again as a covert unit and engage your help in hunting down the source of the monies funneled into Germany." U.S. Attorney Johnson nudged aside his coffee cup and entwined his fingers, his expression earnest. "We need to know how the money is being raised and where. We need to know who's behind the scheme, on the front end and the back end. We need to know if a treasonous plot is in place, and if it is, we need to stop it and have all guilty parties brought to justice."

"Or annihilated," Davis said coldly.

"Whatever it takes." The commander nodded.

"You'll be hired by the Department of Justice," the U.S. Attorney went on. "You'll exist as a private military company whose job will be to protect your country right here at home. You'll work in complete secrecy. By destroying the root of the problem, you'll prevent it from spreading throughout the rest of the world. Germany, especially."

For a moment, silence hung in the room.

"With all due respect," Grant drawled finally. "That's a hell of a plan."

"It's an impossible one," I snapped.

Jarrett rubbed his jaw. "Hard to know where to start."

"Gangsters," the attorney said, glance bouncing between them.

Rico blinked. "What?"

"You're surely aware of how Prohibition has lined the pockets of far too many hoodlums. Why, Luciano Carbano and Al Capone alone--."

"Leave it to the cops," I said.

"Who are far too corrupt to be trusted, and who have profited themselves by graft," the attorney shot back.

My brow lifted. "And that's *our* problem?"

Jesus, I wanted no part of this. The distraction would destroy my own mission to find answers, the truth in my brother's death. And now Drew's.

"Major Malone." Johnson regarded me through the round lenses of his eyeglasses. "There is nothing that pains me more than to see the abuses in our judicial system. Every day, I learn of more judges who are making a mockery of their own courts by succumbing to the very greed they've sworn to thwart. These gangsters are tightening their grimy fists over our city and beyond. Their profits from bootlegging are staggering."

"I read the newspapers, sir," I grated.

"This hotbed of crime and ill-begotten wealth make it prime fodder for *my* imagination"--Secretary of War Davis thumbed his chest--"and convinces me it's not altogether infeasible this explosion of funds could be used for even more nefarious purposes."

"Like treason," the ambassador said flatly.

"Which brings us full circle," Commander Van Fleet said, his voice strangely hushed. "You men have proved yourselves to be disciplined. You're tough. You're dedicated. You know how to survive. Most of all, you're smart. That's why we need all six of you."

In the ensuing silence, my brain worked over the information and refused to accept what they asked.

"It's been eight long years. We've changed since the war. *I've* changed," I said. "I'm afraid you'll have to count me out."

"You'll be paid well for your services," Johnson said. "This endeavor will be backed--."

"It's not about the money," I said.

"--by prominent businessmen who will do everything in their considerable power to protect their investments and those of this city. Hence, the nation."

"If we were to agree," Grant began slowly, his gaze avoiding mine. "When would we begin?"

"Immediately." The three men spoke in unison.

"No." I stood. I'd heard enough. Staying any longer would be a waste of my time and everyone else's. "Thank you, but no."

Kane frowned. "But, Major--."

Damn it, I needed a drink. I grabbed my Fedora, yanked open the door and strode out of the room. The door slammed shut behind me.

In the next moment, it opened again. I kept walking. I'd half expected someone to come after me. Any one of them would, starting from the commander on down.

"I'm not going to let you refuse so easily," Van Fleet said.

Stiff-backed, I turned toward him.

"You already know why I can't be a part of this mission," I said roughly.

"Because of Benjamin."

"Damn right because of Benjamin!"

"Because of Drew, too."

"Yes," I gritted.

Van Fleet didn't move. "There's something you need to know."

I shook my head. "No."

"I've heard from Delilah."

The words rolled through me, giant shock waves that jolted my nerve endings and left me electrified.

Sweet Jesus Christ. Agent Delilah.

For years, I'd all but blocked her from my mind. She was dead. I'd seen for myself what remained of her apartment in Germany, the ruins still smoldering from the explosives that detonated in the middle of the night. I'd seen her body, burned beyond recognition, yes, but pulled from the simple bedroom I knew was hers. I'd seen the death certificate, read the small, impassive article about her in the Munich newspaper.

I'd always believed she was hunted down by the same men who killed Benjamin. Murdered for being a double-agent for the United States government.

Had I believed wrong?

Had we all?

"She's very much alive, Michael," the commander said quietly.

"You have proof?" I demanded.

"Of course."

"Where is she?"

"She's not that stupid. But she wants to avenge what happened to your brother."

"After eight years?" My lip curled. "I'll bet she does."

I knew her only by her code name, a German informant who worked secretly with Commander Van Fleet during the war. Because he'd trusted her, I had, too. Until Benjamin was killed.

Why had she faked her own death? Why would she resurrect herself now, after all this time?

"I have information from her," the commander said.

I didn't want to be intrigued, but damn it, I was. "What kind?"

Slowly, Van Fleet shook his head. "You know I can't say. Not even to you. Not until you commit to the mission with the rest of your men."

"But you told Drew."

"Yes."

"And he was killed for it." My tone hardened. "Like Benjamin."

"Yes." His eyes turned stormy from the admission. "Which convinces me all the more of the caliber of men we must hunt down. They're ruthless tyrants who are without conscience for their own political beliefs." His nostrils flared. "I'll tell you this much, Michael. Delilah's information led Drew to investigate a singing society with ties to Nazism that appear surprisingly... profitable."

I needed a moment to absorb the news. Had Drew stumbled onto a possible lead to the monies funneling into Germany? Or did Delilah have an ulterior motive in leading him to the organization? One that led to his murder?

"What if it's all connected, Michael?"

My thoughts scrambled. "What are you talking about?"

"Think about it."

"You think I haven't been?"

"Not hard enough." Van Fleet's shrewd gaze latched onto me and wouldn't let go. "The two men who were with Benjamin that night disappeared. Years of investigation have turned up nothing. Maybe they're dead. Maybe they're not. But let's assume they're still alive and still heavily involved in the Nazi cause. They could have left Germany. They could have moved anywhere in the world to avoid detection." He paused, as if to make sure I understood the immensity of all he was saying. "They would've heard about the Volstead Act. They would know how appealing that would make the United States. They could've gone underground for the fortunes to be made in every damned bottle of beer and whiskey that's being bootlegged out there." He paused, his regard keen. "It wouldn't have been hard to do, Michael."

The words thundered inside my head. If not for Drew on the night we slipped away from the Wittenberg camp, I'd be dead. Drew had saved me, but we'd both failed to save Benjamin.

Had Delilah given us another chance to learn the truth?

Did she really want to avenge Benjamin's death, like she claimed?

"It's a long shot," I muttered, more to myself than Van Fleet.

"But not an impossible one."

"No." Still, I hesitated.

"You're only one man, Michael. Do you really think you can find your brother's killers and expose an espionage scheme in a country halfway across the world all by yourself?"

"I'll find them," I said stiffly. "Eventually."

The commander shrugged, neither agreeing or disagreeing. "Now, you'll have your men to help you. Hell, you'll have the entire United States government behind you. The damned War Department, at your fingertips." He smiled coldly. "And you'll have Agent Delilah."

I breathed an oath. And trembled from the immensity.

The walls of my resistance cracked. I took in a breath. Let it out again.

I knew, then, what I had to do. For Benjamin's sake. For Drew's. For America's.

But mostly, for my own.

"All right." I felt the weight of the bottled rum against my chest and craved its heat in my blood. Courage for what I was about to do. "I'm in."